OVERNIGHT
SENSATION

TRISH
Cook

nal
jam
books

NAL Jam
Published by New American Library,
a division of Penguin Group (USA) Inc.,
375 Hudson Street, New York, New York 10014, USA
Penguin Group (Canada), 90 Eglinton Avenue East, Suite 700, Toronto, Ontario M4P 2Y3,
Canada (a division of Pearson Penguin Canada Inc.) • Penguin Books Ltd., 80 Strand,
London WC2R 0RL, England • Penguin Ireland, 25 St. Stephen's Green, Dublin 2, Ireland
(a division of Penguin Books Ltd.) • Penguin Group (Australia), 250 Camberwell Road,
Camberwell, Victoria 3124, Australia (a division of Pearson Australia Group Pty. Ltd.) •
Penguin Books India Pvt. Ltd., 11 Community Centre, Panchsheel Park, New Delhi—110
017, India • Penguin Group (NZ), cnr Airborne and Rosedale Roads, Albany, Auckland
1310, New Zealand (a division of Pearson New Zealand Ltd.) • Penguin Books (South
Africa) (Pty.) Ltd., 24 Sturdee Avenue, Rosebank, Johannesburg 2196, South Africa

Penguin Books Ltd., Registered Offices:
80 Strand, London WC2R 0RL, England

First published by NAL Jam, an imprint of New American Library,
a division of Penguin Group (USA) Inc.

First Printing, February, 2006
3   5   7   9   10   8   6   4   2

Copyright © Patricia Cook, 2006
All rights reserved

NAL JAM and logo are trademarks of Penguin Group (USA) Inc.

LIBRARY OF CONGRESS CATALOGING-IN-PUBLICATION DATA

Cook, Trish, 1965–
    Overnight sensation / Trish Cook.
        p.   cm.
    Summary: Having made a surprising new friend while visiting the father she only recent-
ly met, Trace comes to some realizations about how her efforts to please everyone may be
harming her relationship with those she cares most about.
    ISBN 0-451-21758-6
    [1. Interpersonal relations—Fiction. 2. Self-confidence—Fiction. 3. Fathers and daughters—
Fiction. 4. Singers—Fiction. 5. Popular music—Fiction.] I. Title.
    PZ7.C773Ove 2006
    [Fic]—dc22   2005027136

Set in Granjon • Designed by Elke Sigal
Printed in the United States of America

PUBLISHER'S NOTE
This is a work of fiction. Names, characters, places, and incidents either are the product of
the author's imagination or are used fictitiously, and any resemblance to actual persons,
living or dead, business establishments, events, or locales is entirely coincidental.
The publisher does not have any control over and does not assume any responsibility for
author or third-party Web sites or their content.

To my mom,
for her awesome friendship,
love, and support

ACKNOWLEDGMENTS

A big shout-out goes to: Steve-o, for being my soul mate and making our life together a great adventure; Court and Kels, for rocking my world on a daily basis; Brendan Halpin, Erica Orloff, Barbara Govednik, and Jennifer O'Connell (www.brandanhalpin.com, www.ericaorloff.com, www.lizaconrad.com, www.423communication.com, www.jenniferoconnell.com) for always being there with advice, wisdom, and a good dash of humor; Marlene Stringer, for her famous pep talks; Charlotte Walsh, for having the same Fred Flintstone feet as me and filling a huge void in my life; Billie Joe Armstrong, Jimmy Page, and Robert Plant, no need to ask why; Suzanne, Sue, Alison, and Michele for being the most amazing "old" (and by that, I mean lifelong) friends a girl could ever ask for; Julie, Joanna, Lisa, Janice, Traci, Linda, Meredith, and Heather for being the most amazing "new" ones; and to everyone who supported *So Lyrical* along the way. Thanks, I love you all!

CHAPTER
1

"**G**imme some pumpkin ice cream with sour gummy worms, pistachios, and kiwi mixed in." The shaggy-haired kid on the other side of the counter smirked at me while his toady skateboarding buddies jabbed him in the ribs. "In an Ex-Lax-dipped waffle cone, that is."

The zit monsters stared at me expectantly, shuffling their feet and whispering just loud enough so I could hear every word.

"This is so gonna work!"

"Look! She's turning green!"

"Naaah, I think that's just some kiwi hanging off her nose."

"Ex-Lax-dipped cone, *hahaha!* Good one, man."

The combo platter of me potentially getting sick and their fearless leader intentionally giving himself diarrhea was making the entire posse completely spastic. They must've been a real hit in second grade back when toilet jokes ruled the school. Too bad they were currently fourteen and so clueless they weren't even embarrassed by their incredibly stunted sense of humor.

I grabbed a scooper and flexed my muscles in what I hoped was an intimidating manner. If these guys wanted to play with me, I could at least show them that despite my weak stomach, the rest of me was fit to beat the crap out of She-Ra.

Getting a really buff upper body from shoveling hard ice cream and then mashing random substances into it for eight hours at a clip was pretty much the only good thing that had come out of my slaving away at the Mixed-Up Creamery all summer. As for the bad things? Believe me, there were waaayyy too many to list, and any sane person would be snoring before I was even done warming up to the topic.

But just for chucks—no pun intended—allow me to present the worst of the worst: One day as I was pounding an oatmeal-cookie-ice-cream-dates-and-walnuts blend into submission, one of the dates escaped my wrath. Now, I don't have a lot of experience with this sticky, waxy, bizarro fruit—it's not like people order them in mix-ins on a regular basis—but even I should've known this one looked a little funky. When I went to squish it back in with the rest of the stuff, zillions of squiggly little wormy things exploded out of it. One look at the *Fear Factor* horror in front of me, and I lost it. I mean seriously lost it. I started wailing like a banshee—whatever that is—jumped so high my head practically went bashing through the ceiling, and heaved, all in quick succession.

Lucky for everyone around me, I made it to the trash can instead of scoring a direct hit on either the ice cream or the mix-ins. Unlucky for me, the kid who ordered the puke-inducing combination turned out to have a very big mouth. He told all his friends about it, and they told all their friends, and so on and so on until the entire town—and possibly the entire universe—had heard about it.

Within days, there was a sophomore Soprano wannabe taking wagers on who could make me kiss the marble slab again and people started referring to the incident as the Yuke of Earl. As in, *I heard Mindy Smith drank a fifth of Jack Daniels and barfed her guts up at Larry Bender's party last weekend—it was practically a tidal wave but not nearly of Earlish proportions*. By default, of course, that made me Earl.

Though I had pretty much decided to never show my face in public again, Bebe was less than sympathetic when I prepped her on the idea of quitting my job and taking off for the rest of the summer to California or the Jersey shore or, well, pretty much anywhere but here. After she was done laughing, my mom reminded me of some of her more embarrassing moments—most of which ended up fictionalized in her books, so see? mortifying life experiences can be useful—said someday it would be a great story to tell my kids, and encouraged me to just hurry up and get over it.

To which I told her easier said than done, seeing as I'm so not comfortable being in the spotlight even when I've accomplished something noteworthy, no less my propensity to gag over anything remotely gross. Besides, these junior high boys wouldn't let me forget it if I tried. I mean, Ex-Lax-dipped waffle cone, give me a break. Like I hadn't heard that one a million times before this summer.

"You want it, you got it," I said, flashing a fake smile at my customers and completely spoiling their fun. "And by the way, whispering is generally more effective when the people you're talking about can't hear you."

"Sorry," ordering guy mumbled. The only thing he sounded sorry about was the fact that I hadn't retched yet.

I passed him the cone, which now served as a reservoir for neon green and baby-poop brown toxic waste. "That'll be four dollars and fifty cents, please."

The kid took a small bite of the sludge, then shoved a huge pile of change and a lone crumpled bill across the counter at me. "Yum," he said, grimacing. "Delicious."

"Looks it."

I glanced at the clock while I wiped up a few jellified worm carcasses and a sprinkling of kiwi seeds suspended in alien goo. Halle-freaking-lujah. Only a few more minutes and I'd be liberated from this place forever.

After taking one last peek at me, the Lame-o Loser Gang admitted defeat and peaced out. Not surprisingly, the ice cream got tossed before they even hit the door.

"Dudes, I could've really used that cash for some new wheels," Mr. He Who Did Not Make Me Spew said, scuffing the toes of his purple suede Vans against the black-and-white linoleum floor. "What a total jam job. Instead of making fifty bucks on that bet, I'm out five. *And* I'm still hungry."

His buddies gave him a wallop on the back in consolation. "Just wait. You'll get her next time."

"There won't be a next time, suckers," I called happily after them. "Because I'm outta here today!"

"Now look what you did," one posse member groaned, giving his former idol a whack on the head. "You made her quit. You always have to take things one step too far, don't you?"

The guys were still arguing as they glided out of sight on their skateboards. And I was still grinning about my imminent escape from the icy hell better known as the Mixed-Up Creamery.

Dunking my scooper paddle thingie in steaming-hot water, I wondered how my life had gone from so exciting to so . . . so . . . *this*. Though I had kind of figured July and August might be something of a letdown after my mind-bogglingly exciting year—stuffed to the gills with training for and successfully running the Rock 'n' Roll Marathon, masterminding a kick-ass plan that led me to my long-lost dad, helping Brina not only solve the slp mystery but realize it was OK to fall in love with her formerly anonymous note writer, and me finding boy, losing boy, and getting boy back—what I'd failed to recognize was exactly how harsh the crash landing back to reality would be. Most days, it had my head spinning around faster than Bebe's old records.

First up on the turntable: "Who Are You?" by The Who. Now that I'd finally found my father, I wasn't spending all my waking moments daydreaming about what a perfect guy he was anymore—like, let's say a cross of Bruce Springsteen, Danny Tanner, and the Dalai Lama. But I also wasn't the full-fledged expert on the real, live human being responsible for half my genetic makeup I'd fully expected to be by this point, either. The truth was, despite all our quickie phone calls and short but sweet e-mails since the marathon, I still couldn't say for sure which of the fantasy-dad combos I'd pieced together over the years he most resembled. Or whether he preferred ketchup or mustard on his hot dogs, for that matter.

Track two: "September," by Earth, Wind & Fire. Now that I'd decided to attend Fairfield, I wasn't doing the whole wonder-where-I'll-go-to-school-next-year dance—but I wasn't there yet, either, so I had no idea whether I'd made the right decision in choosing it over UCLA. Had I been crazy to shun fun, sunny California in favor of sedate, seasonal Connecticut? Sometimes I woke up in the middle of the night, trying to catch my breath, thinking I must be. Crazy, that is. I mean, no one with a smidge of sanity would trade in long, crappy Chicago winters for long, crappy East Coast ones, would they?

Cut three: "Another One Bites the Dust," by Queen. Now that I'd run twenty-six-point-two miles in just over four hours, I wasn't working toward ticking another big goal off my gotta-do-it-before-I-die list—because I didn't have a clue what the next thing on my GDIBID list might be, or if there would even *be* a next thing. I kept waiting for inspiration to hit me over the head, but so far it hadn't even tapped lightly on my skull.

And for the bring-the-curtains-down finale: "Tainted Love," by Soft Cell. Now that Zander and I had been going out for nearly a year—well, except for that random month or so last spring—long-term togetherness wasn't exactly feeling like the warm, snuggly blanket I'd always imagined it would be. In reality, it felt more like a sock plucked out of the dryer a minute too soon: lukewarm instead of totally hot, less comfortable than I expected, and slightly saggy in key places no matter how much I tugged and pulled to get it back into shape.

It was just that things had never quite been the same—at least for me—since Zander first avoided me like the plague and then dumped me after I spontaneously dropped the L-bomb last year. Even though he admitted later he'd made a total mistake, I still couldn't quite shake the feeling that we weren't back on solid ground yet. That one wrong move— or phrase—might send him skittering off into the distance again. As a result of my paranoia, I'd studiously avoided discussing anything that even verged on serious or mushy-gushy (and therefore scary and skid-mark-inducing) since we'd gotten back together, concentrating instead on cultivating the uber-chill, totally agreeable, and seriously not needy parts of my personality. Most of the time, it felt really mature and highly evolved to be presenting the coolest possible version of me at all times to Zander. Every so often, though, I worried whether constantly mentally censoring myself around him was going to drive *me* mental.

Not that Z seemed to notice either way. He was a guy, making him genetically and blissfully unaware of the crap us females put ourselves through to make a relationship work.

* * *

The vibration of my phone snapped me out of my funkadelic thoughts. I flipped it open and grinned at the message.

Almst FrE 4ever!

It was Zander, texting me from the golf course where he wasn't even supposed to have his cell phone turned on, much less be using it while he worked. For reasons unbeknown to us normal folks, technology invented in the last twenty years—along with anything denim, cutoff shorts, and tank tops—seems to disturb those country club types to no end. I deduced Z must be caddying for old man Frey again, who is as sweet as anything but, let's face it, at nearly ninety needs an ear trumpet and can't see two feet in front of his nose, glasses or no glasses. Mr. Frey wouldn't have noticed if Zander was carrying the clubs buck naked while yodeling the "Star Spangled Banner," so there was no way he'd be tuned in enough to put the kibosh on our twenty-first-century silent messaging.

My fingers flew over the keypad. I'd gotten to be a total expert at texting these past few months after living through long stretches where no one ordered an ice cream and I had nothing else to do but send snarky messages to my friends.

gotta gt outa hre. i cnt lst mch longA!

I tucked the nearly microscopic flip phone back into my jeans and took a sponge to everything in the place until it sparkled, all the while praying that Sanford Paulsen—one of the people Brina and I had added to an early slp suspect list last year, flood-pants-wearing closet nose-picker, and also my increasingly touchy-feely boss this summer—would hurry up and give me my final paycheck. I was so dying to hang up my Mixed-Up Creamery apron and get on with the rest of my life, my butt was practically vibrating. No wait, that was just my phone again.

CW2CU. Cali hre we come!

I was trying to think of a sexy, snappy response to send to Zander about how much fun we were going to have at my dad's for the next week, when Sanford came bustling out of the back room and wrapped me in a bone-crushing hug that melded all my body parts to his.

"Come back whenever you're home on break, Trace," he panted, unable to hide the fact that it was as close as he'd ever come to actually getting laid. "I'll miss you."

"Thanks," I said, thinking there was no way I'd ever set foot in this arctic wasteland again. "But I'll probably be too busy with homework and everything."

"The offer's always there. Remember that." Instead of stepping aside to let me leave, Sanford just stood there staring at me, rubbing his nose and looking thoughtful.

"Sure thing," I said, giving him a quick pat on the shoulder. He was blocking my escape, so I said good-bye again and tried to bob and weave my way around him. Still no yardage. If it hadn't been for Sanford's reedy build and complete lack of athleticism, I would've thought he was trying out for defensive lineman.

"Trace," he finally croaked. "I know you're probably still seeing that Country Day guy—"

"Right," I said. "Zander." I figured the quicker I filled in the blanks, the sooner I'd get out of there.

"And you know how I sort of made a play for your friend last year?"

"Yup. Brina," I said, mentally willing him to get on with it.

Sanford shuffled his feet and gazed at the ground. "Well . . . see, it's like this . . . ahem . . . it's been great getting to know you this summer. I think you're really special. Truly one-of-a-kind. You made me realize girls like Brina aren't my type at all."

"Uh, thanks, Sanford." I said, immediately wondering whether the fact that I felt the tiniest bit pleased that someone besides Zander found me more appealing than Brina also meant I was the world's worst friend. Before I could further contemplate my inner bitch and how to get rid of her, Sanford started rolling again with his well-intentioned but awkward speech.

"I guess what I'm trying to say is, if that boyfriend of yours ever stops treating you like he's the luckiest guy in the world, I'd be honored to take you out."

"You are so sweet," I sputtered, struggling to find just the right words to make Sanford know that while I appreciated his compliments I had no intention of taking him up on his offer of a date. Ever. Even if Z decided to peace out again, permanently this time. I decided the nicest thing to do would be to let Sanford down easy with the old you-can-do-better-than-me routine. "But it's not like I'm Kandy Kane or anything."

Kandy was the latest prepackaged hype to show up in heavy rotation on MTV, and every guy on the planet—with the possible exception of Zander—seemed to have fallen under her techno-pop spell. I figured Sanford was no different, and judging by the way his eyes practically Slinkyed out of his head at the mere mention of her name, I was right on the money.

As for me, I could definitely live in a Kandy-free world. She clearly wasn't a musician, seeing as she didn't play an instrument or write her own songs, was almost certainly a lip-syncher, and, as if that wasn't bad enough, relied on a pathetic *gimmick* instead of good music to get where she was. In my humble (and also completely correct) opinion, Kandy's gleaming pink hair, white makeup with big pink stars outlining her eyes, next-to-nothing outfits, and sky-high platform shoes were all just a desperate attempt to distract people from realizing she had absolutely nothing else to offer. Besides, anyone with eyeballs could see she'd stolen the look from one of Gwen Stefani's Harajuku girls. Seriously, the only thing I could see even being slightly original about the chick—or the retread song she was remaking famous—was that she'd changed the C in candy to a K. And who knows, even that was more than likely a spelling error. There was no way she had higher than a single-digit IQ.

"Don't feel bad, Trace. Not many girls have as much . . ." Sanford hesitated and his gaze came to rest on my double-As. "Uhh-hhh, *talent* as Kandy."

Talent, my ass. We were talking ginormous mammaries here and we both knew it. "Ri-ight," I said, peering at him through squinty eyes. "Have fun at Northwestern this year, buddy. You take care of yourself, OK?"

"You, too," he said, finally stepping aside to let me head on out the door. "And be sure to go easy on that sensitive stomach of yours at Fairfield, Earl."

As I hit the warm summer air, I noticed a super-caffeinated buzz running through my veins even though I hadn't been to Starbucks all day. It took me only a few seconds to realize it wasn't due to coffee beans or lack thereof, but the thought of spending some serious hang time with my newly discovered daddy-o that was making me a jittery wreck.

My anxiety level really wasn't that surprising when you considered Shamus and I had met face-to-face only twice before in my entire life, and one of those times he wouldn't even fess up to being my father. By this point, I'd pretty much forgiven his initial fight-or-flight response. Notice I said *pretty much*, because my dad's actions—just like Zander's sneak attack breakup last year—had stuck with me like a little pebble in my shoe: Sometimes I barely noticed how uncomfortable it made me, and other times it dug straight into my soul.

Still, I was sure once my dad and I made the quantum leap from being merely physically related to spiritually connected, that feeling would go away. I was also pretty sure the reason we hadn't fully clicked yet was because the guy had been so crazy-busy with work all summer—cooking up a deal about which he was extremely long on enthusiasm but short on details—we hadn't had time for the big heart-to-heart I was sure would take us from here to there.

Until now, that is. Now everything was about to change. This trip meant the time had finally come for some serious quantum-leaping, and even a potential stumbling block like the one Shamus had thrown out there during one of our recent blink-and-you-might-miss-it conversations couldn't dampen my hopes. "Wouldn't it be great to invite a friend along on your visit?" he'd asked before I even got past hello. I was so psyched he'd called, it didn't immediately register that his sentence contained a request, not an innocent question.

"I can hang with my friends whenever I want to. I'd actually rather spend time with you while I'm in California," I'd told him.

To which he'd replied, "You're not making this easy, Trace."

Since I had no idea what that was supposed to mean, I'd said, "What's that supposed to mean?"

At which point he'd come clean. "Remember that top secret new client I told you I was working with? And the big business deal we were working on? Well, I'm *this close* to making it happen."

"Congrats," I'd said. "What's it all about again?" So far, all I knew was that it was big. And involved some sort of business.

"Can't really talk about it just yet, for legal reasons," he'd told me.

"How about a hint?" Maybe if I guessed, he could say yes or no until I figured it out for myself.

"Sorry, Trace, no can do. About the only thing I can tell you right now is if everything goes as planned, things will be totally rocking by the time you get here," he'd explained. Sort of. "That means I'm probably not going be able to take you to Disneyland or Universal or Rodeo Drive or whatever you were hoping to see while you're here. I hope you're not disappointed."

I actually hadn't been hoping for anything other than getting to know my dad during my visit, so the lack of mindless entertainment at tourist traps wasn't all that disappointing. I was *family*, after all. I would just jump in and be his right-hand girl. It was so simple, I couldn't believe he hadn't thought of it first. "Shamus, I don't need a friend to entertain me. I can help you," I'd told him.

"Lots of what I'll be doing while you're here is deathly dull. Like watching paint dry, really."

"Maybe I won't think so."

"Believe me, you definitely will."

At that point, I'd gone into totally-understanding-daughter mode, digging down deep to provide my dad an out I really didn't want to offer. "Shamus, would you rather have me postpone my trip until Thanksgiving, when you have more time?"

"No, no. Of course not," he'd assured me.

Had he hesitated for a second, or was that my imagination? "Are you *sure* you still want me to come?" I'd asked again. I needed to be one hundred percent certain he was ready for our emotional bondfest, even if it was going to be more a little more condensed than I'd hoped.

"Positive," he'd told me, sounding completely convinced this time. "I've really been looking forward to seeing you again, Trace. We'll make it work, you'll see."

A honking horn sent the memory flying out my ear and skidding down the pavement. I screamed, threw my hand over my heart, and flung myself back onto the sidewalk. When I dared to look up again, there was Zander in his brand-spanking-new Jeep Wrangler, cracking up.

Though my normal reaction would've been to not so politely mention the fact that he'd almost given me a heart attack, I waved and gave my boyfriend a little smile designed to remind him how laid-back and easygoing I was instead. "Hey, baby!" I yelled.

"Hey, baby, yourself." Z grinned down at me from his too-cool-for-words car, a graduation present from his parents. I was more than a little envious. I mean, the only thing Bebe had given me to mark the end of high school was the latest Duran Duran CD, and we both knew it was going straight into her pile. Never in a zillion years would I let those guys contaminate my music.

"You ready to hit the road?" I asked, a smile plastered to my face despite the fact that I'd been *this close* to turning into roadkill a second ago.

"Yup," he said, patting the seat next to him. "So let's hit it, sweet cheeks, we're running late."

I hopped up, buckled in, and peeked at Zander out of the corner of my eye. The guy was funny, cool, practically oozing with sporty hotness. So why couldn't I just go back to being obliviously in love with him, without all the worry and overanalysis and second-guessing about our relationship? The question bounced around my mind as we drove, the answer finally hitting me right as we pulled into the driveway. *Because it is pretty much impossible to be head over heels for someone when your feet are firmly planted on the ground at all times.* And mine were. Given our history, I felt like I had to be prepared to hit the ground running at the drop of a hat. Or an L-bomb, for that matter.

Z put the Jeep into park, leaned back in his seat, and flipped his sunglasses up on his head.

"You coming in?" I asked, sure he wouldn't be so sluggy he'd just sit there.

"Trace, we're already behind schedule," he said, tipping up his chin to soak in the rays. "It'll be quicker if you'd just grab your stuff without me."

I decided there wasn't time to argue about it, so I gave him a little peck, jumped out of the car, and went to retrieve my things alone. I'd talk to him about what a lazy-ass maneuver I thought it was—not even coming in to say hi to my mom and her fiancé—later, on the plane, when we had more time for an extended discussion.

Oh, sure, I fired back at myself. Just like I'd told him I hadn't exactly loved the way he'd scared me off the sidewalk before. Who did I think I was kidding, anyway? Certainly not myself.

"Hey, Bebe, Mr. Steve," I said, rushing by those lovebirds on my way up to my room.

I stopped dead in my tracks a few steps later, realizing there was something odd about the configuration in the kitchen: There were three lovebirds instead of the usual two. Finally putting two plus one together, I greeted my best friend in the whole world. "Oh, hey, Brina. I didn't see you there at first."

"That's because you came tearing through here like a bat out of the Mixed-Up Creamery," she said, pushing her chair back from the table. "But no worries, I've gotta take off anyway. Big date tonight. It's our three-month anniversary, you know."

I stuck my finger in my mouth, popped it out, and twirled it around. I just loved to yank Brina's chain, especially when it came to her rampant love of Sully. "Is there gonna be a parade?"

"Nope, it's strictly a private affair," Brina said, grabbing an unfamiliar board game from the table. "Thanks again, Bebe."

I must say, she was disappointingly unresponsive to my heckling. "Hold on just a minute there, *chica*," I asked, giving it another try. "What's that you've got hidden under your stinky armpit?" I turned my head to the side in an attempt to figure it out.

"I'll have you know I smell like Teen Spirit." Brina giggled, used to this kind of banter from me after ten years of being friends. "And it's a game. Naked Twister, to be exact. Bebe and Mr. Steve got it as a gag engagement gift and never used it, so I asked if I could take it off their hands."

It was so gross my friends felt comfortable enough with my mom they'd borrow her copy of the Kama Sutra if she offered it. "You were right about the gag part," I said, suddenly not feeling so in on the joke anymore.

"C'mon, Trace," Brina said, the corners of her mouth curling up into an evil little grin. "It's all in good fun. Plus, I only have a week left to show Sully how much hotter I am than all those high school chicks who are going to be after his ass when I'm at school. Naked Twister will definitely seal the deal."

"Brina, the deal's been sealed ever since Sully started sending you those amazing slp notes last year. You don't have to prove anything to the guy—he's already convinced." Really, I was one to lecture after turning myself into Miss Whatever You Say, Dear this summer. Still, smoothing your way through a rough patch was one thing. Using sex to lock someone in was entirely another, and not something I wanted to see my awesome best friend stooping to.

"I am simply trying to give Sully some great memories to go on while we're apart," she said, unfazed by my argument. "What's the big deal?"

"The big deal is this," I told her, surprising even myself by how strongly I was reacting to a ridiculous board game. "He already has all the great times you guys spent together the past three months to go on. How you always laugh so hard at his jokes you end up snorting. The awesome Italian dinners you cook for him. He doesn't need a permanent visual of how you look when you have left hand green, right foot yellow and not a stitch of clothing on to keep him from hooking up with other people while you're at Mount St. Agnes."

"Sully and I are going to have a blast playing this game," Brina told me, blowing off my concerns about her potentially floundering integrity with a flick of the wrist. "What you have to realize, Trace, is that some of us are still in the honeymoon phase of our relationships."

"Zander and I are still in the honeymoon phase!" I protested, ditching my high-and-mighty sermonizing to jump to my own defense. While I may have been having silent doubts about the long-term viability of a partnership that had me biting my tongue half the time, it definitely remained off-limits for anyone else to say out loud. Especially when said partner was waiting right outside the door, obliviously getting himself a tan.

"That's my cue to leave," Mr. Steve said, grabbing his coffee cup and running for the den before we could elaborate any further.

"Trace, just chill," Brina told me, waving me off again. "All I'm saying is maybe Sully and I are a little more adventurous in the fooling-around department than you and Zander."

I wanted to grab the game out of Brina's hands and tell her she couldn't borrow it because Z and I had been planning on playing it the entire week we were in California. Except then I might actually have to do just that—and not only did I totally disagree with everything the game stood for, the thought of contorting my naked body into goofy positions was way too embarrassing to even consider. So what I said instead was, "I'll call you later on this week to check in."

"No need, 'cause here's the message you'll get. '*Beep!* Brina and Sully can't come to the phone right now. They're totally tied up—and I mean in each other—playing Naked Twister. Please leave a message at the moan.'"

Much as I knew I should drop it, I somehow just couldn't. Since I wasn't getting anywhere with Little Miss Hot Pants, I decided to appeal to Bebe, who usually had pretty solid feminist leanings. "Do you really think girls my age—or women of any age, really—should demean themselves by playing sex games?"

"Brina's eighteen now, honey," Bebe said, a bemused little smile on her face. "She can vote, she can drive, and she can choose to play Naked Twister with her boyfriend if she feels like it."

I took the opening and ran with it. "Did you ever consider the fact that even though she's legal, her boyfriend is jailbait? Sully can't drive *or* vote yet. He's only going to be a junior this year, for God's sake."

"Trace, calm down," Bebe said, yawning and making a big show of stretching her arms above her head. "That silly game is PG-13 at best. Are you trying to tell me they wouldn't be making out if I didn't let them borrow it? That anything different than what normally takes place on Saturday nights is going to happen because of it?"

"So true," Brina chimed in.

"Forget I said anything," I muttered. "Have a great time, Brina."

"Oh, I will," she said, nodding enthusiastically as she hit the door. "You can bet on it."

As soon as Brina took off, Bebe hit me with one last appeal to come home a day earlier than expected from my dad's place. "Trace, would you please just consider heading back for Steve's big family reunion on Saturday night? It would mean a lot to us if you were there."

Let me see: lounging in Cali with my newfound dad, or hanging at the Winnetka Country Club with Mr. Steve's tightly wound family at an affair everyone neglected to mention to me until the last minute anyway? Oh, that took about negative two milliseconds. "Can't, Bebe. You bought me a nonrefundable, no-changes-allowed, Saturday-night-stay-required ticket, remember?"

"Right," she said, going into widemouth bass mode again, letting out a yawn so huge I could practically see inside her brain this time. "Why am I so exhausted lately? I feel like I got hit by a Mack truck."

"Grab another cup of decaf and come snuggle with me in here," Mr. Steve called to her from the den. "I'll make you feel better."

Bebe immediately popped up from her seat, let out a girlish little giggle, and padded into the other room in her fuzzy pink slippers. I swear, sometimes it felt like the whole world was a happily paired-off Noah's Ark, and in some weird mix-up I was hanging with the wrong kind of animal. Like maybe a wolf in sheep's clothing, for all I knew.

CHAPTER 2

Snap, crackle, pop. I forced a smile onto my face and gently placed my hand on top of Zander's. It didn't even slow him down. Luckily, I was wearing sunglasses, or for sure he would've seen the look in my eyes that was shrieking, *If you don't stop that right now I'm going to push you out the emergency exit without a parachute.*

Pop, crackle, snap.

Next, I tried throwing my arms around my boyfriend and kissing him softly on the lips. While I usually find PDA completely appalling, I was willing to let my standards slide just this once. If Z reacted the way I hoped he would, he'd have to use his hands for pursuits other than cracking his knuckles.

No such luck. "Trace, nice thought, but we're in a public place," he whispered out of the corner of his mouth, going right back to his bone-snapping activities. "Everyone is staring at us."

I looked around, trying not to feel rejected. One little kid was gaping in our direction, all bug-eyed and slack-jawed. I silently conceded that might be a little distracting, if I were Z and had been trying to kiss me back.

"Did you ever see *European Vacation?*" I asked, trying once again to find a nice and not so critical way to let him know his bad habit was driving me freaking nuts.

"You mean the flick where Matt Damon does a cameo as a punk rocker?" Zander started whipping his head around and singing whatever lyrics he remembered to "Scotty Doesn't Know." Which consisted mainly of, well, Scotty doesn't know. And nothing more.

Way more people were staring at us now than when I'd kissed Zander a few seconds ago, not that he seemed to notice. "Nope, that was *Eurotrip*," I said, trying to get back to the issue at hand—no pun intended. "The movie I'm talking about is really old, starring Chevy Chase."

"I must've missed that one. Why?"

The real reason was this flight was beginning to remind me of the scene where the Griswold family is on a train trip and the brother and sister start doing things to annoy each other because they're so bored. Like, the girl starts flicking the ashtray in the armrest open and shut, open and shut, open and shut. Then the brother puts on his Walkman and is half humming, half singing the songs while pounding out a beat on his legs. Anyway, it's really funny if you don't happen to be actually experiencing it. Which I was.

I was just about to bottom-line it when I decided better of it. "Never mind."

Crackle. Pop. Snap. Zander was clearly headed for crackhead rehab. I tried to smile again but my head was pounding too hard by this point. "Z, could you stop doing that, please?"

"What are you so uptight about?" Zander asked, scowling and stuffing his hands in his pockets. Now muffled crackling noises were coming from the vicinity of his balls. Gross. "Is this about your dad?"

"Yeah, probably," I said, even though I knew my uptightness was definitely more about the annoying noises than Shamus. "I guess I'm kind of nervous. I want everything to go right, you know?"

"It will," he said, forgiving me with a little smooch on the cheek. "I mean, what could go wrong?"

Thousands of possibilities flooded my head, though I kept them to myself. "I guess nothing," I finally said.

"Trace, all that's going to happen in LA is that your dad will find out once and for all what I already know," Zander said, giving my knee a little squeeze. "That you're the coolest chick around."

I leaned my head on his shoulder and sighed into his Coldplay T-shirt, hoping I could continue to live up to my hard-earned reputation without losing an important chunk of myself in the process.

At the baggage claim, I assigned Zander the position of luggage watcher so I could search for Shamus. It was time for the moment of truth—my dad and I together, finally. My nerve endings felt like they were on fire, and every hair on my head was standing at attention. I took a few deep cleansing breaths, just like that annoying lady on Bebe's yoga video was always telling me to do. I hate yoga, by the way. And I hate the annoying lady on the video even more.

After searching high and low, up and down, in and out, my jitters were replaced by the acid pit of doom. It would be a very definite bad start to this vacation if Shamus had forgotten we were coming. Or even worse, blew us off for his business deal, whatever it was. Frustrated, I made my way back to carousel number nine.

"Any sign of him?" Zander asked from his perch on top of my Roxy suitcase.

"Nope," I said, scanning the crowd one more time for Not So Famous Shamus, as I'd come to think of him after finding out he wasn't one of Bebe's former eighties idols, after all. It always made me laugh whenever I remembered how far I'd been into the my-dad-must-be-a-rock-star-and-that's-why-my-mom-hid-his-identity-for-so-long fantasy last year. I mean, at one point I'd actually convinced myself that I was Bruce Springsteen's daughter. And let's get serious here. There was no way someone as lyrically challenged as me could possibly share genes with a gifted songwriter like that.

I craned my neck in every direction, spotting only a uniformed man resembling a Weeble headed our way. "You Tracey?" he asked us once he reached our spot. "And Zander?"

"We might be," I said, immediately suspicious. "Depends on who's asking." I added the last part because I thought it made us sound street-smart—like we weren't going to be an easy target if this guy was looking to take us for everything we had. Which wasn't much, believe me. Ice cream scooping and caddying both paid minimum wage, and Z wasn't allowed to so much as sniff at his mongo trust fund for another decade, so we were both basically broke.

"I'm the official driver for KRP," the Weeble said, ignoring my fake tough-girl answer and heaving our luggage onto his waiting cart. "Here to take you to Mr. McDonohue's house."

"KRP?"

"Mr. McDonohue's company," he slowly explained, like maybe he thought I was new to the English language. "You know? Kandy's Room Productions?"

"You didn't tell me that was the name of his production company," Zander whispered as we followed the waddling little egg-shaped man through the airport.

"I couldn't," I whispered back. "Because I didn't even know he *had* a production company."

"So I guess you guys still have a lot to learn about each other."

I decided *duh* might not be the sweetest, most mature response, so I went with, "I guess you're right." As psyched as I was about finding my father, life had been definitely less complicated prediscovery. "I wonder why he calls it Kandy's Room, anyway?"

"Come on now, Trace," Z said, looking at me with a lumpy mixture of concern and disbelief. "Think."

"What?" I scrunched up my face, trying to brainstorm a logical explanation. Full seasons flew by.

"Think," he urged yet again.

"I already tried that," I said, shaking my head. I was surprised there wasn't a rattling noise or dust pouring out of my ears.

"It's the name of a Springsteen song," Z told me triumphantly.

"Ri-ight." The truth was, I didn't even vaguely remember a Boss song with that title—probably because he's so Bebe's guy and so not mine. "Well, at least that makes sense. The big business deal still doesn't, at least to me."

"Shamus still hasn't told you anything more about it?"

"Nope," I confessed. "My best guess so far is Vegas. People pay big bucks to see some god-awful things there, like ancient Botoxed men playing with their pet tigers and Celine Dion warbling the *Titanic* song for the fourteen millionth time, right? Even a semidecent tribute band could probably pack 'em in."

"If that's the case," he said, "then at least it'll be fun to visit him there, right?"

"Right," I agreed, trying not to feel embarrassed by the fact that now not only did I have an eccentric, romance-novel-writing mom, but I'd added a cheesy-Vegas-performer dad to the mix. I pushed the not so nice thought right out of my head before it even came close to entering the discussion. And I was such an expert at that by now, it went away without even saying boo.

* * *

We followed the Weeble man outside the doors to a sleek black limo. I immediately added trying harder to understand Shamus's work to my list of goals for the week. Based on my limited understanding of his career, I'd assumed he'd pick us up in an old beater van and drive us to his bachelor pad located in the same seedy neighborhood all the wannabe musicians, actors, artists, and other entertainment types crashed in one-room apartments while waiting for their big break.

Obviously, I'd been way off the mark. See how much I actually knew about my dad? Next to nothing. And that realization put me this close to having a full-blown panic.

"Sweet," Zander whistled under his breath as he slid across the seat of the car, not noticing my near-hyperventilation.

"Po-teet," I added in breathy voice that sounded nothing like mine, and then started giggling like a crazy person over my nonsensical rhyme. When I saw Zander eying me like I was an escapee from an insane asylum, I bit the inside of my cheek and tried to settle down.

As we eased out onto the highway, the glass partition buzzed down to reveal the Weeble. "Mr. McDonohue stocked the bar with soft drinks for you two," he announced. "You'll also find some snacks back there along with a clicker for the TV and a DVD Mr. McDonohue thought you kids might enjoy."

It had been a long time since our last meal—the minuscule bag of peanuts they served us on the plane didn't count—so the snackage sounded great. While Zander rummaged through the minifridge, I scavenged for food. I got all choked up when I saw what Shamus had bought for me: Cheeze Doodles. Not Cheetos, fake-o bake-o cheese puffs, Pirate's Booty, or any of the other pretenders, but the honest-to-goodness real thing. I'd told Shamus during one of our more recent phone calls if I ever got stuck in a *Cast Away* kind of situation and by some freak of nature a crate of food washed ashore with me, I would want it to contain Cheeze Doodles. We never got around to his answer—his call-waiting had clicked in and he had to hop, as usual—so I had no clue what his answer would've been or how I'd ever be able to reciprocate.

"You want Coke, Diet Coke, Sprite?" Zander asked. "Or this?"

I did a double take: Z was holding up a bottle of posh-looking champagne. I pointed at it, unable to answer more directly because I was too busy shoveling not-found-in-nature orange curlicues into my face.

"This probably wasn't meant for us, you know," he said, giving me an are-you-sure? kind of look.

I nodded, trying unsuccessfully to remove the massive glob of Cheeze Doodles that was now glued to the roof of my mouth. "No worries," I said after I was finally able to swallow. "We'll plead ignorance if anyone says anything."

"Sounds like a plan." Z peeled off the foil cover and untwisted the wire cage. Positioning his thumbs under the cork, Zander gave a big push. Nothing happened. He tried again. The thing didn't move an inch.

"Need some assistance, babe?"

"You think you can do better, go for it," he said, looking slightly annoyed but still handing over the bottle.

Did I think I could do better? Uh, yea-aahhh. If I'd had control of the cork-popping from the start, I was sure we'd already be halfway through our first glass of bubbly by now. Positioning the bottle between my legs, I tugged gently, fully expecting the cork to slide out with ease. My plan was to shrug coyly at my instant success, give a Z a semicondescending smile, and say something cute, like, "Sometimes, it just takes a woman's touch."

Instead, absolutely nothing happened, knocking my unspoken

bravado down more than a few notches. Frustrated, I wiggled harder. Still nada. "What the hell . . . ?" I said, bending over to get a better view of the situation and attacking the thing with more violence than I'd intended.

This time, my effort was a little *too* successful and the cork came flying out at warp speed. The insane trajectory definitely would've taken it all the way to the moon had there not been a little thing like my forehead getting in the way. The aftermath was immediate: My brain slammed into the back of my skull and everything faded to black. It was like someone had suddenly pulled down the shades and turned off all the lights. "I can't see!" I screamed.

The scene was so right out of one of Bebe's books, I could almost hear the teaser copy—which was good, since I'd never be able to see it now that I was blind. *When a young woman loses her sight in an underage drinking accident, a mother must sacrifice her career—not to mention the greatest love of all—to teach her daughter how to navigate a darkened world. After many trials and tribulations, the two find new life lobbying Congress to offer CD track listings in Braille.* I added the last part because I knew Bebe always had to have something musical going on in her stories.

"Shhhhhhh," Zander said as the window came buzzing down again. Just in the nick of time, he tucked the bottle behind his legs.

"Everything OK back there, kids?"

I carefully probed the tender spot on my forehead for any signs of blood or brain oozeage. As far as I could tell, all my vital organs were intact, so I tried peeking through the cracks of my fingers. Discovering my sight had been miraculously restored, I dropped my hands from my face only to find the Weeble's concerned eyes staring at me in the rearview mirror.

"Absolutely," I answered.

"If you're sure then, miss," he said, the divider buzzing back up. "Just let me know if you need anything."

Once the Weeble was out of sight, Zander handed me a plastic cup full of champagne. "You OK now?"

I took a sip and nodded, still feeling a little deer-in-the-headlights-y. "Did it leave a mark?" I hoped the answer would be negatory. I'd spent the entire summer daydreaming about how great this reunion was going to be, and not one of my fantasies had starred Tracey Tillingham, deformed rhino. I didn't want to have to add an ugly little detail like that in now.

"Come on, you're totally fine," Zander said, sliding down the seat until he was nearly on top of me. "Not a scratch on you."

His sudden movement sent something sharp jabbing into my cheek—and I don't mean either of the ones on my face. "Oww," I yelped, reaching down to retrieve the offending butt-invader.

"What's wrong?" Zander asked. It sounded like maybe the cork drama had already filled his quota of tolerance for kooky injuries for the night.

I held up a hard, flat, square package. It was clearly the DVD Mr. Weeble Man had told us about, though it was too dark to make out exactly what movie we were about to enjoy. I started pushing buttons randomly in the hope of shedding some light on the subject. After the first few flicks, it was still dark, but Kenny Chesney's "Guitars and Tiki Bars" came blasting out of the speakers.

I shuddered and went to spin the tuner, but before my hand hit the dial, Zander stopped me. "This is my new favorite song! Remember how we were dancing to it down at the beach last weekend?"

Much to my dismay, Z had gotten on a total country music kick this summer. And while I love, love, *love* rock and pop-punk beyond all words, the truth is, I'd rather listen to a vacuum cleaner than country. But I guess in my effort to keep everything all peace-and-love-y, I'd kind of "forgotten" to mention that fact when Zander had me shimmying down into the sand with my back facing him during the song's chorus because he thought it made us look like two faces on a tiki.

Yeah, yeah, *I* know a tiki has only one face. He was probably thinking of a totem pole. But Zander? Apparently not so much. At the time, I'd chosen to let the whole tiki-totem thing slide, not wanting to ruin a perfectly fun afternoon by having to give Zander a lecture on semantics and the vileness of country music. Funny thing was, though, now didn't seem like the best moment to clear up my lack of love for Kenny and his crowd, either. It would be seriously hard to explain why I hadn't just said so in the first place. Anyway, expanding my musical horizons wouldn't kill me, I thought. In fact, it might actually turn out to be a valuable educational experience.

Yeah, right.

"Right," I said, leaving the tuner alone and shifting my attention to the next row of buttons. A touch here and a push there ended up activating the air-conditioning, which blew icicles into my face. After another few flicks, the AC went off and a blast of hellishly hot air nearly melted the hair off my head. Undaunted, I kept punching and flicking until that pesky divider started coming down again.

"Oh, crap, did I do that?" I asked, hitting every button in sight that might make it go back up. No such luck.

"Something I can help you with *now*, miss?" the driver asked, turning on the lights so I could finally make out that the DVD I was holding on to was a compilation of Kandy Kane videos. Where Shamus had gotten the idea I even remotely liked songs that featured computer generated bleeps and bloops instead of real instruments and the wailing of a girl dressed like some random

Yu-Gi-Oh character was beyond me. I'm way more Liz Phair, Sleater-Kinney, and The Donnas—all of whom bring slashing guitar riffs, serious musical chops, and ballsy lyrics to the table—than Hilary, Lindsay, or Ashlee. Oh, well, add another item to my to-do list: Tell Dad about musical preferences. I thought for a second and then added a mental asterisk: *When Z isn't around, so I don't have to commit either way to Mr. Chesney and the country crew.*

"No, thank you, Mr. Wee—" Oh, God, now I'd gone and almost called him a Weeble to his face. I had to think quick. "Mr. Wee-mousine driver, I just pushed the wrong button. Sorry."

This time, the divider didn't immediately slide right back up. Instead, the driver held my gaze in the rearview mirror. I panicked, thinking we were completely busted about the champagne.

"I can explain . . ." I trailed off, running circles around in my mind in search of a reasonable explanation as to why two underage kids might think it was just fine and dandy to bust open and drink an expensive bottle of alcohol that was not rightfully theirs. I was trying to decide between "I thought the drinking age in California was eighteen for beer and wine" and "Oh, this? Isn't it sparkling grape juice?" when the driver interrupted me.

"No need for explanations," he said. I heaved a silent sigh of relief that was cut short when I heard his next comment. "I was just wondering if you'd like some ice for that."

I stared into my drink, thinking it was pretty gauche of him to offer ice for champagne—I mean, even *I* know you don't do that—when I realized he hadn't taken his eyes off me in minutes. Or, more specifically, my forehead. I peered into the mirror and saw an angry red circle smack between my eyes. It looked like maybe my loony grandparents had gotten a little off track with their dotty dabbers at the senior center's Bring Your Granddaughter to Bingo night.

"No, thanks, it's just some marker from a belated Father's Day card I was writing to Shamus, nothing a little soap and water won't fix," I babbled nervously, even though I realized that a) talking way too fast and b) giving way too many ridiculous details were the top two surest signs of lying.

"Mmm-hmm," the driver said, closing the divider for the final time of our ride.

As soon as I was certain the guy was back in his own habitat, I shot Zander a look that wasn't usually part of my repertoire with him. "Why didn't you tell me about the cork hickey, dude?" I asked, digging through my bag looking for some heavy-duty cover-up. It was obvious the sweet and agreeable persona I'd so carefully crafted this summer was ready to take a very long hike, leaving the dark side in charge for a while.

Zander shrugged, seemingly oblivious to the fact that I'd almost outed myself as a person who might spin her head around and spit pea soup if her boyfriend neglected to tell her there was a horn growing between her eyeballs. "I didn't even notice. It's so small you can barely see it," he said, popping in the DVD. A second later, his eyes began growing a size a second. "Just like that smokin' Kandy's little outfits."

A weird pain stabbed me somewhere between my heart and my gut. "You think Kandy's hot?"

Zander glanced over at me in disbelief. "I'm a guy, aren't I?"

"Since when?" I demanded.

"Since I was born."

"I meant, since when do you like her?" I knew it wasn't like she was going to come over and smear her pink and white grease paint all over Zander's body, but still. He wasn't supposed to be rhapsodizing about other girls in my presence, was he?

"Since who cares and why does it matter?" he asked, looking truly perplexed now.

"It matters because there are a million talented musicians out there, and Kandy isn't one of them," I insisted, opting for a less embarrassing musical argument rather than admitting I was plain old jealous. "She has no right being famous when so many other bands deserve the recognition."

Z shrugged. "I'm a musician, and I don't hold it against her."

"I'm talking about *musician* musicians. People who can play more than just A, E, and D." I'd been completely disillusioned about Zander's artistic abilities when I finally figured out he always used the same three chords no matter what song he was playing. When I questioned him about it, Z finally had to admit they were pretty much the only ones he knew.

"Still not buying it," Zander said with a little half grin, like he found my sudden conviction amusing and was trying not to laugh at me.

His reaction only served to spur me on, so I switched tactics. "Well, what about the fact that she's completely brainless? Doesn't that bother you? 'Hee hee hee, is this chicken or tuna? I didn't know buffalos had wings. I can't even say Massa-twoshits.' Give me a break."

"You're thinking of Jessica Simpson, Trace."

"Same difference." All the teen queens ran together in my book, whether they wore weird makeup or not. "I mean, what is it you find appealing about her, anyway?"

Z slung his arm around me and started ticking things off his fingers. "Number one: She's beautiful."

"You have a bizarre cartoon character fetish, is that it?"

Zander ignored me and kept going. "Number two, and I hope

you're taking notes because this is a biggie: She's got a killer body. Number three—"

I interrupted him midsentence with another inane, completely obvious question. "Don't you even care that there's nothing natural about her body?"

"Nope," Z grunted, mesmerized. "Anyway, it looks completely natural to me."

I looked down at my so not big chest, which was by now bubbling in an uncomfortable vat of envy. "Really? Even though her boobs never seem to move?"

"Move, schmove," he said, never glancing my way. "The chick's top half is tremendous. Same goes for her bottom half."

I sighed, feeling small and insignificant and amoeba-like. "I hear she has major zits, and that's why she's never seen without all that goop on her face."

Zander finally managed to pull his eyes away from the video long enough to note my major psychic pain. "You're cute when you're mad, you know that? And I think you're hotter than Kandy any day, if that's what all this is about."

I didn't really care that he was lying through his perfectly white teeth, it was just what I needed to hear at that moment. "Hmmmm-mmmm," I said, trying not to smile but not really succeeding.

"And who needs big boobs anyway?" Zander added, back-pedaling even more. "It's like that old saying. More than a handful is wasted."

Feeling very lucky to have Z in my life—even if he made slightly gross and completely false analogies about how much he preferred little chests to big ones—I planted a grateful smooch on him that just kept on going for the rest of the ride.

CHAPTER
3

The limo took a sharp turn and slowed to a stop. Without the forward motion to lull us into a false sense of security that we were all alone and somewhere other than the backseat of a car, reality set in—we were finally at Shamus's place—and our little lovefest came to an abrupt halt. We frantically tried to tuck and fix and pat everything back into the right place, and had just about gotten ourselves presentable by the time the Weeble opened the door.

"We're here, miss," the Wee-mousine driver said, offering me an outstretched hand. "I do hope everything was to your satisfaction."

I reviewed the last hour quickly in my mind. Things I could've done without: Kenny Chesney, Kandy Kane, and the near-blinding incident. Things that rocked: the Cheeze Doodles, champagne, and making out with my boyfriend in the back of a limo. I decided, on the whole, it had been the ride of a lifetime. "It certainly was," I assured him.

We followed the driver as he hauled our bags and dropped them on the front porch. His finger was just about to ring the doorbell when I realized I was holding my breath. Please, please let everything turn out OK, I prayed. Please, please let my dad and me like each other and get along and want to stay connected after this little visit. Please, God. Please.

Just as I was about to move on to the amen part, Shamus opened the front door and pulled me into an awkward hug. "You made it!"

"Yup," I said, finally exhaling as he patted my back in staccato bursts.

"So how was the flight? And the drive here?"

I pulled back to look at him. Just as I remembered. A little bit Springsteen, a little bit me. "Awesome, thanks so much," I said, my smile practically splitting my face in two. "It's so great to see you again."

"Me, too. I mean you, too. I mean . . . you know what I mean," my dad laughed.

My dad. It was so weird to be able to say those two words, even if it was just in my head, after so many years of wondering who he was and whether he ever thought about me. And now here we were, together in the same place for a whole week, staring at each other like two goofy idiots. And we probably would've stayed like that for hours, or maybe even days, if a completely jarring crackling noise hadn't broken the magical spell. It was Zander's knuckles again, of course.

"I almost forgot," I said, fumbling around for the proper way to make the introductions. "Shamus, this is my boyfriend, Zander. Zander, this is Shamus."

The guys stuck out their hands and shook competitively, as if whoever pumped harder would be crowned my hero. "Heard a lot about you, man," Shamus said, giving Zander the once-over.

"You, too," Zander said, his eyes taking a walk all over Shamus. So far, the conversation was like two cavemen grunting at each other. Men are so weird.

"I trust you're taking good care of my daughter," Shamus said.

"Definitely. And I trust you intend to be a good father to her," Zander replied. "Better late than never, you know?"

I blushed even harder than when I split the seam of my pants in second grade and everyone saw my Rainbow Brite underwear. Because as great as it was to feel the love on both sides, it was also totally embarrassing to watch Shamus trying to cram eighteen years of Papa Bear watching over his cub into this moment, and Zander coming right back at him with his very own protective boyfriend routine.

"Come on," I said, trying to reduce the ridiculous level of testosterone flying around out there. "Let's all go inside and be good to each other."

"Welcome to the disaster area," Shamus joked as we walked in the house. Cardboard boxes lined the walls, and everything looked sparkling, shiny, and new. Not to mention empty. "I just moved in last week and things have been so crazy I haven't had a chance to organize anything yet."

"It's a great place," I told Shamus as he escorted us from room to unfinished room. "And it will be even better once you're unpacked."

My dad laughed. "It's probably going to be a while before that happens. I'm a pretty busy guy these days."

Seeing the echoing expanse of empty rooms, I remembered my misguided thoughts about where I'd be spending the week. "I don't know why, but I had it in my head you lived in a studio, somewhere more cityish," I admitted.

"That's because I used to," Shamus said, flashing that warm grin at me again. "I just moved in here last week. Part of the super-secret business deal, you know."

I was about to beg my dad to just spill it already when Zander butted in. "Supersized is more like it. This place is totally blinged out."

I thought Shamus might take offense to Z's assessment, but

instead his chest puffed out like a proud peacock's. Men. Again. "It is, isn't it?"

"Yup," Z replied, back to caveman conversation again.

"And now, for the pièce de résistance," Shamus said, flinging open a door to reveal the one fully decorated room in the house. It was clearly mine, an exact replica of page twenty-five of the PB Teen catalog—the one I'd told him featured my dream digs.

"I don't know what to say," I said, forgetting all about Shamus's mysterious business stuff and focusing on trying not to choke on the lump that had spontaneously formed in my throat instead. So he *had* been listening to me, even though our conversations never lasted very long.

"Say you love it," Shamus said, slinging his arm around my shoulder and squeezing me tight. "Say you're surprised and happy and want to stay in it every time you visit. Say it makes up in some little way for us not knowing each other until now."

"All of the above." I threw myself at Shamus and hugged him so hard he nearly fell on his butt. It was still a little awkward, but definitely getting less so every time.

"Believe it or not, I have one more surprise for you. And it makes this one look like small potatoes."

I couldn't imagine something that would make my dad not only *saying* he wanted me in his life but actually *proving* it seem anything less than humongous, but I was willing to give it a shot. A minute later, when we were standing in front of the glistening freeform pool complete with a waterfall, my suspicions were confirmed. I mean, for sure it was cool, but nowhere near as personally big for me as the Cheeze Doodles and customized bedroom had been.

"Sweet," Zander said, dipping a big toe in the water.

"Yeah, it's totally awesome, Shamus," I added with an enthusiasm I wasn't feeling. "I'm sure we'll spend a lot of time out here."

My dad laughed. "This isn't the surprise," he said, motioning for us to follow him. "This is."

Shamus led us down a moonlit path and there, hidden among the palm trees and tropical shrubbery, was the coolest little guest-house I'd ever seen. It was exactly the kind of a place the *Real World* cast would get to live in. "This is unbelievable!" I screamed, jumping around like one of those overly excitable game show contestants.

"You ain't seen nothin' yet, sister," my dad said from behind me. His voice sounded like it had a smile in it.

With a loud clap, Shamus magically turned on all the lights both inside and out of the place. With each step we took, something more incredible would appear. First it was the his-n-hers Roxy and Quicksilver surfboards leaning against the fence. Then it was a trampoline built into the pristine lawn, followed by the swings suspended from the roof of the front porch gently banging in the breeze against the tiki bar.

"It's so . . . so . . ." I trailed off. Whose place was this, anyway? It was too full of stuff kids my age liked to be my dad's, no matter how young at heart he seemed to be. And it couldn't possibly be mine, not with the designed-just-for-me room back at the main house. Could it?

"So not over yet," he said, shushing me. "The biggest surprise is yet to come."

Bigger than everything out here? I might have a heart attack. Oh, well. At least I'd die happy.

"Here it is," he said, making a big show of putting the key card into the front door before he swung it open. "Tah-dah!"

I gasped. The inside of the place was even more incredible than the outside. A whole wall of windows aimed directly at the water made me feel more like I was on a yacht than on land. A silver juke-box that looked like an alien spaceship beckoned from the corner, begging me to punch a few buttons and get it rocking. The most enormous plasma television I'd ever seen was on the east wall and in the shelves to the right, what must've been the world's most comprehensive DVD and Xbox library. To top it all off, my most favorite arcade game ever—Dance Dance Revolution—sat in the far corner, just waiting for me to come and play with it.

"Holy shi—" Zander started to say. I stomped on his toes before he could complete his thought. No way was I going to let a potentially offensive swear word ruin what might seriously turn out to be the best moment of my life.

"How did you know—" I began again.

"Uh, uh uh. Please hold all questions until the end of the tour," Shamus said with a smile so big his eyes had all but disappeared. Then he turned to Zander. "That goes for all curses, too, however appreciative they may be."

On to the bedrooms. The first held two bunks that looked like they were suspended in thin air. As I got closer, I saw they were actually held up by a network of clear cables. Everything in the place was cutting-edge and futuristic, from the podlike furniture to the Power Macs on the twin desks. The other bedroom was the polar opposite of the first: soft, fluffy, fit for a princess. The sumptuous king-sized bed even had a flowing canopy. I had always wanted something like it as a kid, but my room at home was too small for anything but a twin sans headboard. Now, really, how had my dad known my deepest little girl desires? It was like he was a mind reader or something. Maybe the place *was* mine after all?

Next up: the bathroom, complete with huge Jacuzzi tub and steam shower and the plumfiest towels I'd ever felt. Then a loft carpeted in white fake fur that was practically begging for people to take off their clothes and roll around on it. And finally, the kitchen. Not something I'd normally care much about, seeing as my idea of making a meal consists of pouring cereal into a bowl and adding milk, but this was different. The main attraction here—a soda fountain complete with cups and lids and straws and crushed ice and everything else I love but usually have to hit 7-Eleven to get—was a total dream come true.

The place was definitely mine, mine, all mine. Why else would Shamus choose Pepsi products—my favorite—rather than Coke, which most people prefer? I was completely speechless. Blown away. Ready to crash to the floor in a grateful heap and kiss my dad's feet for caring so much he'd not only personalized a room in the main house for me, but had built his only daughter this cool mini crash pad and stocked it with everything she loved.

"Check this out," Shamus said, flipping a switch. Instantly, the lights dimmed, "I Want Kandy" blared from every speaker in the house, and the words KANDY'S ROOM lit up the west wall in neon pink.

The blatant advertisement for his company splashed all over in laser lights hit me as a little over-the-top in terms of self-promotion. And as for the musical accompaniment to the big unveiling? The best I could figure it, either my dad a) was a way creepy fan of the fake Harajuku girl or b) thought I might be. Before I could thank Shamus for the amazing apartment while kindly setting the record straight about my opinions about Miss Kandy Kane, Zander busted in again with his own unrelated musings.

"With a spread like this, your company must be insanely successful," Zander said, his mouth hanging open. "Are you producing the real Springsteen now or something?"

Shamus shook his head. "That's your best guess after everything I've shown you?"

"Get serious, Zander. It's a Vegas deal, right?" I said, testing out my theory from earlier in the airport.

"You're getting warmer," Shamus told me. "Because that might be one stop on the tour, though it's definitely not going to be the only one."

"You mean you're hitting the road with Born to Run?" I asked, feeling totally let down and wishing he'd at least stay in one place long enough for us to get to know each other before heading off into the sunset. "A real extended tour? Europe, Asia, the works?"

"You think I'm talking about *my* band?" he laughed, pointing to his chest. "That's just what I do for fun, not my career."

"Really?" I realized I had *zero* idea what my dad did on a daily basis.

Shamus shook his head. "Nope."

"And it's not The E Streeters you're touring with, either?" Zander reiterated.

"Now you're approaching a Chicago in winter kind of cold," Shamus said, wrapping his arms around his body and pretending to shiver uncontrollably.

Zander and I stared at each other and shook our heads. "Give us a hint," I said.

"Think, kids. The DVD, KANDY'S ROOM spelled out in lights, 'I Want Kandy' on the jukebox . . ."

"You mean that wasn't just because you named your company after your favorite Bruce song?" Zander asked.

"No. In that case, it would've been candy with a C, not a K," Shamus told us.

We both stared at my dad for a long time, mouths gaping open and shut like beached little fishies. Certain pieces of the puzzle were becoming clear, though I couldn't quite put them all together yet. I assumed Z was feeling the same way.

"Fine, I'll tell you," Shamus said, breaking the silence. "The big surprise is that I'm the creator and executive director of Kandy

Kane's new reality show—*Kandy's Room*. She'll live here with her mom and we'll film their lives. Kind of like a cross between *The Ashlee Simpson Show* and the *Gastineau Girls.* Cool, huh?"

"Whoa!" Zander said, his eyes big as Frisbees. "Awesome!"

Speaking of reality, something that should've been obvious before finally became clear to me: This amazing house was hers, all hers, and not even a measly straw or to-go cup of it was for me.

"So what do you think?" Shamus was looking at me expectantly.

Not wanting to seem ungrateful about the amazing room that *was* mine or less than impressed with my dad's big coup, I struggled for something positive to say. "That's . . . wow . . . Kandy's so . . . uh . . ." After a few torturous seconds, I finally found a word. "*Popular* these days."

Zander shot me a look. "Actually, Trace ha—"

I shot him a look right back. "H-h-has been listening to her CDs lately, you mean?" I interrupted before Z could utter the word hate.

Zander furrowed his brow so much it looked like caterpillars were invading his eyeballs. "But we were just talking in the car about how—"

"How h-h-hot Kandy was, right?"

"Right," he said, looking completely confused.

Shamus beamed, so I felt like I'd done the right thing, trading my harsh reality for a more polished, albeit skewed, version of it. "Her career certainly is sizzling, isn't it?" he asked us.

"On fire," Zander agreed, dropping his attempt to get a confession out of me, though he was still giving me the evil eye. "So can you introduce us to her?"

"Absolutely," Shamus said, giving Z a little wink.

I looked around the place again. What had seemed overwhelmingly exciting just a few minutes ago now just seemed overwhelming. I decided a change of scenery might help me get a better perspective on everything that was happening.

"How about we all grab a Pepsi and head back up to the pool?" I said.

Shamus looked at me in surprise. "I was kind of thinking you guys might want to hang out here for a while. You know, without the old man watching over you."

"Don't be silly," I said, instantly jumping to his defense. "And anyway, you're not old."

Shamus cleared his throat. "The truth is, I actually have some last-minute shit to get done," he said, his hand flying to his mouth after dropping the S-word. "Oops, sorry. I meant stuff. Get some stuff done."

It was so totally endearing—his thinking he had to censor himself around me, the veritable queen of foul language before I quit last year with lots of help from Brina—it almost made me feel better about his having to take off already, before we got the chance to kick back together. "I've heard the other word before, Shamus. Quite a few times."

He gave me a sheepish little smile. "I guess we're going to have to make up the rules as we go along, huh, honey?"

"That sounds like fun." And it did, because it was something we'd be doing together.

"How about this for our first rule?" Shamus proposed. "Let's make sure to break one every once in a while. For instance, the crew was very serious about everything in here being spotless for when Kandy and her mom move in tomorrow, but I say go for it. Why don't you guys stay here, play the games, use the computers, do whatever while I get back to work? Just remember to clean everything up before you leave."

"That's such a rad idea, Shamus," Zander said, hopping around in excitement. Or who knows, maybe he just had to pee. "Thanks!"

"Yeah, it is," I said, opening the door and leading us all back out onto the porch even though I was still hoping my dad would reconsider and postpone his work until the a.m. I mean, wasn't the point of my being here so we could get to know each other, not so I could have the chance to roll around on the fake fur rug with Z? "But maybe we could help you get your stuff done first? You know, six hands are better than two and all?"

"Actually, I'd rather you just have a good time while you're here. There's no reason for my job to interfere with your vacation," Shamus said as he started up the path back to the house. He was totally not getting the fact that I'd flown halfway across the country for spiritual quantum-leaping, not a vacation. I was about to yell after him, to try to clarify the deal, when he called over his shoulder, "Now don't do anything I wouldn't do."

Superglueing our souls together clearly wasn't going to happen tonight. "Of course not," I called back.

As soon as Shamus was out of sight, Z took my face in his hands and started attacking me. "You're totally delicious, did you know that?" he whispered between kisses.

I was grateful for the cover of semidarkness so he couldn't see the humongous blush parading up my cheeks and over my ears. "But not as tasty as Kandy, right?"

He stopped kissing me and sighed. "Why do you always do that?" he asked, ducking behind the bar. A few sloshes, whirrs, and clink-clinks later, he popped back up with two blue frozen drinks in hand. "Can't you ever just accept a compliment without trying to find some kind of hidden meaning in it?"

It was a tricky question I couldn't begin to answer, so I changed the subject instead. "How do you know how to make these?"

"When I was little, I used to watch every episode of *MacGyver* with my dad."

"And how can one drink be so freezing and so toasty at the same time?" It was cold yet somehow still burned a path down to my stomach.

"It's the rum float," he told me. "Gets 'em every time."

After a few more sips of the yummy concoction, all the tension in my body started easing out my fingertips and toes, and it hit me that Zander was totally right. I really did need to stop stressing, to stop searching for ulterior motives when it came to him. "And by the way, thanks for the compliment before."

"You're welcome," he said, swirling the little umbrella around in his glass. "And here's one more. I'm really going to miss seeing you every day when we're at school."

I grinned, his words melting my resolve to always keep it cool. "Me, too."

I'm not sure if it was the rum float making me feel so reckless or just that I didn't want to waste what was basically a perfect storm of a situation—the unbeatable setting, being unexpectedly alone in it, and Zander spewing nice stuff about me left and right—but either way, a brilliant plan had just popped into my head. Even if it *was* a strategy I'd just advised my best friend against implementing for a plethora of valid reasons. "Know what we should do after this drink?"

He let his head fall back and sighed. "Play Xbox?"

"Not even close," I whispered, strategically placing a hand on his thigh.

"Don't tell me you want me to try DDR again," he said, completely missing the point.

"Nope again."

"Thank God. You know how bad I suck at it. Not to mention it's a total chick game."

I was hoping he'd get my drift without me having to spell the whole thing out. "Remember when I snuck over to your house last New Year's Day?"

He opened his eyes a crack and peered at me. "The time you were so mad at Bebe, you mean?"

"Yeah."

"And?"

Clearly, he was not deciphering the message just yet. Taking a big slug of my drink, I said, "You know . . . I was wearing the pink bunny slippers?"

Zander's eyes nearly shot out into the ocean. "Are you serious?"

I nodded. "Yup." I really didn't know when hanging on to my virginity had turned into such a big deal—especially after hearing all Brina's swinging-from-the-ceiling sex stories—but at this point, it was getting ridiculous. Anyway, I was going to make it onto the endangered species list if I kept it up much longer. Technical name: collegius freshmanus virginus.

We chugged the rest of our drinks in record time, then semifell out of the swings and kissed and stumbled our way to the front door.

"I need the key card," Zander said, coming up for air for just a second.

"I thought you had it," I said, nuzzling his earlobe, afraid to let myself think for fear I'd totally bail.

"You're kidding, right?" I could almost hear the sound effect that would've gone along with our predicament—a record needle being pulled off an album, leaving only silence where cheesy love songs had been playing seconds earlier.

"Sorry, no," I said. "Didn't my dad give it to you?"

Z shoved his hands in his pockets. "I thought he gave it to *you*."

Zander looked so pathetic—like he was about to cry, really—I just couldn't help but laugh. Giggles that started as tiny bubbles in my stomach poured from my lips, and there wasn't a thing I could do to stop their sudsy escape plan.

"What's so funny?" Zander asked, kicking the gravel like some angry little kid.

"I was just thinking maybe it was a sign. Like, maybe the timing's not right, no matter how much we want it to be."

"Either that," Zander griped, slouching down even farther. "Or maybe your dad just forgot to give us the key card."

Or maybe some higher power wanted to stop me from doing something I might regret, I added silently as we walked back up to the main house. Like, maybe the Goddess of Passion knew it wasn't just pure, unadulterated love prompting the big move on my part; it was basically just a desperate attempt to get over the hump—no pun intended—of all the lame-o insecurities I still had about our relationship. Not exactly the best reason for giving up your virginity, even I had to admit.

"Hey, kids." Shamus's voice floated up from a lounge at the pool where he was tapping away on his BlackBerry, startling us out of Z's pity party and my giggle party. "What happened to your big night in Kandy's room?"

"We decided we'd rather hang with the old man," I teased, giving my dad a little chuck on the shoulder.

"That's nice. And a good thing, too," Shamus said, getting up from the chair. "Because I just got a message from my crew. They need to do some emergency diagnostic testing on the sound and video tonight, and I wouldn't want you to be embarrassed by having to see an instant replay of your evening in the editing room tomorrow morning."

A flash of relief lit up my entire being. I mean, come on now. What if I had actually gone through the plan? My dad would have been witness to my deflowering, the whole horrifying scene committed to tape, and I'd become the next in a long line of people caught doing the nasty on camera—though I hardly thought we'd garner as much interest from the buying public as say, Tommy Lee and Pamela or Paris Hilton and What's-his-face.

"That was a close one," I whispered to Zander.

This time, it was Z's turn to laugh. "Maybe you were right. Maybe it was a sign, after all."

CHAPTER
4

"Yo, sweet child of mine," Shamus called through my bedroom door. "You interested in being on *Kandy's Room* while you're here? You could be an extra in some scenes we're shooting this week or be interviewed for a montage of fan shout-outs we're filming for the opening credits."

"Mmmmppphh," I mumbled into my pillow, trying to regain consciousness but not quite succeeding.

When I failed to add anything further, Shamus added, "Or if you're not ready for something up close and personal quite yet, you could be part of the audience at the free concert later on today."

Me, the girl who couldn't even stand getting my school picture taken, on TV? Me, the one who babbled and stammered and blushed my way through my shout-out on *TRL* last year, being interviewed? Me, who flipped the channel every time "I Want Kandy" came on, watching her "sing" live? I didn't think so.

"Maybe later, Shamus," I croaked, throwing the pillow over my head and pulling the comforter up over my shoulders. I'd have to remember to fill him in later about my usual sleeping habits (late, late, late) and level of interest in grabbing my fifteen minutes of fame (I'd happily donate them to someone else so they could have thirty).

"We'll come down later, after we've gotten some more shut-eye and taken showers and had breakfast and everything."

"Who's we?" he called back. "The Z man is already dressed and ready to go."

I should have figured Zander would be way too awake and way too intrigued by the whole situation to wait the requisite four or so hours more I normally would have slept if it hadn't been for all the knocking and conversation.

"On second thought, maybe I'll join you."

"No rush. We'll wait," Shamus called from outside my door, as if I'd even considered for a moment that maybe they wouldn't.

I quickly hopped into the shower, shaving, exfoliating, and moisturizing every body part within reach whether it needed it or not. After I finished my head-to-toe naked makeover, I dumped the entire contents of my suitcase on the floor, surveying all my options before pulling my most casually sexy outfit from the pile—Joe's Rock Star jeans, chunky funky espadrille updates, and a silky halter top. Then I dried my hair until it shined like those Pantene commercials and glommed on more makeup than I'd worn to the prom. *Extradom, here I come,* I thought.

"Whoa," Z said, whistling as he caught a load of my unusually decked-out self. "Look at the hottie who just walked out of Trace's room."

I rolled my eyes at him and smiled. "Cut it out."

"Just take the compliment, remember? The appropriate response is 'Thank you,'" Zander said with a grin.

"Thank you," I corrected myself.

"You look stunning, hon," Shamus said, glancing up from his bowl of cereal. "But a bit overdressed. Did I forget to mention the concert is on the beach? A bathing suit would've done the trick."

I looked over at Zander again and saw he was wearing his Reef sandals, Jams, and an ancient Abercrombie T-shirt. I sighed—all that effort for nothing. Turning around, I walked back into my room and shut the door, reemerging a few seconds later in the same outfit, minus the jeans, plus one Chip and Pepper miniskirt.

"OK, now I'm ready to rock," I said, still overdressed for the beach, but what the hell. At least I'd look as good as possible when Zander inevitably started comparing me to my dad's little protégé.

We all hoofed it down to the guesthouse together, at which point Shamus immediately excused himself with an apology. "We've still got some work to do on the sound in here. Totally boring stuff. So why don't you guys head on down to the beach? Much more exciting things are going to be happening down there."

I peered down the very long, steep flights of stairs from Kandy's Room to where the stage was set up, and saw it had already become a temporary home away from home for an enormous crowd of teenyboppers. Everyone was waving signs and posters and whatever other Kandyphernalia they could get their grubby little hands on.

"Don't these kids have parents?" I wondered out loud, then immediately hoped my dad hadn't heard me.

Apparently, he had. "It's summer, Trace," Shamus told me gently. I loved the way his eyes crinkled at the corners when he smiled at me. "Time for surf, sun, and sand. Besides, we've been promoting this event nonstop on WHOT all week in the hopes we'd get a turnout like this."

"Right," I said, realizing how crabby my last comment had sounded—and, well, who wouldn't be crabby, getting up hours earlier than usual and not even having my daily latte yet? Still, I wished I could suck the words right back into my lungs. Since that wasn't an option, I tried to make up for it by being overly enthusiastic, adding an exclamation point after everything I said next. "I mean, what a great idea! This is so exciting for Kandy's fans! And it must be really exciting for you, too!"

"It is," my dad agreed, seemingly unaware I didn't normally talk like a cheerleader on a sugar high. "The truth is, this show is the break I've been waiting for my entire career. I'm just crossing my fingers that everything goes perfectly."

"I'm sure it will, Shamus," Zander told him, giving him a manly slap between the shoulders.

Shamus beamed at Zander, giving him way more than the little eye crinkles I'd gotten just a second ago. I was just going to have to learn to love Kandy, that was all there was to it. "Yeah. You're going to be a total A-lister from now on," I added, all fake confidence. I went to give my dad the same kind of pat Zander had just bestowed upon him, but unfortunately I misjudged my own strength.

"I'm sure you're right," Shamus said, still coughing from what had actually turned out to be more of a whack. "I'll come find you guys later, when we've met all the technical requirements in here."

After my dad disappeared inside the house, I turned to Zander. "So, are we really going to hit Lipsynchapalooza?"

"Of course we are," Z said, looking just as excited as the kids in the crowd even though we were a good five years older than most of them. "Didn't you hear Shamus talking about all the cool stuff going on this afternoon, like the DJs and the crazy contests? It's going be just like MTV *Spring Break*, only maybe a little less racy, since most of these kids are underage."

"That's an understatement," I said as we took our places on the back of a depressingly long line.

Z let out a sigh so long and loud it sounded like a leaky tire. "If you'd rather we did something else, why don't you just say so?"

"I didn't say I want to do something else," I said, knowing full well I was having a hard time covering up the fact that I actually did. "I think this is going to be tons of fun. Though maybe more like Nickelodeon's *Slime Time Live* than MTV's *Spring Break*."

Z peered at me out of the corner of his eye. "Why do I get the feeling you're not being a hundred percent truthful?"

"Not a clue," I said, taking another half shuffle forward. "Maybe you're just paranoid?" Ha. As if I didn't already have that territory covered.

"Trace, what's the deal with you lately?"

"Huh?" The unexpected question had me pretty much shaking in my completely inappropriate high-heeled sandals.

"I'm not a mind reader, you know," he said, sounding even grumpier than I had before about the kiddie crew on the beach. "And neither is your dad."

"Make that three of us. So why don't you just tell me what's bothering you so I don't have to guess?" My heart was pounding so loudly in my ears by this point, I wondered if I'd even be able to hear his answer.

"What's bothering me is you being so evasive all of a sudden," Zander said. "Like last night, when you wouldn't admit Kandy's music really isn't your style. What's that all about?"

"It's called being polite," I explained, wondering how such a smart guy could be so slow. "And besides, it's not like I actually came out and told my dad I liked Kandy or anything. I just failed to mention that I *didn't* like her. There's a big difference."

"Give me a break," Zander said, rolling his eyes. "I know you're nervous because this is the first time you've really hung out with Shamus, but saying stuff you don't mean—or not saying what you do mean, or whatever it is you just told me you did last night—isn't going to help matters."

"Okaaayyy," I said, feeling like I'd just gotten sent to the principal's office for something I didn't do. "But didn't you hear how excited he was about his big announcement? I didn't want to be a buzzkill."

"He'd still be excited, even without you pretending to be a fan. And he'd still like you, too, if that's what you were worried about."

"I guess I can see your point," I said, not sure if I was really on board with what he was saying or just pretending to be so we could stop talking about it quicker. "I'll try to sit him down and explain it later, OK?"

"OK."

"So everything's cool now, right?"

"Actually, there's one more thing I've been wanting to ask you."

Damn it, my plan to just move on already was so not working. "What's that?"

"You don't do that to me, do you, Trace?" Zander was looking so deep into my eyes I felt like he was trying to cram his entire body inside my brain. "Pretend to like stuff to make me happy?"

I considered spilling the beans right then and there. Really I did. It would've been such a weight off my shoulders, letting Z in on a few key facts. Like the one about not really wanting to play foosball every time I was over his house. Or that I thoroughly hated any music with a fiddle and upright bass in it. And that, sorry, like it or not, I really *did* love him—or at least I thought I had, until he scared the feeling into some dark recess of my body that felt like it was located closer to my intestines than my heart. But then I saw the look in his eye, and I just couldn't bring myself to admit any of it, not a single thing.

"Of course not."

"Good. I would've thought we were in serious trouble if you did."

And at least this way, only I was. "Nope, things are totally co-pasetic."

"Double good," he said, giving me a sweaty hug. "Because if we weren't being honest with each other now, I can't imagine we'd very good at making the long distance thing work once we're at school, either."

Since the line we were stuck in was barely moving, I had plenty of time to think about what Zander had just said, and what I was going to do about it. It was hard to strategize exactly where to begin, though, because even if the line was creeping forward slower than a sleeping snail, it was way louder than one. The ever increasing throng of kids surrounding us seemed to punctuate every sentence with a shriek or an "Oh, my God, look! It's Kandy!" Which, of course, it never was—just some other girl in war paint.

A million shrieks and *oh, my God*'s and no progress on my plan later, we finally made it to the paperwork table and signed pages and pages of forms, all of which I assumed gave Shamus and MTV the rights to televise anything we said or did during the concert. Not that I actually read the thing. I mean, what was the point? I knew I was going to stay as far away from the camera as possible, and if forced into the spotlight, anything I said wouldn't be fit for tweener consumption, anyway.

"Would you be interested in participating in one or more private, invitation-only events with Kandy this week? For example, there's a party Thursday that would be perfect for you two. Clips of it will air with the first episode," she said, dangling out the possibility of being on TV like it was a priceless treasure. Not knowing, of course, that we could be front and center in any of 'em just by asking Shamus, though that didn't dampen Zander's enthusiasm even one iota. He was so caught up in the excitement of having unlimited access to Kandy he could barely keep his feet on the ground.

"Definitely!" Zander said a nanosecond before I was about to shake my head no.

"What kind of party?" I asked instead, stalling for time.

"A very cool one at an extremely hip club. There'll be refreshments, music, foam dancing, that sort of thing."

Zander scanned the information Release Form Lady had shoved under our noses more closely. "Whoa, you get paid for it, too?"

"Yup, a small stipend for your time," she told us. "Even more if we end up using any interviews we do with you, or footage of you interacting with Kandy."

"We are so in," Zander said.

"Make that *he's* so in," I told the woman. "Sounds way too close to an acting gig for me."

"I forgot about how you hate being in the spotlight," Zander said, looking a little disappointed but definitely not like he hated me or anything. "I should probably bag it too, right?"

"Naaah, you go ahead," I told him.

"You sure?" Zander asked, still riffling through the packet of information. "It says here the shoot is going to take all afternoon."

"Afternoon?" I was momentarily distracted by how lame it all sounded—Kandy deigning to hang with regular peons like us at a supposedly hip club on a Thursday *afternoon*? Didn't she know normal people partied at night?

Release Form Lady looked a little embarrassed. "We had to schedule it for the daytime because so many of Kandy's fans have early curfews, especially on weeknights."

"Oh." So it was even lamer than I'd originally thought.

Z took his pen to the forms more than once, but never quite got around to putting ink to paper. Finally, he looked back up at me and said, "Trace, this is crap. You invited me here so we could hang out, right?"

"Right."

"So then we're going to hang."

"Come on. It's only one day," Release Form Lady said. "You don't have to sign up for any other events if you don't want to."

"Sorry," Z said, slinging his arm around my shoulder and breaking into a grin. "But I'm sticking with her."

I slid my hand in his back pocket and pulled him close to me. Why had I ever doubted him?

"Keep moving, keep moving," a girl in a neon green WHOT baby-doll yelled into a megaphone as we were escorted into a fenced-in pen of crazy Kandyaholics. The crowd of kids was smushing and shoving each other so hard in an effort to get closest to the stage it almost seemed like a mosh pit at a Slipknot concert. Until you saw how young everybody was, and how they all were made up like they were headed for an animé convention. "We want to get as many people as possible in here for Kandy's performance later on this afternoon."

Just then, a way too perky DJ jumped onstage and started working the crowd into an even bigger frenzy. "Who are you guys here to see today?"

"Kandy!" the crowd called back.

"And what do you want?" she yelled, practically inciting a riot.

"Kandy!" everyone screamed as Kandy's signature song came blaring out of the speakers.

I looked around and saw I was the only one putting my hands over my ears. Everyone else was singing along—even my boyfriend.

He was actually so caught up in the festivities he was pumping his fist in the air along with the rest of the eighth-graders. Yikes.

The music abruptly stopped after the first few bars. "That was good, you guys, but nowhere near as good as I know you can do," the DJ said, acting all disappointed.

"Awwwwwwww," groaned the crowd.

"So let's try it again!" she continued. "WHO . . . ARE . . . YOU . . . HERE . . . TO . . . SEE . . . TODAY?"

"KANDY!" the crowd exploded, a zillion decibels louder than before.

This kept going and going until I felt like Bill Murray in *Groundhog Day*. To make matters worse, the girl in front of me kept bonking me on the head with her sign every time she started dancing along to the tune; the noonday sun had me sweating so profusely my way too dressy silk halter top had turned from lime to hunter green; and my feet were killing me, both from the sky-high shoes and being stepped on by random people trying to get a better view of the stage.

I was tired and annoyed and bored and . . . *quitting*. Of course, that was it. "Let's blow this popsicle stand," I yelled into Zander's ear while simultaneously trying to dig my toes out from underneath the three-inch-high Rocket Dogs of the kid in front of me.

"Huh?" Zander shot me a surprised look.

I chucked him on the shoulder. "C'mon. Let's head back up to the main house for a while."

"And do what?" Zander asked, like he couldn't believe I'd rather not wait around here all afternoon pretending to be thrilled to see Kandy when she wasn't actually going to appear onstage until the evening. Especially since I wouldn't be thrilled even when she *did* finally appear.

"How about change clothes, grab some lunch, hang out at the pool, and relax, for starters?" Z looked totally unconvinced, so I threw caution to the wind. "And then maybe fool around a little . . . ?" I know, I know, totally cheeseball, tossing that one in, but he looked so cute standing there all sweaty and rumpled.

"Honestly, Trace, I'm having a great time here watching the crew, seeing how this stuff actually gets filmed."

It was obviously time to pull out even heavier artillery than a potential nooner. "You'd probably get to see more behind-the-scenes action if we went to visit my dad before lunch. What do you say?"

"I guess that *would* be pretty cool," Zander said. "But I kind of got the feeling it was a closed set after he told us to come down here earlier. Do you think it would be OK if we popped in now?"

"Absolutely," I said, not having a clue whether I was right, wrong, or somewhere in between, and not particularly caring. "Let's cruise."

Before he could change his mind, I grabbed Zander's hand and we turned back from the crowded stage.

When we came to the stairs leading back up to Kandy's Room, a ginormous lump of a man stopped us dead in our tracks. "This here's private property," he barked. "See the sign? No trespassing allowed."

"I'm not trespassing," I told him. "I'm Mr. McDonohue's daughter, Trace."

"Mr. McDonohue don't have no daughter," he said, crossing his beefy arms over his humongous chest and standing his ground without moving a muscle, just like one of those British dudes with the tall, fuzzy hats who guard Buckingham Palace.

"Actually he does," I said, trying to sound sweet yet firm. "And she's me."

"No . . . he . . . don't," Beefy Man said, practically spitting out every word. I could see he hadn't been hired for his manners or grasp on the finer grammatical elements of the English language. "And I suppose now you're going to tell me this here's his son, too."

"Nope, nothing like that," I said. Fighting with the Surly Mean Giant clearly wasn't going to get me anywhere, so I tried turning on the charm instead. "I know you're only doing your job, and I don't want to get you in trouble, so why don't you just call Shamus on your walkie-talkie and ask him if it's OK to let us back up?"

The guard grudgingly agreed to check our credentials, and a minute later grudgingly allowed us to pass. "Better carry an ID or something next time," he grunted as I walked through the barricade.

"Sure thing, Cro-Magnon man," I muttered once I was positive I was far enough away the dude couldn't hear me. "I'll make sure I have my daughter's license with me."

Zander cracked up. "You're bad. And I mean that in the best possible way."

"That I am."

"I like that in a girl."

"And I like that you like that in me," I said, glad he was seeing my ballsier, more definitive side for a change, and not the hard-to-pin-down girl he was so annoyed with earlier.

Z and I busted through the front door of the guesthouse arm in arm—and were greeted by deafening silence. Uh-oh. Maybe Z was right about us being uninvited. We just stood there stock still as a bunch of guys holding cords and lights and cameras and microphones and who knows what else listened to nothing, at least as far as I could tell. I nervously searched each face, trying to find Shamus. Nope, nope, nope, nope—*aha!* There he was, crouched over in the corner of the living room.

Putting a finger to his lips, my dad motioned us over. I tiptoed over the cords, ducked under the hot lights, and avoided all cameras as I made my way to where he was, with Zander following close behind. Not knowing what else to do once we were huddled down next to my dad, I settled for not making a sound and holding my breath. Finally, Shamus broke the silence. "I think that one's OK. Let's move onto the next."

Z's face lit up. "Did you find it yet?" he asked Shamus.

"Not yet, but we will," Shamus answered, all eye crinklies, like they were sharing some special secret.

They might as well have been speaking Klingon for all I knew. I looked over a Z, hoping he'd clue me in, but just then my dad flicked a switch and everyone went quiet again.

After what felt like an eternity, Shamus said, "Got that one, too." And then the process started all over again. It was like a quieter version of the who-are-you-here-to-see? thing we'd been doing on the beach a little while ago.

Finally, I couldn't stand not knowing any longer. "What are we doing?" I whispered in between my dad's declaring whatever it was we were listening to OK and pushing another lever.

"Trying to find the mike that's picking up extraneous noises," Zander explained before my dad could utter a word.

Shamus smiled over at my boyfriend. "Right on. How did you know?"

Z's chest jutted out with pride. "I'm majoring in television and film at NYU," he announced loud enough for all the crew to hear. "And back in high school, I volunteered at the campus TV station a lot."

"Well, then, don't just sit there. Make yourself useful," one of the crew guys told him, shoving a big microphone on a long stick thingie at Zander.

Z stared at it in awe, like it was some sort of treasure. "A boom? Are you sure?"

"Of course," Shamus told him. "We could actually use the extra help."

The deathly dull things they were doing in here made being an extra seem like my dream job. "How much longer will you guys be working on the sound stuff?" I was hoping my dad would say maybe they were almost ready to break for lunch and we all could go grab a bite together or something. I was positively starving by this point.

Shamus glanced at his watch. "Probably another hour, and then start setting up the lighting."

"Oh," I said, hoping the disappointment didn't show on my face.

"I told you this stuff was like watching grass grow." His understanding comment at least made me feel like I didn't have to pretend I thought what they were doing in here was fascinating.

"I think the green stuff might be more exciting than this," I admitted.

Shamus rewarded me with a smile yet again. "Kind of makes you want to head back to the beach, huh?"

I cocked my head toward Boom Boy. "Actually, we were thinking more along the lines of heading back up to the main house for lunch and then hanging at the pool for a while. The truth is . . ." I said, getting ready to let him in on the fact that I wasn't exactly a huge Kandy fan.

"Trace?" Zander interrupted before I got the words out. "Would you mind if I stayed here instead? I'm actually totally into this, and anyway, I'm not really all that hungry."

After almost having left the building—finally—Mr. Doubt turned right back around and made an encore appearance. "What? I thought we were going to hang."

"We will. After this, I promise," he said, giving me that irresistible puppy dog look. "Please? It would be such a great experience for me."

"Fine," I reluctantly agreed, though the words didn't come out sounding as nice and lighthearted as I'd intended.

"Thanks, Trace. You're the best!"

Shamus raised an eyebrow my way. The familiar gesture—it's big in my repertoire, too—made me feel much more connected to my dad. "You sure you won't be lonely?" he asked. "You're welcome to stay here with me, you know."

I gave him my own version of the ol' eyebrow right back. "Thanks, I know," I said. "But I can take care of myself, and if I get bored, I know where to find you."

"True," Shamus said, still eyeballing me, like he was trying to figure out whether I was really OK with Z staying or just pretending to be (the answer to which was somewhere in between). "Well, just in case you don't make it back before then, Kandy's performance is at six. You and Zander can watch from backstage, and then we'll all head back up to the house for dinner."

"Sounds great," I said, beginning to make my way back through the tangled mess of cords and cables.

One of the crew guys called for silence, and I quickly backed out the door right before he slammed it in my face. The noise startled me so bad that I jumped and lost my footing. And the next thing I knew I was sprawled all over the stairs—and some poor lost Kandy fan.

Or something like that.

CHAPTER
5

"Oh, my gosh," the girl's muffled voice said from underneath me. "I sure wouldn't want to meet you in an alley at night."

"Sorry, I'm not usually such a bruiser," I said, brushing myself off and then reaching out my hand to her in a belated peace offering. "Here. Let me help you up."

"Thanks." She scrambled to retrieve both her glasses and the book she'd been reading before I so rudely mowed her over. The girl's blond ponytail and freshly scrubbed, naturally-beautiful-without-makeup face seemed prime for landing a Neutrogena commercial. I felt like maybe I'd seen her somewhere before—who knows, maybe it *was* on a Neutrogena commercial.

"You hurt?" I asked, hoping I hadn't broken anything on her.

Miss Natural Beauty shook her head, so at least I knew her neck was OK.

Feeling like I should somehow make up for my lack of grace, I reached into my arsenal of inane pleasantries. "Beautiful day, huh?"

She nodded vaguely, like I was some sort of pesky gnat buzzing around her head.

"So how come you're not down there with everyone else?" I tried again, pointing toward the craziness on the beach.

The girl stopped reading for a second and pushed her glasses up her nose. "All that yelling and screaming was making me totally nuts, so the powers that be said I could leave and come back later, when the concert starts."

"I was going crazy down there, too, but I did you one better—I totally bailed."

"At least that means you can take off now," she said, burying her nose back into the book. "I'm stuck here until after the show."

"Actually, I can't leave, either—at least not farther than the pool. My dad is the producer of this show." Or was that director? Or Kandy Kane's manager? No matter. Pride swelled up in me faster than a balloon animal gets blown up and twisted into a semirecognizable form at a kid's birthday party. I mean, I half expected a colorful latex wiener dog or bunny rabbit to come shooting out my butt.

"Lucky you," she said, glancing up at me, then back down into the pages of—what was it she was so engrossed in, anyway?

"What's that you're reading?" I asked, noting I should probably give up on the polite conversation thing, seeing as I'd already more than excused my roller derby entrance with small talk, and she was clearly more into her book than me.

The girl held up the cover so I could see it.

"Body Outlaws: Rewriting the Rules of Beauty and Body Image," I read out loud. "Is it any good?" Jeez, why couldn't I just shut up and walk away like a normal person?

"Oh, it's great," the girl said, nicely continuing to tolerate my big mouth and sudden lack of control over it. "Too many girls today buy into the idea that they have to look like Barbie to be beautiful. This is all about empowering women to find their own definition of beauty, without plastic surgery or starving themselves to death."

"Wow," I said, impressed. The last book I'd read was *Tommyland*, Tommy Lee's autobiography, sometimes narrated by his legendary schlong. Not exactly the mind-expanding, worthwhile subject matter of hers.

"Hey, since we're in basically the same boat, do you want to kill some time together?" The girl was squinting at me now, like she was trying to figure out whether I had a high enough IQ to hang with her intellectual, feminist self.

I considered the offer for a moment before tossing away my original plan—which was pretty much head back up to the house and figure it out from there—for this potentially more stimulating one. "Why not?"

"Cool. So what do you want to do first?"

My stomach rumbled ominously.

"How about we grab a bite from the food services table while we're deciding?" she said before I could either excuse myself or think of a good answer.

I hesitated. "Are we allowed to?"

"You're the producer's daughter, aren't you?"

"Producer, director . . . something like that." The titles—never mind the job duties that went along with them—were way too confusing to me, and I just couldn't keep them straight.

"So it's fine then," she declared.

As we piled salad and fruit onto our plates, I tried to think of a topic of conversation that might interest my deep-thinking new friend. When nothing momentous came to mind, I went with the very second-grade "Want to know a secret?" instead.

She glanced over me, probably regretting that she'd asked me to keep her company already. "Sure."

"The thought of being on TV, even just as part of a crowd, was practically sending me into convulsions," I confessed. "I mean, I'm the girl who used to get horrible stomachaches every time I had to give a book report in school."

The girl let her mouth curve up into the beginnings of a smile. "You're kidding, right?"

I laughed and plunked myself down at a deserted picnic table. "Nope. I have really bad stage fright. I mean, you should've seen me when I had to do a shout-out on *TRL* last year. Long story, but I could barely croak out the words, never mind the *woo!* at the end."

The girl sat down across from me. "When I was out east looking at colleges this fall, I hit *TRL*, too. It was a lot more fun than I expected."

Well, well, well. If Ms. Smartypants had spent an entire day waiting in line to get on the MTV show like I did, she must have another side to her, one that could totally appreciate pop culture and cool tunes. Interrresting. Before this piece of info cropped up, I would've pegged her as a classical-music-listening, Baroque-art-appreciating museum-lover. "So where did you decide to go, anyway?"

"Huh?"

"To school, I mean."

"The University of Nowhere," she said, plunking her head into her hand with a sigh.

"The local community college?" I guessed, shoveling food into my face.

"Not even close. But it's not worth talking about anyway, since my mother's making me defer my admission until further notice."

"Why?" I asked through a mouthful of pasta salad.

"She's got me booked for so many jobs, I can't do both. 'Might as well make the most of your opportunities while you still have them,'" the girl said, totally mimicking her mom. She hadn't so much as taken a bite of her food, and I'd already practically cleaned my plate.

I shook my head in disbelief. "Bummer."

"I know. I keep hoping she'll change her mind or the work will fall through," she said, absentmindedly nibbling on a strawberry. "The truth is, I went ahead and sent in all the paperwork for the fall semester anyway. There's still a spot waiting for me in Broadway Hall in case a miracle happens."

"So what are the chances?" I asked, moving on to the gigantic Rice Krispie Treat I just hadn't been able to pass up.

"Slim to none," she said, putting the half-eaten berry back on her plate.

I racked my brain for some goofy tidbit that might jolly her into a better mood. I came up blank. Finally, I settled on my biggest issue of the moment. "Hey, I just thought of another secret I can tell you. Guess what I hate even more than the being in the spotlight?"

"What?"

"Techno-pop singers who probably can't even sing," I told her, scrunching up my nose in distaste.

"I have to say, I'm getting pretty sick of Kandy myself," the girl said.

"I mean, what kind of a role model is someone who dresses like that and can't even string a sentence together?" I added, the girl's heavy reading material still on my mind.

"To be fair, I'm sure there's a stylist picking out the outfits," she said. "And all that makeup probably makes it hard to talk." Great. Now not only had the girl shown herself to be smarter and more profound than me, but she was also more compassionate. I was really going to have to get on a self-improvement kick once I got to Fairfield.

"Hmmmmmm," I mumbled, my mouth full of marshmallows and cereal.

"And sorry to break it to you, but none of that's a secret."

"I know," I said, plunking down my trump card. "The secret is, I haven't exactly gotten around to telling my dad any of this stuff yet. He's so pumped up about being involved with Kandy's show, I didn't want to bring him down."

The girl looked up at me, surprised. "That's just like me, with my mother," she admitted. "She's sacrificed so much to help me make it in this business, I can't bear to tell her how much I want to quit. So I just slap a smile on my face and pretend I still love it."

"So you know exactly how I feel?"

"Yup, but not for long," she said fiercely. "I'm gonna have a long talk with my mom tonight. Help her see that improving my mind is way more important than making money. Or promoting the superficial stuff this industry values, for that matter."

"That's cool. Maybe I'll have a talk with my dad, too."

"Oh, you totally should," she said. "Honesty is the key to any good relationship, whether its with your parents or friends or boyfriend or whoever. Don't you think?"

I agreed with her in theory. It was just that real life seemed to call for omissions here and there. "Sure. Hey, I just had an idea for what we should do this afternoon. How would you like to help me get my dad's stuff unpacked? He just moved in and the place is a total mess."

"A little volunteerism? Sounds great," the girl said, dabbing her mouth with a napkin, though I'm not sure what she could possibly think was there except maybe a tiny strawberry seed. She hadn't eaten a thing.

"Cool," I said, folding my empty paper plate into quarters, like that would hide the fact I'd completely stuffed my face. "Let's hit it."

"Hey, if we're going to be hanging out together, you should probably know my name. It's K.C.," she said, sticking out her hand.

I shook it enthusiastically. "Is that C-A-S-E-Y or K-A-C-E-Y?" I asked. I'd known girls at school who'd spelled it both ways.

"Neither," she told me. "Just a K and a C."

"Short for?" I asked

"Nothing I'd care to admit right now," she said, smiling.

It was probably something horrendous, like Karla Clementine, I thought. Or even worse, Karma Chai. "Well, I'm Trace. Short for Tracey. Nice to meet you."

"You were right about your dad needing help," K.C. said once she had a chance to survey the very messy state of affairs back at the main house.

"I know, nightmare city, right?"

In the daylight, the task seemed even more daunting than it had the night before. No wonder Shamus hadn't made much headway yet. Still, I didn't want the mayhem in there rubbing off on my dad's fledgling show and giving it crappy karma or foul feng shui or whatever the latest new age curse might be, so I was determined to forge ahead no matter what. I certainly wouldn't blame K.C. if she ran out of the place screaming, though.

"Where should we start?" she asked, surprising me with her staying power.

"In the kitchen, I think. But first things first, I've got to change. Wait right here."

Running down the hall and into my PB Teen haven, I threw off the hottie-tottie extra outfit, tossed my hair into a casual ponytail, and pulled on my comfiest cutoffs and a vintage Sublime wife-beater. Instantly, I was transformed back into Trace, normal girl. I headed back to the disaster area of a kitchen, feeling much more like myself.

"Where do you want me to put these?" In the few minutes it took me to change, K.C. had already busted open the first box and unearthed gobs of barware. Her willingness to get down and dirty impressed me even more than her reading material.

"Here, don't you think?" I said, pointing to the cabinet closest to the beer fridge.

"Per-fecto."

After we'd made our way through the pint, wine, and shot glasses, I said, "You know what would make this more fun? A Big Gulp full of Pepsi and some good tunes."

"Make mine a diet and life is cool."

Since I had no idea where the nearest 7-Eleven might be, I decided to check out the regular refrigerator to see if our beverages of choice might be in there. No such luck—a tumbleweed practically blew out when I opened the door. Inside held only a nearly empty carton of milk, an even emptier container of OJ, a browning head of iceberg lettuce, half a jar of mustard, and a few 7-Ups. Typical bachelor, I thought—the beer fridge is full but the one for food is more barren than Siberia in a snowstorm.

"Looks like we're going to have to stick to water for now," I said, taking out two of the glasses we'd just unpacked and turning on the tap. "Unless you want to sneak down to Kandy's place to get us some contraband sodas."

K.C. shook her head. "I'm staying away from that whole scene for as long as possible. So water's fine. Not too cold, please."

I handed K.C. her lukewarm drink, added tons of ice to mine, and then flicked on my dad's XM radio. Typical bachelor times two: His gas probably wasn't even turned on yet, but his satellite and cable had already been hooked up. Cranking up the volume on Alt Nation, Green Day's "Wake Me Up When September Ends" filled the room. Even without the Big Gulp, things had already improved one million percent. Not that they'd been so bad to begin with.

Piling forks into the appropriate slots in the divided drawer, I found myself vaguely singing/humming along to the tune, depending on whether I definitely knew the words or maybe just thought I did. Pretty soon, there was K.C., harmonizing alongside me. Brainy girl had perfect pitch and a crystal clear tone, too. Was there anything she didn't do well?

"Amazing."

"What?" she asked, stacking spoons in the drawer.

"Your voice. It's awesome."

K.C. shrugged. "It's no big deal."

"It's a very big deal," I insisted, breaking open another box. "A total gift. I'm gonna tell my dad he should let you open for Kandy at her next concert. Or at least sing backup vocals for her."

"Thanks," K.C. said, pulling out a bunch of everyday dishes and stacking them neatly into another cabinet before adding, "I think."

"It was definitely a compliment," I laughed. Funny how even a young feminist like her had trouble accepting one gracefully.

The Bravery came on just as we were busting into a box of pots and pans, and we started rocking out, singing at the top of our lungs as we worked. It was like one of those ridiculous movie montage scenes, only this was real life. *My* life. And it was starting to feel like real fun.

Soon, we were making real progress, too. K.C. moved on to putting away all sorts of decorative thingiemabobbers while I dealt with random plastic cups from long-forgotten frat parties and sporting events. "Hey, look at this," I called to her, my voice echoing from inside a box. "'UCLA Freshman Orientation, September 1986.' This thing is older than I am."

Instead of answering with a "Me, too" or a "Not me, I'm XX years old," there was total silence. I looked up to see what cat had gotten K.C.'s tongue, only to find her running for the sink, her hand covering her mouth.

"Are you OK?" I asked once she'd stopped gagging.

"Oh, Trace, I'm so sorry. There was some kind of dead rodent in the bottom of that last vase, and the smell was just awful," K.C. said, wiping her mouth. Correction: It seemed a mouse had actually gotten her tongue. And uvula.

"No worries," I said. Thinking warm water probably wasn't going to cut it in a crisis like this, I opened the fridge again and handed her a 7-Up. It wasn't a Diet Pepsi, but it would have to do. "I would've had exactly the same reaction."

"I highly doubt that," she said, popping the top and taking a small sip. "I swear, I must have the world's most overactive gag reflex. Once I even puked because I picked up what I thought was a Raisinet off the floor that actually turned out to be a rabbit turd."

"No way," I said, a very unladylike snort escaping me.

"Way," she said, squishing up her whole face and nodding in embarrassment. "I was working at the time, and everyone thought it was so funny they just about laughed their asses off. Even worse, they called me Ralph for the next month."

"No *way*," I said yet again, practically whooping now.

"Way," she insisted. "And you want to know the funniest part about the whole thing?"

I nodded.

"I almost ate it."

I stared at her, my eyes practically bugging out of my head. "What?" I screamed.

"The Raisinet," K.C. said, finally giving in to how funny it was and choking out the words between giggles. "That was really bunny boo-boo."

That got us completely hysterical, and we howled until we were both holding our stomachs and rolling on the floor. Once I could speak again, I decided to let K.C. in on the Yuke of Earl story. Even though I'd sworn myself to lifelong secrecy, I figured I was a long way from home, and anyway, she'd just told me *her* most mortifying gagging moment. So I spilled it, and we cracked up for another five minutes.

"It's such a relief, hanging with someone who's not in the business," she said after we'd finally composed ourselves. "It's like, I don't have to worry about how I act and what I say all the time. I can just be myself, you know what I mean?"

Did I ever. As we continued to unpack, I found myself admitting a *real* secret to K.C.: How Zander's post-L-word dumping had gotten me so paranoid, my tongue practically tied itself into knots on a daily basis trying to spit out just the right words at the right time, as well as keep the wrong ones in. And that even though I was starting to work on getting the kinks out, I still had a long way to go.

When I'd finished my pathetic little tale, I felt so unburdened, so light and airy, I was surprised I didn't just float away. The feeling didn't last long.

"You know what you're *really* doing with all that, don't you?" K.C. asked.

"Yeah, I'm making sure the guy doesn't burn rubber again."

"Good try."

"Just taking things slowly, then?" I guessed, searching for the answer she wanted to hear. "Being the coolest girlfriend on the planet? Never being his beast of burden?" All were correct as far as I was concerned.

K.C. shook her head. "You know as well as I do you shouldn't have to change who you are for anybody—even the hottest guy in the world."

"Seriously, it's not like I've changed," I said, trying to explain my position. "I'm just trying to give him the best of me. Isn't that what people who really care about each other do?"

K.C. put down the barbecue tools she'd been unpacking, leaned back against the kitchen island, and crossed her arms. "If you really cared about him, wouldn't you trust him with all of you and not just the quote-unquote cool parts?"

I shrugged and stared at my feet. I felt completely deflated, like she'd taken a pin to my feel-good balloon and popped it. On purpose.

Then she added the topper. "And did you ever consider that pretending to be someone you're not isn't fair to either one of you?"

An hour ago, I'd been admiring K.C.'s more cerebral qualities. But now her know-it-all-ness was really starting to get on my nerves. "I'm not *pretending* anything. I'll have you know I totally hate fake people."

"I'm sure that's true, and that's why you need to seriously reconsider what you're doing," K.C. persisted, despite the fact she had to know I was getting irritated. "Let me put it this way. Do you honestly think agreeing to do things you don't necessarily want to do or telling your boyfriend you're fine with things when you're not is being real?"

"Maybe it's a just different kind of reality than you're used to," I insisted, tucking the pieces of hair that had fallen out of my ponytail behind my ears with a shaky hand. It sounded ridiculous, even as it came out of my mouth.

"Like, pseudo-reality or something?" she asked.

I slammed a bunch of wisks and mixing spoons into a drawer. Who did this girl think she was, anyway? Ms. Always Right? "Something like that."

"Look, I'm not trying to make you mad," she told me. "If you and your boyfriend are happy the way things are, that's totally cool and there's no need to change a thing."

"Things are totally cool," I muttered, piling bowl after bowl into the drawer below the other cooking stuff. "And I'm not changing a thing."

"Fine," she said in an annoyingly soothing tone.

"Fine," I said, in a not so soothing one.

"Great."

"Great."

"It's just that . . ." she trailed off.

Oh, jeez, here we went again. "It's just that what?"

"If everything was so cool, then why the big confession? And why act so embarrassed about it?"

I sighed. Much as I hated to admit it, she was right. She knew it, I knew it, and my gut knew it. Seriously, my stomach felt suddenly gurgly, like maybe the dead mouse from the vase was haunting *me* now. "I guess I just never thought of what I was doing as being fake before," I finally said. "I mean, that definitely wasn't my intention."

"Oh, you'd be amazed how far people will go to protect themselves, and how far into denial they can be about it," K.C. told me. "Don't worry, Trace. You were just being human. And you can also fix things pretty easily, from the sound of it."

"Thanks." There didn't seem to be much else to say . . . until K.C. spit out her next proclamation, that is.

"And the answer to my earlier question is this: What you're *really* doing when you hide your emotions and opinions from your boyfriend is making sure he doesn't get too close to you. It's almost like you've been telling him, 'You don't know me,' all summer."

I thought about that one a moment. Damn. Right again. "You don't know me . . . so you can't hurt me, right?" I asked quietly.

She nodded. "Now you're getting to the bottom of it."

"So you think I haven't been saving our relationship this whole time, I've actually been sabotaging it?" It came out in a whisper, as if if I didn't say it out loud, it wouldn't be true.

"It doesn't matter what I think. What do *you* think?"

"I think you sound like a psychologist," I muttered.

K.C. broke into a humongous smile. "I do? Awesome! I'm going to be a psych major once I finally get to college."

I was distracted enough by her revelation to stop focusing on my much more uncomfortable one for a minute. Psychology, huh? I'd reviewed the list of majors at Fairfield a thousand times, only to find myself bleary-eyed and still without a clue. At this point, I was counting on a lightning bolt of inspiration to strike me as I was sitting in freshman orientation. "What made you choose psychology?"

"I've definitely had my own issues, so I feel like I have a lot of empathy for what people are going through," she told me, all revved up from our impromptu therapy session. "Especially teens. You know, girls struggling with anorexia, bulimia, low self-esteem. Things like that."

I wondered which one on the laundry list of problems had been K.C.'s. And I was just about to ask when she grabbed her T-Mobile Sidekick out of her pocket and flipped open the screen. "Looks like I have to get back down to the beach now. Catch you here tomorrow? I could help you finish whatever rooms are left."

"You'll be back tomorrow?" I asked. "I mean, since you're going to have that talk with your mom tonight?"

She nodded. "Oh, you can bet on it. She won't let me bag anything I've already committed to. I'll just have to make sure she doesn't book anything else so I can start Columbia second semester."

"Columbia? As in University?"

"None other."

"I'm going to Fairfield," I told her. "It's only an hour away from New York City. Maybe we can stay in touch."

"I'd like that." She looked like she meant it.

CHAPTER 6

After K.C. left, I found homes for the remaining utensils, corkscrews, and other random things that apparently served some purpose, though I had no clue as to what that might be. With every carton I opened and every tchotchke I placed just so, I felt closer to my dad, more a part of his life, and more like this could really become my home away from home.

I'd just finished breaking down all the boxes and putting them in the recycling bin in the garage when Zander came bursting through the door. "Let's go, Trace! Everything's already totally rocking down at the beach!" It sounded like bad dialogue from one of those corny old surfer movies.

I glanced up at the Elvis clock I'd unpacked fifteen minutes before. His legs were practically glued together: six thirty. "Whoa, look at the time. I've been so busy, I didn't even notice how late it had gotten," I said, totally fishing for compliments about the kitchen magic K.C. and I had performed.

"Well, you better get a move on," Zander told me, either not noticing the results of my hard work or not mentioning it if he had. "This is your dad's big moment."

I sighed. "Fine, just give me a minute to get ready."

As I was throwing back on my extra outfit—minus the silk

halter top and plus a light blue James Perse tube top—Z called to me from the hall. "So, what'd you do all afternoon? Sit at the pool and catch rays?"

Without waiting for an answer, he launched into the details of his exciting day—all of which involved equipment I've never heard of and tasks that sounded vaguely pornographic. He cranked a something-or-other. Assisted a grip. Did something with a puller. Zander wrapped up his seemingly sordid story with, "Shamus is such an awesome guy. You're really lucky he's your dad."

Even though I knew I'd accomplished something far more useful for Shamus than pulling a gripping cranker or whatever it was Z had done, I still felt left out of their apparently budding buddy-buddy relationship. "Yeah, I know. That's why I totally worked on making his life better today," I said, grabbing Zander's hand and dragging him toward the kitchen. "You gotta check it out. And as an added bonus, I met—"

Zander stopped short before we'd made it two steps down the hall. "Whoa, sorry to interrupt, but did I tell you who I just met? Kandy Kane! And she looks just as beautiful in person as on TV!"

Why had I never noticed before that Z's voice rose three octaves and got all breathy when he was excited? It was hardly an aphrodisiac. "Bully for you," I said, sarcasm just dripping off my lips. "I mean, the girl I met wasn't a star or anything, but she was totally cool and she helped me—"

"That's awesome you found someone to hang out with while I was working," Z said, interrupting me yet again. If he kept cutting me off like this, I was going to start hemorrhaging. "I was worried you were going to be mad at me for being gone so long."

"Well, I'm not," I said, definitely sounding mad. Maybe feeling it a little, too. I guess ditching me for the day was stirring up old wounds, and gushing about how beautiful Kandy was was just icing on the emotional cake.

By the time Z got back around to asking about my afternoon activities it was like he'd already sucked the life out of me, and I shrugged off his halfhearted question. Needless to say, I skipped the big tah-dah tour I'd planned on giving him, and we went whizzing through the kitchen and set off for Kandyland instead. In his excitement, Z basically ran ahead of me, not even stopping when he hit the huge flight of stairs down to the beach. I had to take them much slower in my stacked sandals, and I must've looked like a little peanut by the time he hit the sand.

"You don't look very tan," he said when I finally made it down to where he was waiting, tapping his foot impatiently. "For someone who baked in the sun all afternoon."

"That's because I didn't," I said, completely exasperated by our lack of communication now.

"You didn't?"

"No, I actually busted my ass."

Before I could explain once and for all that I'd been doing manual labor and not lying around a pool for the past four hours, Shamus sidled over to us. "Trace, I'm so glad you're here. I've got a big surprise for you," he said, giving me a little squeeze that made me feel both missed and wanted. "Caden Collins agreed at the last minute to do a three-song acoustic set to open for Kandy. He's about to get started, so let's head backstage."

"That *is* a surprise," I said, following close behind my dad. Caden was the exuberant lead singer of a Simple Plan–like band that was as well known for the pranks they played as for their music. I was definitely interested in checking out his solo stuff, along with however he was planning on punking the audience while he was playing. I didn't think the rest of the teenybopper crowd and their moms were going to be quite as open to hearing songs they wouldn't know every single word to already, though. Or getting stinkbombed—which was what his band had done on their last tour during a song called "Blowin' in the Wind (A Gaseous Tale)"—for that matter.

Escorting me and Zander onto the stage, Shamus plunked us just behind the stacks of speakers. I'd never had such an up-close-and-personal view of what it's like to be a rock star before, so I peeked out into the crowd—and my entire body immediately started shaking. Yeah, I knew I wasn't the one performing, but apparently my knees didn't. "Thanks, Shamus. This is definitely the best seat I've ever had at a concert."

"Anything for my girl," Shamus yelled into my ear over the din of the crowd. "I've got to go check in at command central now. Since it's so packed out here, I think it probably makes the most sense for us to just meet back at the house after, don't you?"

"Sure."

Shamus walked two paces away, then turned back around again before I could gloat to Zander about the surprise I had waiting for my dad. "Hey, mind if I borrow your boyfriend for a bit more?" Shamus yelled into my ear this time. "One of my camera guys looks like he could use some help."

I shook my head. What was one more hour apart from Mr. I'm So Excited I'm Not Even Listening, anyway?

"Great, thanks." Shamus crooked his finger at Z, who looked like he was in seventh heaven a minute later despite the fact that his entire position seemed to consist of trailing behind the camera guy making sure the cord didn't get caught on anything.

Just then, the WHOT DJ hopped onstage. "We're just about to get started with the concert, folks!"

Cheers of approval rang out all around.

"But before we welcome Kandy Kane to the stage, I'd like to introduce the lead singer of The Menace Men, Caden Collins!"

There was a smattering of applause, but mostly a large "Awwwwwwwwww!" from the crowd. Feeling sorry for the guy, I stuck two fingers into the sides of my mouth and practically blew my brains out. And I had worked myself up to a completely piercing noise level when I felt someone brush by me. I whirled around to see who it was—figuring the most likely candidate was Zander, back from his exciting flunky experience—and found myself face-to-face with the opening act. "Thanks," he mouthed at me.

"Hey. It's great to be here," Caden said into the microphone a moment later. "Most of you probably think of me as a total wild man, but tonight, I'm going to start out with some mellower stuff."

Without any more fanfare—or practical jokes—he began strumming. While he'd always been known for his manic energy onstage, the solo Caden seemed completely serious and mature. Even more disappointed now, the audience went back to talking and tossing beach balls around.

I was another story entirely. Though I'm not normally a ballad lover, deeming most of them cheesy and wimpy, the hairs on my arms were completely standing on end. Caden's music felt innovative but still as comfortable as an old T-shirt; his lyrics raw and yearning yet still managing to maintain just the right amount of cocky optimism. The combo platter was insanely appealing to me.

As the final chord rang out, Caden stood motionless, head hanging over his guitar for what felt like an eternity. Without even thinking, I began whistling again like a possessed teakettle.

"Thanks," Caden said, looking directly at me and smiling. "I thought you might like that one."

I completely froze, grinning back at him with four fingers still stuck in my mouth. Realizing what a dork I must look like, I dropped my hands to my sides and wiped the residual spit on my pants. When I finally composed myself enough to look up again, Caden was back to addressing everyone and not just me.

"Here's one that's really close to my heart. It's called 'A Place of My Own,'" he announced, launching into another plaintive ballad to much the same results. The crowd didn't care, but I was bowled over—especially by the lyrics.

> Tried to do it your way, now it's time for mine
> 'Cause nothing is sacred when everything's fine
> Just gotta make it across that line
> Leave this limbo for something divine
> Yeah, I'm looking for a place to call my own
> Funny how you can be together and feel so alone

It was like . . . well, it was like the words to one of Bebe's most depressing favorite songs, "Killing Me Softly"—you know, the one about the stranger strumming the girl's pain with his fingers, singing her life with his words. I totally knew what Caden meant. When the song was over, I clapped so hard my hands stung. It still didn't wake up for the fact that not many other people out there were.

"Seems like you guys might want a return of the wild man," Caden said, pulling out the biggest Super Soaker water gun I'd ever seen. He shot it out into the crowd to roars of approval, then kicked into The Menace Men's most popular song, "Cat 'n' Mouse Game." Everyone bopped around like maniacs, chanting along to the infectious chorus. Success, finally.

It didn't last long, though. As soon as the music ended—and before Caden had even made it off the stage—the audience started screaming for Kandy again. I shook my head in disgust. "Those people have zero taste in music," I said out loud, to no one in particular.

"But you do." It was a statement, not a question.

"I'd like to think so," I said, looking up at Caden, a weird combination of bravery tinged with the teensiest bit of shyness mixing up inside me. "I mean, your songs are really powerful. Not to mention unexpected."

"You thought I'd be writing 'Girly Go Round' for the rest of my life and encouraging the audience to spin around so fast when I was singing it, at that least one or two of them would puke?" Caden asked with an expression that was half smirk, half sad.

It was one of his old band's more happily immature songs, though I actually liked its goofy lyrics and crunchy guitar riff. "Not that there would've been anything wrong with that. It was a fun one."

"Fun while it lasted, I guess," he said with a shrug. "But I needed to move on. Be taken seriously, you know?"

"Well, that certainly shows in your solo stuff," I said, hoping he didn't think I was just kissing major ass. "You just blew me away out there."

The smirky frown turned into a genuine smile. "For real?"

"Yup."

Before I could fill him in on all the details, Kandy flounced onto the stage to a standing ovation. Just as I expected, lights flashed, a deafening beat pumped madly, and dancers starting contorting their bodies in the most unlikely ways.

"So, you wanna head back to my dressing room?" Caden yelled into my ear at the exact same moment my boyfriend happened to come hunching by clutching the camera cord. Though there was no way he'd heard Caden's offhand invitation, Zander still glared at me before stalking off.

Not wanting to get into an unnecessary fight with Z, I decided the easiest thing to do would be to put an end to the conversation with Caden, no matter how interesting it had been so far. "My mom was the groupie, not me," I yelled back, thinking my line was pretty clever. "And even she wasn't a very good one."

Caden laughed. "You're funny. And I'm way less dangerous than you might think. So how about a walk on the beach instead?"

I was just about to say no when I caught a load of Zander out of the corner of my eye. He was all the way on the other side of the stage by this point, mouth hanging open even wider than P.Diddy's usually is. For a second, I couldn't figure out which he was drooling over more: the camera equipment or Kandy.

No wait. It was definitely Kandy, after all. She was shaking her big bazongas right in front of his face, dancers mimicking her actions in the background, while Zander stared down into her grand canyon of cleavage. He looked like maybe he was even considering blowing big raspberries between her boobs. The big dork had clearly forgotten that I, the camera cord, and anything else in the world existed.

I turned back to Caden, an evil glint in my eye. "Just a walk, huh?"

He nodded, shaggy blond hair falling into his face.

"Sure. Why not?" My dad would never know I'd bailed after the first song, and judging by the hypnotized twirligigs that had replaced Zander's pupils after his recent brush with the big bosom of fame, I didn't think he'd notice, either.

Minutes later, it felt like Caden and I were miles away from the crowd, even though it was probably more like a few blocks. I'd successfully shaken the jealousy thing off my back, too. I mean, it was kind of hard to be upset when warm sugary sand was tickling my toes, sandals were dangling playfully from my fingers, and a semi-famous, slightly goofy musician decided to make me his evening stroll partner.

"So, did you write 'A Place of My Own' about a relationship?" It was a question that had been rolling around my mind ever since he'd stopped playing it.

"You could say that."

"Well, I could totally relate," I said, plunking myself down in at the ocean's edge and staring out at the waves. "Especially the line about how you can be together and still feel alone, because that's kind of how things are with my boyfriend right now."

Caden stared out at the water along with me, hands stuffed in his back pockets. "It's cool the song spoke to you."

"It did. And I'm sorry your girlfriend made you feel that way."

"I actually didn't write it about a girl."

"Oh," I said, feeling extremely stupid. I had no clue Caden played for the other team. "Guy, then."

Caden plopped himself down next to me and laughed. "Not a guy, either," he said. "It was about the troubles I was having in the band. I wanted us to grow up, both personally and musically, and the rest of the guys totally weren't into it. Thought we'd be alienating our fans. So mostly, the chorus is about realizing we'd have to break up if that was the only way I could be myself."

"Wow," I said, locking the piece of information into my memory bank forever. I don't know quite what was making it so easy for me to have such a personal conversation with a guy I barely knew when I couldn't manage one with someone I supposedly knew so well, but it was sure fun. "Thanks for sharing."

Caden picked at remnants of shells, examining each before tossing them aside. "I don't know what it is, but something about you just makes me want to be honest."

"Not your usual MO?" I felt special, chosen. And maybe like this guy wasn't so goofy after all.

He shook his head. "My first instinct is to lie like a rug, just for kicks. To keep people guessing."

"Well, then, I'm guessing I'm either very lucky or you're lying to me right now."

"I'm not lying," Caden said, leaning over to brush some sand off his elbow. He was so close, I could feel his breath on my shoulder. "And I also don't think my last girlfriend the supermodel would say you're lucky to be hanging out with me."

I held my hand to my arm. I wouldn't have been surprised if it was glowing. "Things didn't work out, I take it?"

He fell back in the sand with a soft thud, clasping his hands behind his head. "She was so worried about how she looked all the time, she never wanted to do *anything*. I mean, God forbid she get sweaty or ruin her makeup and have a less than perfect picture show up in the tabloids. What I need is a girl who knows how to hang out and have fun, you know?"

"Maybe you just need to date normal people," I said. "Not actresses or models or singers, but regular girls."

"Got anyone in particular in mind?" he asked, propping himself up on one elbow and grinning at me.

"No," I said, smushing my toes into the sand and blushing like crazy. I hadn't meant to imply he should consider me for the role. Even though that might be fun—in another lifetime, that is. "No. Not at all."

Caden's grin got even bigger as he sat all the way back up. "Well, you better think fast, because my manager is trying to set me up with Kandy Kane. And there's no way I'm going for that."

I stopped burying my feet for long enough to look up at him.

"Why not? I mean, every other guy seems to think she's the hottest thing going."

"Let me paint you a picture here," Caden began, treating me to my very own private Vh1 *Storytellers* session. "When I was five, my mom hired a clown to perform at my birthday party. He showed up late, smelled something awful, and swore at us kids when my mom went in the kitchen to get the birthday cake."

"Why do I feel like you should be launching into some very sad dysfunctional family song right about now?"

"Because you're totally right. Something along the lines of 'Clowns are freakish, so are the little clown cars they drive, / still have nightmares of the drunken birthday clown from when I was five,'" he riffed. Despite the ridiculous lyrics, the tune actually sounded pretty good.

I laughed. "It's your next single."

"Want me to make up one about you now?"

"I've already had a song written for me, thanks," I said, trying to play it cool, to ignore the hot-hot heat I'd felt before when he'd almost touched me.

"Courtesy of the boyfriend that's currently making you feel so alone?" he teased. "Or one of the many that came before him?"

If Caden only knew Z was the first guy I'd gone out with for more than three months, and the song he'd written about me wasn't romantic at all—it was called "She Can't Sing to Save Her Life." "That's top secret," I teased right back. "And what does your tragic fifth birthday party have to do with Kandy, anyhow?"

"I was just getting to that. To this day, I'm scared to death of clowns. Or anyone dressed up in a costume, for that matter. I mean, who is this Kandy underneath all that makeup, anyway? A drunken, foulmouthed dude, for all I know."

"I kind of doubt that." I laughed. "Most dirty old men aren't as stacked as she is."

"Even so, Kandy's probably just as neurotic about her looks and less fun than my ex was," Caden said, casually taking my hand and flipping it over, tracing the lines of my palm as he spoke. "So was your song called 'Heartbreaker'? 'Devastating Darling'? 'The Queen of Cool'?"

"None of the above," I said, pulling my hand back. Caden's laid-back moves were sexier than any kiss I'd ever gotten. Which of course made me wonder what it might be like to kiss him. Which of course I wasn't even supposed to be thinking about, since I had a boyfriend of nearly a year waiting for me a few blocks away. Who of course was most likely wondering where the hell I was right this very moment.

"I should get back now. Z—Shamus is probably looking for me." Zander, Shamus . . . whatever. Caden already knew I had a boyfriend. No need to keep reminding him.

"Why do you need to report in to Shamus like he's your dad or something?"

"Because he actually *is* my dad," I said, standing up and brushing myself off.

Caden nodded slowly. "It all makes sense now, you being backstage during the concert. So you're the infamous Trace, huh? Shamus has been bragging about you ever since I met him."

"He has?" Could my dad really have been talking me up to anyone and everyone? Wow. Maybe we were already more bonded than I thought.

"Yup. And you know what else? You should tell Shamus you want to hang out on the set tomorrow. I have a bunch of scenes to do at the house and it would be nice to have a friendly nonclown face around."

"I'll try to make it," I said, already plotting ways to sneak in a few snippets of flirty conversation with the guy even as warnings went off in my mind about how it probably wasn't such a smart idea.

"You do that."

We parted ways with a wave and I ran back toward the stairs. I knew it was silly, feeling so giddy over hanging out with Caden Collins. That nothing—and I mean nothing—could ever come of it. But I still couldn't help but think this was exactly the same way I'd felt after meeting Zander.

And that I hadn't felt the same for a long time since.

CHAPTER

7

I took the stairs in twos, tore up the path to the main house, and burst through the back door. Shamus was already standing there in the kitchen, shaking his head. "This is incredible. Utterly amazing. I don't know how to thank you, Trace."

"The psyched reaction was thanks enough," I laughed.

"No, seriously. I can't believe you got this done all by yourself. It's nothing short of a miracle."

"I'm glad you like it, but the truth is I had a little help. And tomorrow, the two of us are going to attack some of the other rooms—"

"Absolutely not," Shamus said, shaking his finger at me, semijoking, semiserious. "You are not doing any more work while you're here. This is your last hurrah before college, and I'm not going to have you locked in the house acting like Cinderella."

"But I *want* to help you," I told him. "Just like you let Z help you today."

As if I'd summoned him just by uttering his name, Zander appeared. "Today was great, Shamus. Can I be your apprentice again tomorrow?"

Shamus threw his hands up and laughed. "I've never met two more motivated teenagers in my life. When I was your age, Bliss and I could've won gold medals for the gymnastics we went through to *avoid* work. I must say, we pulled a lot of disappearing acts."

Kind of like me and Caden, I thought, and then gave myself a stern warning: Stop thinking about Caden! "I'd love to hear more about that summer," I told Shamus, trying to get my mind onto other things.

"Let's see, hon, it was full of concerts, long walks on the beach," he began, but was interrupted by the doorbell almost immediately. "Just wait a sec while I go see who that is. . . ."

So Bebe and Shamus had liked concerts and long walks on the beach just like Caden and I did, huh? *Aggggggghhhh!* I simply *had* to get my mind onto other, more important things. Like why Zander had just planted himself right in front of me, and why he looked so mad, for starters.

"So where'd you take off to, Trace? One minute you were talking to that goofy Menace Man, and the next you were gone. Or, should I say, you were both gone."

"The truth is—" I started fake coughing, trying to figure out my next move. Was I really going to tell him what I had been doing while he was busy salivating over Kandy? It probably wouldn't go over big, regardless of the fact that nothing had happened. Unsure of how to explain my adventure without Z getting totally pissed off, I opted for more coughing.

"You need some water?" he asked. He looked like he'd be about as good a caregiver as the Grim Reaper.

"No, no," I said, clearing my throat and moving on to Plan B—not an accurate accounting of the facts, or even a facsimile thereof. "The truth is, I felt like I was missing out on the choreography from where I was standing, so I went out front to get a better view."

"Really," Zander said. He might as well have said *bullshit.* I wasn't exactly known for my interest in dance moves.

"Really."

"Funny. That doesn't sound like your style," Z said, his mouth set in a sharp, straight line.

Since my defense wasn't working, I went on the offensive instead. "Z, you're freaking out about nothing. I mean, so I said a few sentences to Caden Collins backstage. You met Kandy today and told me how beautiful you thought she was. I even caught you ogling her while you were helping the camera guy, and I didn't get all nuts on you, did I?" I reached up and stroked his cheek, hoping it would distract him from asking any more questions.

"I guess not," he finally admitted, wrapping me in his arms. They felt sturdy, familiar. Not as exciting as Caden's palm-reading maneuver had been, but I knew that kind of crazy electricity had nothing to do with love and everything to do with lust—and that I was lucky to have found the former, even if the latter had kind of fallen by the wayside over the course of the past year.

"You know what? You're cute when you're mad, too," I said, relaxing into his chest.

He pulled back and looked at me in all seriousness. "Thanks. But let's get one thing straight—I wasn't ogling. I was just trying to find the best angle for the camera operator."

"Got it," I said, not believing it any more than he'd gone for my missed-choreography routine.

Before we could try and sell each other any more little white lies, my dad walked back into the kitchen with a million and one cartons of steaming Chinese food. "Grab a plate and load it up, everyone," he said. "I'm declaring tonight movie night, featuring my favorite from when I was your age. I saw it with your mom, Trace."

"That's so cool," I said, plopping egg rolls, vegetable fried rice, and lettuce wraps on my plate.

Shamus dove into the chicken lo mein. "So what's your favorite?"

"Probably the lettuce wraps."

"I meant *movie*," he said, throwing his head back and laughing. "What's your favorite movie?"

"Oh," I said. Now I knew how Jessica must've felt after the whole world heard her "I didn't know buffalos had wings" comment. "I guess *Almost Famous*. Or maybe *Ferris Bueller's Day Off*."

"You're kidding, right?" Shamus's jaw just about dropped to the floor. "You've already seen Ferris? That was my pick for tonight!"

I nodded, a huge grin spreading out toward my ears. Now I knew why the flick was one of Bebe's favorites, and why we'd watched it together so many times over the years. "Life moves pretty fast. . . ." I said, throwing out one of best lines.

". . . If you don't stop to look around once in a while, you might miss it," Shamus jumped in. "Well, we're definitely related, aren't we, Trace?"

"Looks that way," I said. Could smiles be permanent, I wondered?

Zander certainly answered that one for me fast enough. (It's no, by the way.) "My favorite is *Philadelphia*."

"Cream cheese?" I asked, giving him a look like *Who are you kidding?* I knew for a fact his favorite movie was *Old School*, not the sensitive drama about AIDS.

"I haven't been there in years," Shamus said at the same time.

"I'm talking about the Tom Hanks film with the Bruce song in it," Zander persisted, trying to save his dying brown-nosing mission. "You know, of the same name?"

"Oh," Shamus said, dropping the topic and moving on quickly.

"Come, guys, bring your plates and drinks into the theater. We're going to do a little brew and view—with the brew being these root beers, of course."

Soon we were all settled into the cushy big Barcaloungers, me between the guys, sucking up globs of Chinese food and taking big swigs of our sodas. As the credits rolled, I was surprised to see that instead of Matthew Broderick showing up for his opening mono-logue, the screen flickered with a bunch of vaguely familiar actors while a song no one in their right mind—much less someone my age—should know blared in the background.

" 'Simple Minds,' right?" I said to no one in particular.

"How do you know all this retro stuff?" Shamus asked, his voice brimming with amazement.

"Have you ever met my mother? You know, the queen of bad eighties music?"

"It's not so bad, Trace," he said, patting my hand. "Or at least it didn't used to be. Now maybe it sounds a little dated."

"Aka bad," I said, just loud enough for him to hear it.

"All right, you got me there," Shamus admitted after another verse, and we shared another laugh that seemed like it might just have some sticking power to it.

I hadn't seen Shamus's new pick, *The Breakfast Club*, before, but I was glad he'd chosen it. It was another eighties flick about five to-tally different kids stuck in detention who get to know each other by fighting, getting high, and, eventually, kissing. Not only was it funny, but it also provided good fodder for the big heart-to-heart I'd been hoping to have with my dad while I was here.

So somewhere around the middle of the movie, I turned to Shamus and whispered. "Which character were you most like in high school? The jock, the wastoid, or the nerd?"

No answer. I could hear my dad breathing, so I figured he was thinking. "Come on now, Shamus," I said, busting his chops for taking so long. "You're not going to tell me you were the princess or psycho case, are you?"

Still nothing.

"Shamus? I really want to know more about you, and for you to know more about me. Seriously."

Suddenly a loud snore exploded out of his mouth, exiting with a gust of air that somehow wound its way back up his nose and started the process all over again from the beginning. Sigh. The big bondfest would not be tonight.

Still, it didn't have to be a total waste. "Hey, Zander," I whispered, even though we were the only ones in this movie theater and it wasn't like we were going to disturb anyone, least of all my comatose father. "I have a confession to make."

I'd only been planning on spilling the beans about chatting it up with Caden earlier, asking forgiveness for the lie, and leaving the past in the past. But then I decided to take an even bigger leap—into our future—even though I had no idea where we'd end up. I figured it would be either a) a much better place than we were currently in, and maybe even that somewhere divine Caden had sung about or b) Splitsville. I'd finally come to the conclusion, thanks to both Caden and K.C., that either one had to be better than limbo.

Staring straight ahead so I wouldn't see the look on his face and chicken out, I started my speech over. "Z, I actually have a couple of confessions. I'm going to start at the beginning and make my way through them, and I don't want you to say a word until I'm done, OK? When you broke up with me last year, I basically lost my trust in you. In us, really. But instead of telling you how I felt about that—really, how I felt about a lot of things—I just held it all in and acted like everything was cool. And since I was too afraid to ask, to get all serious because maybe then you'd decide we were over again, I settled for hoping things were cool over actually knowing.

I stopped for a quick breath, then plunged right back in before I lost my nerve.

"I finally figured out today—with the help of that new friend I was telling you about—that I wasn't being fair to either of us. So from now on, I want us to be able to say whatever's on our minds, whenever it's on our minds. Even the hard stuff. I'll start, OK? Tonight after the concert, I didn't want to get a better view of the dancers. I actually saw how into Kandy you were and it drove me insane with jealousy. So I went for a walk with Caden Collins, kind of in retaliation. Now, before you go ballistic, I need you to know nothing happened and I won't talk to him again if it makes you uncomfortable. And I also need you to know . . . to know . . . I really l-l-l-like you, Zander. And I really want to make things right."

Though my heart was *ka-chunking* around my chest like it was looking for an escape hatch by the time I finished my speech, I felt calmer than I had in ages. I'd gone and spilled my guts—well, most of 'em, seeing as I weaseled out on using the big L-word, settling for the littler one instead—and it felt completely liberating.

"OK, Z, I'm done. Your turn now."

Silence. Jeez, these men of little words tonight.

"Zander, I swear. Nothing happened with Caden. You've got to believe me."

I finally turned to look at him and found he was in the exact same position as my dad—head tilted back, eyes closed, mouth wide open. Shamus and mini-Shamus, snoozing away while I blabbed on and on about my feelings to them. When in hell was I going to learn to just keep my mouth shut?

* * *

I watched the rest of the movie essentially alone, occasionally poking Shamus and Zander to see whether either would wake up. Neither did, until the closing credits came on and I turned on the lights.

"Did I fall asleep?" Shamus asked, rubbing his eyes. "I'm sorry, hon. Long day. Mind if I hit the sack?"

"No problem."

"Hey, I forgot to ask before, I was so stunned by the kitchen. What did you think of the concert?"

"It was awesome," I said. "I loved Caden's new songs. And Kandy certainly puts a lot into her performance. I mean, the crowd seemed to love it."

"What about you?" Shamus asked, searching my eyes. "Did you love her performance?"

Zander crossed his arms and gave me a piercing stare, like, *If you don't tell him I will.*

I closed my eyes so I wouldn't have to look at either of them and went for it. "The truth is, I'm really not that into dance music," I said, the words spilling out of my mouth in a single wave.

The best part about the complete honesty thing was that Shamus didn't seem angry or shocked by what I'd said. In fact, he laughed. "Me, neither. But those kids out there today? They eat that shit up."

Relieved, I went to give my dad a hug. "You mean stuff, don't you?"

"Nope," he said, patting my back and still laughing. "This time, I really did mean shit."

A minute later, Shamus shuffled off to his bedroom, leaving just me and mini-Shamus—who of course gave me a similar speech about being exhausted and needing to go to bed. But I was still hoping to do some serious making up and/or out before the night was through, so I followed Zander to his room and lay down on the bed while he brushed his teeth, threw on sleep pants, and turned off the light.

As soon as Z slipped under the comforter, I scootched over and snuggled into his back. He didn't flip over and attack me like I expected. Next I tried kissing his neck, sucking on his earlobe, and running my fingers through his hair. Still nothing.

Now this had never happened before. Zander was always up for fooling around. Maybe he hadn't forgiven my disappearing act down at the beach yet? Or worse, maybe he *hadn't* been sleeping while I poured out my heart and just hadn't like what he'd heard? "Are you mad at me?" I finally whispered.

"Not mad, Trace," he said, lacing his fingers through mine and pulling me even tighter to him, so there was no mistaking we'd just be spooning tonight and nothing more. "Just tired. I worked a lot today."

I *wanted* to say, *Me too*. I *wanted* to say, *You're not the only one*. But what I actually said was nothing. Absolutely nothing.

CHAPTER
8

"Time to get up."

"No, thanks," I mumbled into my pillow and rolled over. I hate getting up. "Start without me, Shamus. I'll be there in a while."

"I'm definitely not Shamus. And does the rise-and-shine method work any better with you?" The way too wide-awake person threw open the curtains so sunshine streamed in the windows and onto my still very sleepy eyelids. "It's a beautiful day."

I knew my mom was half a country away, so that couldn't be who was bugging me. I cracked my eyes a slit, but it did little to solve the mystery. The half-blind-without-contacts thing was getting so old.

"Hey, Earl. It's me, Ralph."

Who? I didn't know any guy named Ralph—especially one with such a high-pitched voice. Maybe if I closed my eyes again I'd figure it out. Or go back to sleep. Either sounded fine.

"Trace, do you want me to come back later?" The voice was sounding decidedly less perky at this point. "Or did you change your mind about unpacking some more stuff today?"

Hello, now I got it. It was K.C., just doing what I'd asked her to do. I sat up and fumbled around the nightstand until I found my glasses. "Sorry. I can be pretty hard to wake up sometimes," I said, sliding the frames up my nose until a clear image of my new friend appeared before my eyes. "All the time, if you want to know the truth. Sorry."

"No apologies necessary," she said, handing me a gigantor Starbucks cup.

I took a slow sip and found she'd gotten it completely, one hundred percent right. "How did you know my drink order?"

"You told me when we were putting the coffee mugs away, remember? Grande nonfat vanilla latte," she said. "One thing you should know about me if we're going to be friends—I'm a really good listener."

I nodded. "I already figured that out yesterday when you were being my therapist."

K.C. plopped herself down on the bed next to me. "I hope you're not still upset about that."

"Nope. You actually inspired me," I told her. "I totally spilled my guts to my boyfriend last night."

K.C.'s eyes lit up. "That's awesome! How did it go over?"

"Not so great."

"He was totally pissed off?" she guessed.

I shook my head.

K.C. clapped her hand over her mouth. "Don't tell me he broke up with you."

"Worse," I said, giggles overtaking me. "I looked over when I was done with my big confession, and he was sound asleep. Didn't hear one word of it."

"Consider it good practice, then," she said, joining in with that little tinkling bell laugh of her own. "And try again tonight."

"You'll be glad to know you even inspired me to tell my dad I'm not exactly a Kandy lover."

K.C. picked at one of the little balls on my Yummy Puff quilt absent-mindedly. "I've been meaning to talk to you about that," she said.

"I'm all ears," I said, though the only thing I could hear at the moment was a crinkling noise every time I moved. I finally reached under my thigh and pulled out the offender—an adorable note from my dad. "Wait, hold that thought for a sec while you listen to this. 'Darling Daughter, You are a true dynamo. How can I ever thank you enough for all the work you did in here yesterday? I thought maybe letting you sleep in would be a start—we'll figure out the rest later. Come visit me at Kandy's Room when you wake up. I promise it'll be much more interesting today—we're filming scenes with Caden Collins after lunch. Much love, Shamus. P.S. No worries—Zander's offered to help me out until you come to retrieve him.'"

"So sweet," K.C. said. Her mouth was still smiling but her eyes were two big balls of worry.

"Yeah, and so cool, Caden being at the house today, don't you think?"

Pick, pick, pick. At the rate she was attacking my bedding, my Yummy Puff was going to turn into a Yucky Rag in no time. "He doesn't really interest me all that much."

"I didn't think he would interest me, either," I said, a little thrill-chill going up my spine just remembering our walk on the beach. "Until our big conversation last night, that is."

K.C. looked up at me, surprised. "Conversation?"

"Yeah. After his set, we started talking and he asked me back to his dressing room," I told her, trying to act like things like that happened to me all the time.

"And you went? I mean, what about your boyfriend? Isn't that relationship worth more to you? You've certainly invested a lot of time and energy in it."

"No, I totally didn't," I said, smiling at her mother-hen act. "We just took a walk and talked."

"And what happened? No, let me guess. He shared his recipe for fake vomit with you? Or asked you to pull his finger a couple of thousand times?"

"No, he was actually totally cool," I said, jumping to Caden's defense. "Mature, too."

But K.C. was having none of it. "Come on now, Trace. No guy who thought up the *Punk'd* episode about blow-up dolls can be mature."

"He was, really. We talked about important stuff, like about the meaning of his lyrics."

"Decoding 'We're playing a cat and mouse game, let me come into your hole' isn't exactly rocket science."

"We dissected his solo stuff, not Menace Men lyrics," I said, trying to explain how special Caden had made me feel. "And then he told me how disappointing his relationship with his old girlfriend was."

"Rock star dating a supermodel. How cliché can you get?"

"I know, but he broke up with her because even though she was beautiful, she wasn't any fun. And then he told me a story about his fifth birthday party where this clown came to entertain the kids—"

"Wow, that does sound serious," she said, being totally sarcastic now.

"It was actually more serious than you might think," I plowed ahead, trying to get her to see that Caden wasn't anything like his reputation. "The bottom line is, Caden's way more interested in what's inside people than what's on the outside. And that's why anyone in costume scares the crap out of him to this day, because it's like they're hiding who they really are."

K.C. rolled her eyes. "Deep."

Even though I knew this next piece of information was probably not for public consumption, I went for it anyway. "Well, it's definitely why he's too deep to date Kandy, even though his manager is trying to set them up."

"I'll bet Kandy wouldn't give a class clown like Caden Collins the time of day."

"You sound like you've got inside information."

She shrugged. "Not really."

"Well, I don't think Kandy deserves a great guy like Caden, anyhow," I said. "Honestly, I think you should go for him yourself." The theory here was, maybe if K.C. and Caden got together, then I'd be able to get the guy out of *my* head once and for all.

"No, thanks," she said, not even considering my suggestion. "I have enough on my plate already without adding a goofball like that into the mix."

So that strategy to get Caden unstuck from my brain wasn't going to work—maybe changing the subject would? "Hey, what were you about to tell me before I so rudely interrupted you before?"

K.C. bounced up off the bed and offered me her hand. "Oh. Uh, just that I'm sorry I can't help you with the unpacking today. I have to get to work earlier than I expected."

"That's OK. I actually got it all done last night after everyone sacked out on me," I told her, feeling super-proud of what I'd accomplished while my dad and Z snoozed away. It helped that my dad had come from a much smaller place—the kitchen was the most involved unpacking job by far. In comparison, the guest room, den, and bathrooms had been a piece of cake. "So what are the extras doing today?"

She gnawed on a perfectly manicured nail. "I'm not really sure."

"Well, want to head down to the set together and find out? I just have to throw on some clothes and makeup."

K.C. glanced at her watch. "Sorry, I should probably get going now. In case we don't hook up later, want to have another coffee date tomorrow?"

"Sure," I said, glad for the female bonding. "I promise I'll set my alarm this time."

I have to admit, I took waaayyy longer than usual getting dressed after K.C. left. Every outfit I tried on seemed wrong—this one was too casual, that one too frumpy, another too dressy, the next one too obvious. I was going for a look that screamed *I'm hot without even trying!* but unfortunately nothing even approaching that existed in my wardrobe. And let's not even get started with the crazy stunts my hair was trying to pull.

After too many unsuccessful attempts at "effortless" hotness to count, I finally gave up on trying to impress anyone. After all, Zander knew what I looked like, and nothing was going happen with Caden even if I wanted it to—which I didn't, I kept trying to convince myself. So in the end, I settled on my destroyed Abercrombie jeans, a tight pink Junk Food T-shirt, and black Chuckie T slides (which I absolutely love because no one else has them). Then I pulled my crazy bedhead into a ponytail, plunked a black baseball cap on top of it, and made my way down to Kandy's Room.

I spotted my dad and Zander as soon as I walked in the door. Both were sitting side by side in identical director's chairs. I swear, if Zander shrunk about four feet and started holding his pinkie to the corner of his mouth while saying "One meeeeeelllllllion dollars," people were going to start mistaking him for Verne Troyer.

As soon as he saw me, Z jumped up and ran over to me. "Hey, I was just about to come and wake you up," he said. "In a very special way, I might add."

It actually sounded like a pretty good idea. We hadn't so much as kissed since the first night on the front porch when I'd been plotting something much more involved, and between that and my encounter with stardom last night, my hormones were going crazier than they had since Z and I first got together. "Yum. So maybe I should run back up to the house, hop under the covers, and pretend I'm still sleeping?"

Zander shook his head. "I'd rather it be a surprise, you know? And anyway, the stuff going on here today seems like it's gonna be awesome. Rumor has it Caden and Kandy already hate each other."

Shamus waved us over to where he was sitting. "Hey, hon. You got here just in time," he said, gesturing to the chair next to his. "Have a seat."

My eyes welled up. It said Trace in block letters. "For me?"

"Mais oui," he said and called for silence. "Quiet, everyone. Filming starts in just a minute. Caden and Kandy, just pretend we're not here, OK?"

"OK, Mr. McDonohue," Kandy said. Along with her trademark makeup, she was wearing white Daisy Dukes with pink piping, a white-and-pink-striped belly shirt and pink platform sandals that must've been two feet high.

The doorbell rang, and Kandy clomped over to answer it, a cameraman trailing her the whole time. She obediently acted like she didn't notice and opened the door. It was Caden.

"I didn't order a pizza," she said and slammed the door in his face.

Zander chuckled softly. Shamus shot him a look. "Lesson number one: No reacting to the action," he whispered.

Zander nodded like an out-of-control bobblehead. "Got it," he whispered back.

Kandy was heading for the loft when the doorbell rang again.

Sighing, she went to answer it. Caden pelted her with Silly String the minute she opened up this time.

"Very funny, Pizza Boy," she said, not locking him out again but not exactly inviting him in, either.

Caden walked inside anyway and picked a few stray Silly Strings out of Kandy's gleaming pink wig. "Looks like we got off on the wrong foot, huh?"

Kandy pretty much ignored the guy.

"So let's start over again. I'm Caden Collins, pleased to meet you," he said, sticking out his hand.

"Hi," she said, shaking it limply before retreating to the kitchen.

Caden shrugged and followed her. "So, what do you want to do today?"

"Nothing," she said, barely looking up from the magazine she was reading at the counter.

"I can see why. I mean, there's absolutely nothing for you to do in here," Caden said, walking over to the Dance Dance Revolution machine and hopping on. "Like this, for example. You probably can't figure out how it works, right?"

Kandy scowled at him. "I'll have you know I'm amazing at DDR. No one can beat me."

"Is that a challenge?" Caden asked, totally mugging at the camera even though he definitely knew he wasn't supposed to be.

"Yeah, it totally is, buddy," she said, sounding much tougher than her impractical getup would lead you to believe. "So how do you want me to hand your ass to you—going head-to-head or versus?"

"Anything that involves your hands and my ass is just fine, darling," Caden laughed.

Both Zander and I exchanged a look and tried to hold in our giggles as a woman I hadn't noticed before yelled, "Cut!"

Shamus rolled his eyes. "Mrs. Kane, it's *my* job to yell cut. Things were just getting rolling."

"But my baby said a bad word, and then that boy made a lewd comment. . . ."

"It's OK, Mrs. Kane. We can edit anything inappropriate out of the show," he told her gently. "But quite honestly, it's MTV, and the word *ass* is no problem."

"Are you sure?"

"Positive. Now can we get started again?"

Mrs. Kane tottered over and took Kandy's face in her hands. "Just one moment, Mr. McDonohue," she said. "I need to talk to my baby briefly."

As Kandy got a whispered lecture from her mom, I noticed Caden was motioning for someone—maybe me? naah, couldn't be—to follow him.

I looked behind me. No one was there. Glancing back over at Caden, I saw he was laughing and motioning more wildly at me. Luckily, Zander was too busy checking out the camera equipment to notice, and by the time he looked up Caden had disappeared down the hall.

" 'Scuse me a sec."

"Where are you going?" Zander asked sharply.

"To the bathroom," I ad-libbed.

"Well, hurry up, Trace," Shamus told me. "We're going to start shooting again just as soon as Mrs. Kane gets over hearing her baby utter a baby swear."

I sprinted out of my seat and was just passing the bathroom door when an arm reached out and pulled me inside. "Check this out," Caden said, placing a small black plastic contraption in my hand. I had no clue what it did, and wasn't about to start pushing buttons to find out.

"Cool," I said, trying to act all casual even as I flirted with danger. "So what is it?"

He reached out and put a hand on the wall behind me, so our bodies were practically touching. "Something very naughty."

"R-r-really?" Much as I was trying to keep my cool, I was losing it. Fast.

Caden leaned in even farther. "Don't worry, I'm not going to make you try it out. It's actually a surprise for Kandy."

"I'm not so sure she's going to let you close enough to use that thing on her," I said. My voice sounded foreign to my ears, like it belonged to someone else. Maybe this was what it was like to have an out-of-body experience.

Caden laughed. "That's the best part, Trace," he said, backing off with the sexy stuff and chucking me in the arm like a buddy instead. I felt strangely let down. Like, I knew I shouldn't hope he was about to make a move on me, but was still kind of disappointed when he didn't. "It's remote controlled. God, this is going to be so funny. Kandy and her mom are going to blow a fit."

"I can't wait to check it out," I said, slipping out the door and heading back to my chair, which Zander was temporarily occupying. I prayed he'd stay completely absorbed in whatever Shamus was saying for long enough to miss Caden coming out of the bathroom a few seconds after me. I heaved a sigh of relief when I realized I had gotten away with it.

"Everyone ready?" Shamus yelled into the bullhorn as I stuffed myself into the seat next to Zander. "And action!"

"So let's do it." Caden said, leaning against the bars of the DDR machine. "You first."

"You're on," Kandy said through gritted teeth. She programmed in all the information, chose a song, and waited for the machine to power up. "Watch and learn, dude."

The music started and Kandy, true to her word, got every step right in the first verse. Just as I was wondering when Caden was going to make his big move with the little black contraption, Kandy did a double-footed hop, which was unexpectedly accompanied by a quick little farting noise.

"Something you ate?" Caden asked, grinning.

"That was not me and you know it," Kandy said, still concentrating on her dance moves.

The next time she did a complicated left-right-hop-hop combination, it was supplemented by burp-puke-dry-heave-loogie-snort sounds.

"You are completely disgusting," she told Caden, never missing a beat.

"*I* am?" He was practically doubled over he was laughing so hard by this point.

"Yes. Repulsive," she said, never once cracking a smile.

When Kandy finished her dance, a symphony of scatological noises rang out, concluding with one humongous fart. Kandy shot Caden the most evil look I have ever seen and stalked off while the entire crew roared with laughter.

During the riot that ensued, Caden strolled over to where Zander and I were sitting and held up the noisemaker. "Didn't I tell you this was going to be a howl?"

Zander eyed both the gadget and me while Shamus gathered Kandy and Caden into a little huddle.

"What?" I asked Z.

He looked disgusted with me. "You were in on planning that gag?"

"No, of course not." And I wasn't, really. I'd just gotten an early heads-up, and even then I didn't really know what was going to go down.

"Kandy didn't deserve that," he said. "She's one of the nicest people I've ever met. Caden Collins is such a loser."

Oh, yeah? Two could play that game. "Actually, Caden is one of the nicest people *I've* ever met."

Before Z and I had time to get into it further, Shamus got things rolling again.

"Just a little icebreaker, Kandy. No hard feelings, right?" Caden stuck his hand out to shake.

"What, you've got a buzzer hidden in your palm? No, thanks."

"No, really," he said, holding up his bare hand. "I'm sorry for embarrassing you."

"Apology not accepted until you make an ass out of yourself on DDR."

"Fine," he said, chuckling.

It was all over in a matter of a minute. "You really suck," Kandy told Caden after he'd tripped over his own feet for the last time. "I beat you by five hundred thousand points. Ready to quit yet?"

"Not so fast," Caden said. "Let's try another game where we're more evenly matched. Like, say, Karaoke Revolution."

Kandy hesitated. Now we were going to find out once and for all whether the lip-synch rumors were true. "You're so on," she finally answered. I had to give her credit for having been basically unflappable thus far. "Just let me grab some water."

"Will you go get her some?" Shamus whispered to Zander. "She likes it room temperature."

Caden set up the game while Kandy headed back into the kitchen. When she got there, Zander was waiting with a smile, looking even happier to be her water boy than he had being camera-cord holder. While Kandy took dainty sips, Zander stared on in awe like he couldn't believe how well she could swallow or something. I wanted to barf.

"Ready!" Caden called from in front of the big-screen TV, and started singing Jet's "Are You Gonna Be My Girl." He pogoed around, hitting all the right notes at the right time while his cool character did the same on-screen. He scored platinum—mostly perfects, with just two goods thrown in there.

When Caden was done, he handed the microphone to Kandy. He'd programmed her character to be this big, fat guy wearing flippers and a duckie inner tube, and the song he'd chosen for her to sing was The Darkness's "I Believe in a Thing Called Love"—a bizarre, almost "Bohemian Rhapsody" kind of thing sung half in falsetto. I mean, no one can make that song sound good.

But somehow, Kandy did. Actually, it was better than good. It was great. I was floored, and from the looks of it, so was Caden. In the end, Kandy edged out Caden's score by five hundred points— she'd gotten only one good in the midst of a billion perfects. "I don't think you can beat me in anything, Mr. Collins. Do you?" she asked, looking all smug.

"What else you got, sister?"

"Trampoline, baby," she said. "Best tricks win."

Caden and Kandy ran outside like two little kids, the crew following close behind.

"They're either gonna kill each other or fall in love," Shamus whooped on the way out. "And either one is going to be great for ratings!"

"That's awesome, Shamus," I said. "Hey, where are the extras today? I was hoping to see my new friend here."

"She might be down on the beach. They're shooting a bunch of fan interviews there today. Want to go and see?"

"No, thanks," I said after thinking about it for a second. "This is way too much fun."

Caden was already bouncing on the trampoline like a maniac by the time we got outside, doing crazy flips and drops. His best sequence: a doggy-seat-doggy-front-flip combo.

"Is that all you've got?" Kandy called, arms crossed over her pneumatic chest.

"You can do better?" Caden asked.

"You better believe it," Kandy said, hopping on the tramp while Caden hopped off. She immediately launched into Caden's doggy-seat-doggy-front flip . . . and then added a back-flip-left-side-aerial-right-side-aerial-twisting-layout to the end.

She'd won again.

"Forget these chick games," Caden said, looking a little flustered. "How about wiffle ball? There's no way you can beat me. I am the absolute king of wiffle ball."

Kandy readily agreed. "Fine. One pitch each, whichever ball goes the farthest wins."

"You're on."

Kandy gave Caden a pitch straight down the middle. He got a good piece of it, sending a line drive whipping at Kandy's head. Most people I know would've automatically ducked and let the ball go flying by, but not Kandy. She casually plucked it out of midair right before it was about to smash into her pretty, overly made-up face.

"Gotcha, goofy boy. My turn now."

"She's gonna whiff," he said, full of bravado, though it looked like he might've been sweating it out at this point.

Caden took a full windup and threw her a fastball that was high and inside. Instead of taking the ball and asking for a better pitch,

Kandy calmly readjusted her stance and took a whack at it. Everyone watched as the thing soared over our heads and down to the beach below.

"I win again," she crowed.

Caden pretended to shake his head mournfully, but I could see he was smiling underneath it all. "You surf?"

"I've tried a couple of times," she told him.

"Well, grab a board and let's go. All or nothing. First one to ride a wave in is the declared the winner of today's decathlon."

"Quintathlon, you mean."

"Huh?"

"This is only our fifth event," Kandy explained. "A decathlon has ten. And *quint* is the Latin root meaning *five*."

"What-ever," Caden said. "You're still going down."

"That's what you think."

We all started for the long flights of stairs, Mrs. Kane rushing ahead to get to Kandy. "Darling, I don't want you surfing," she yelled after her daughter. "I just don't think it's safe. We can't have you getting injured now, with the tour just around the corner."

Kandy ignored her, board in hand, following right on Caden's heels.

"Yeah, are you sure you want to do this?" he called back at her. "I mean, you might mess up your makeup or something."

"It's waterproof," she shot back.

As soon as they hit the beach, both raced into the waves, paddling like crazy to get out to where they were breaking. Almost immediately, both got up on their boards and stayed on them until they were back at shore. It was a tie. At least Caden hadn't outright lost again, I thought.

"Face it, not so menacing man," Kandy said, looking even more beautiful wet and wild from the surf, if that was possible. "Anything you can do, I can do better."

"Oh, yeah?" he shot back. "We'll see about that. Because tomorrow we're tackling songwriting. Come prepared with your best song—a new one, not something you've been working on a long time. And we'll get some impartial judges to pick the winner."

"Deal."

Kandy was walking back toward the steps when Caden grabbed her arm. "Did anyone ever tell you you're a lot more fun than my ex-girlfriend?"

Kandy's smile softened her words. "Don't go getting any ideas, buddy. I still don't like you."

I felt a quick flash of jealousy, followed by a dull throb of relief. If Caden was suddenly changing his mind about Kandy, at least I wouldn't have to worry about how to resist his sexy maneuvers anymore.

Caden sounded off the fart machine again, cracking himself up.

"Hilarious," Kandy said, the smile disappearing from her face.

"How come you're not laughing, then?"

"I don't find juvenile humor funny," she announced. "And therefore I don't find you funny."

Another challenge. As unlikely as it seemed, these two were practically made for each other. "Are you saying I could never make you laugh?" Caden asked.

"That's exactly what I'm saying."

"Just you wait. I'll have you peeing your pants tomorrow."

"Are you always this crude?" Kandy said, heading back into the house and locking him out for real this time.

"Yeah," Caden yelled at the closed door. "Pretty much."

* * *

OK, so maybe Caden's getting sucked in by Kandy's charms and my dad being her manager—or whatever the heck title he had in her life—*was* going to be fun after all. Despite my twinges of jealousy, I couldn't believe how bummed I was when shooting wrapped after Caden and Kandy's parting shots. And I could barely wait to see what was going to happen tomorrow.

CHAPTER 9

"So how'd you get involved with Kandy, anyway?" I asked my dad as we were digging into the awesome barbecue dinner he'd ordered—ribs, chicken, cole slaw, mounds of fries. The way I was eating here, I was going to put on the dreaded freshman fifteen before I even set foot on campus.

"I actually discovered her in a mall, singing her heart out to maybe five people," Shamus said, licking his fingers. "She was trying to make it as a singer-songwriter—kind of along the lines of early Jewel—and she just wasn't making any headway."

"Why not?" Zander asked.

Shamus shrugged. "She's certainly a good-looking enough girl, and she has a great voice. But girls like Kandy are a dime a dozen around here. What she needed was something to set her apart. So I came up with the idea of the makeup and the outrageous outfits, hired The Matrix to cowrite a couple of songs with her, and here we are."

"Brilliant move," my boyfriend added. I didn't know whether I'd ever be able to make out with him again. I mean, he might be too busy kissing my dad's ass to use his lips for anything else for the next couple of years.

"I can't believe you came up with that look, Shamus," I said, completely surprised it was a guy's invention. "Were you inspired by the Harajuku girls?"

Shamus shook his head. "Who?"

"You know, the stylish Japanese girls from Tokyo that Gwen Stefani was so impressed by she had them follow her around for the entire *Love Angel Music Baby* tour?"

"Oh, gosh no, honey," Shamus said. "My inspiration came from Kiss."

"Who?" Zander asked.

"You know, the band that wore all the makeup and crazy costumes and platform boots back in the day? And one of the guys had a really long tongue? Am I ringing any bells here?"

Zander and I shook our heads.

"Well, they were huge when I was a kid—they even had their own Saturday morning cartoon. So I just thought, maybe I'll bring back that kind of look, but in a more feminine way."

"Well, judging from the way everyone was dressed down the beach yesterday, your instincts were right on," Zander said, becoming toadier by the second. "The kids love it. Maybe you should do some articles with before and after pictures of Kandy, to show kids how to perfect the look."

"Well, here's the thing. We're actually trying to keep Kandy's real identity hush-hush, to build the brand—the illusion, you know. She's like a superhero to her fans. They may be too old to worship Batman or Spiderman, but they can certainly plaster posters of Kandy on their walls and still be cool."

It was an interesting perspective. "I never thought of it that way. Honestly, I used to think Kandy's style was just a way to distract people from realizing she had no talent. But after hearing her sing on the set today, and now listening to you explain the thought behind it, I'm impressed."

"Thanks, Trace," he said, passing the red-and-white-checked bucket of fries around the table again. "To tell you the truth, Kandy doesn't necessarily agree with the look, either—she'd rather be judged solely on her talent. But I told her to just go along with this for a while, make her mark, and then do her own music on her own terms. See? Zander was right. Your old man's brilliant."

I shoved a few more fries into my face and patted my stomach. "I knew I got it from somewhere."

"We're a lot alike, Trace," he said, smiling at me.

I saw my opening and went for it. I had only four more days here and needed to get to that heart-to-heart soon if I was going to stick us together forever on this visit. "Well, I'd definitely like to find out how alike we really are. For instance, do you like mushrooms on your pizza?"

It was a trick question—I hate them, but didn't want to influence my dad's answer. Unfortunately, his cell rang before he could clarify his position on the slimy fungi.

"Let's pick up this conversation where we left off later," he said when he got off the phone. "Right now I need to go see dailies—my editor is howling, and he says the footage we got today is so good it can't wait. In the meantime, start the game without me."

"What game?" I asked.

"Our weekly Texas Hold 'Em game," one of the camera guys announced as he and the crew came piling through the back door.

"Cool," Zander said, pulling up a seat. "I need cash for this semester. My parents are on a big pay-your-own-way kick. They want me to learn how to manage money better and think making me use my own is the way to go."

"You have to admit, they're probably right," I said.

"Yeah, but it still totally sucks."

"Stop whining and start dealing," the galoot who had been guarding the beach the other day told Zander, tossing him the cards.

I tried to figure out the rules for a while, then gave up and headed off in search of something else to do—like maybe call Brina or check in with my mom, neither of whom I'd talked to since I got here. But first I'd need to locate my cell phone, which was located somewhere in the depths of my messenger bag, which was located somewhere in this house, though I had no idea where. I'd unceremoniously dumped it when I'd walked through the door a few days earlier and hadn't seen it since.

After a half hour of unsuccessful searching, I gave up and headed back out to see what was happening in the living room. Shamus was back, Zander had a pile of chips in front of him so high it nearly reached his eyeballs, and there was no end in sight to the game.

"See, Trace, told you I'd make sure we had fun this week," he said, puffing away on a stogie. Z was practically turning green from the one stuck in his mouth, but that didn't stop him from trying to act like one of the boys.

"Yeah, it's been totally great so far, Shamus," I said. "But I'm a little tired, so I think I'll head off to bed now." Anything to stop me from gagging on all the fumes in here.

"So soon?"

"Yeah, I'm totally beat," I told him.

"OK, come on down to the house sometime around eleven tomorrow. That way, you can catch a few extra z's and not have to sit through the boring setup. You'll get there just in time for the good stuff."

"Can I help with the setup?" Zander jumped in, close to hacking a lung up by now. "It's not boring to me, you know."

"Sure," Shamus replied. "Maybe we can even get you behind a camera to do some test shots, if Trace doesn't mind."

"Really? That would be amazing!"

"I thought we had plans tomorrow morning," I said, giving Z the evil eye before heading out of the room.

"Can I take a rain check?" Zander asked, trailing me into the hall like a puppy.

I let out a heavy sigh. "It seems like you've been doing that ever since we got here."

Z went to kiss me, but I turned me head so all he got was cheek. Besides me being mad at him, his cigar breath was too disgusting for words.

"Please, Trace. It would give me such a leg up on other guys at NYU," Zander said, a pleading note creeping into his voice. "Film school is so competitive, and this is such a unique opportunity."

"So it's not just because you want time alone with Kandy Kane, without me there to see you flirting?"

Zander wrapped me in his arms. "Not even one bit. And if I was the jealous type, I'd be asking you the same question about Caden Collins."

"No worries there," I said, though maybe Z should've been a little worried. Something about Caden had grabbed me by the bazongas and wouldn't let go.

"So it's cool, then?" Zander said, wrapping his arms around me. "I'll go to work with Shamus early tomorrow and I swear I'll make it up to you when we get home."

I was practically gagging on the smoke smell in his shirt by this point, so I cut our hug short. "When we get home, we have one day to finish packing and then hit the road," I reminded him.

"The following weekend, then. We'll do all the touristy stuff in NYC together, all weekend, just me and you. What do you think?"

What I was thinking was that while the plan sounded good, it probably wouldn't be the brightest thing I'd ever done to take off the very first weekend of school. I'd be, like, a social leper by the time I came back, with everyone speaking a different language about all the fun stuff they'd done while I was gone. And I'd be forever known as the girl who simply couldn't bear to be away from her boyfriend for more than a few days at a time—you know, the type who transfers second semester, so no one bothers to make friends with her in the first place. What I was thinking was that this whole going to different colleges thing was going to be tougher than I thought.

But what I said right before I headed off to bed and Zander headed back to the poker game was, "Sounds good."

CHAPTER 10

I was already up and dressed by the time K.C. got to the house with my coffee the next morning. A few sips into my highly caffeinated drink, I launched into the tale of what happened between Kandy and Caden the day before.

"See, I told you the guy was a joker," K.C. said as my story wound down. "And you wanted me to get involved with him?"

"I have to admit, Caden acted totally juvenile yesterday. But you can't help but laugh—he's so funny. And anyway, Kandy didn't take any crap. It was an even match."

"Well, there's a silver lining, then," K.C. said. "Most reality shows are so soulless, they have no moral value. At least this way, kids can look up to Kandy as a strong female role model."

I nodded at her insight. "Yeah, and maybe she really can be a superhero to them, just like my dad is hoping. And anyhow, forget morals and role models—it's great TV. I can't wait to see how the songwriting contest and the laugh-off go today."

"Laugh-off?" K.C. asked

"Yeah, Caden said he's going to totally make Kandy laugh and she said he couldn't."

K.C. gave me a look like, *That's so lame.*

"I know it sounds stupid, but I'm telling you, there's definitely a spark between those two," I told her. "And it's a good thing, too, because I can barely breathe when I'm around the guy."

"You're kidding me. You think Caden Collins is attractive?"

I shrugged, a little embarrassed. "Maybe it's not so much his looks, but more the fact that he's devastatingly magnetic and sexy."

"Really?"

"Really."

"Hmmmm," she said. "I guess I'll have to check him out more closely today."

"Did you even catch a glimpse of him yesterday?" I asked. "I mean, I never saw you at the house."

"Just a quick one," she mumbled. "I was there for just a few minutes, and then I had to go."

"Right, the fan interviews on the beach," I said. "I forgot about those. So, where are the extras going to be today?"

"Who knows?" she said. "It's something different every day. I should go check in now."

"I'm just going to pick up a bit in here for my dad before I head down to the house," I told her. "Hopefully I'll see you there." The Texas Hold 'Em crew had left disgusting piles of half-eaten chips, cigar butts, and dead beers in the living room, and I didn't want Shamus being bummed out about having to clean the house after a long day of work.

K.C. opened the back door. "Things are really going well with your dad, aren't they?"

"Yeah," I said. "I'm guessing you still didn't have that talk with your mom yet, though."

"I'm still working up to it. She's just really gung ho about me getting a lot of jobs, so it's been harder than I thought to bring up the subject."

"Columbia is worth it. So keep trying, OK?"

"I know, I will."

By the time I got to the house, Caden and Kandy were already circling each other like boxers before a fight. Caden was tuning up his guitar, Kandy was noodling around on a keyboard, and neither had anything to say to the other. A bunch of extras sat off to the side of the room, all nervous laughter and poking each other. I scanned the faces for K.C.'s but couldn't find her.

"OK, who's going first?" Shamus asked.

"I am," Caden said before Kandy even had a chance to answer, and started strumming. The tune, from what I could tell, was called "Do Over," and was about a kid who kept losing at all the playground games and wanted another chance to kick ass. The song reminded me of the clown riff Caden had gone off on while we were hanging out at the beach—it was funny and catchy, but a total throwaway.

That didn't stop him from acting like he'd composed the next "Stairway to Heaven," though. When he was finished, Caden got up and high-fived the extras, bowed to the crew, and kissed Kandy's hand. "Let's see you top that, sweetheart."

"Oh, you will. This is called 'The Girl Behind the Mask,'" she said and launched into her song. The tune was haunting, beautiful. So was her voice. But the words were way too preachy to be catchy.

> *Won't you come out*
> *Come out from behind the mask*
> *Let others see your brilliance*
> *How you shine, how you glow*
> *Girl, leave the mask behind*
> *And you'll grow, and you'll grow*

When Kandy was done, she avoided the theatrics Caden had gone through and simply stood up and nodded graciously.

"Let's hear it now!" An extra who'd been appointed emcee yelled. "Who thinks Caden's song was the best?"

There was a smattering of applause and a few catcalls.

"Come one, dudes," Caden goaded them. "You can do better than that."

"And now who thinks Kandy's song was better?" Mr. Emcee guy asked, eliciting the same amount of polite applause.

"There's no way you could think her slop was better than mine," Caden complained.

"Slop?" Kandy said, totally offended. "My song about personal growth is slop, and your song about getting a do-over is gold?"

Caden shrugged. "I didn't exactly say it was gold. But at least it's fun."

"And at least mine had meaning," she shot back.

They were in a standoff, staring each other down.

"Well, what would you have done differently with my song?" Caden finally asked. He even looked serious, like he really wanted to hear her answer.

"I'm going to start playing and you'll get out your fart thrower, is that it?" she asked.

"No, I'm totally serious," he said. "Promise."

Kandy still looked suspicious, but went for it anyway. "I'd slow down the tempo, replace the power chords with open ones. More like your solo stuff instead of a Menace Men song."

"So you have been listening to me, after all?" Caden asked.

Kandy nodded. "You're definitely capable of more than you'd care to let on. Like, how about this?"

Kandy instantly transformed Caden's silly pop-punk anthem

into more of a ballad. Zander, the cameraman with the biggest under-eye circles in the universe from staying up way too late playing poker, caught every moment of it on film.

Once the chorus hit, Caden started singing, changing his words to be more of a love song.

> *I want to go back and make a better impression*
> *Meet you again and make a better suggestion*
> *Act in a way so you'd never have questions*
> *I want a do-over, gotta make a confession*
> *I want to do it all over with you*

When they were done, Kandy and Caden eyed each other like each was waiting for the other to start the razzing. But neither did.

"That was amazing," Caden said instead.

Kandy played with a clump of pink hair. "Really?"

"Yeah."

"Well, I really liked your lyrics, too."

"Maybe we could work on the song more later?"

"How about now?" Kandy asked.

Caden shook his head. "Now it's time for me to make you laugh."

I glanced at Shamus, whose mouth was hanging open at this point. "This is even better than yesterday!" he whispered to me.

"I'm so happy for you," I whispered back.

Kandy plunked herself down next to Caden on the couch, holding a pillow to her chest for protection.

"You're not how I thought you'd be," Caden said, sliding closer to Kandy. "And I mean that in a really good way."

"I could say the same for you."

"Did anyone ever tell you you're completely gorgeous?"

She smiled and shrugged. "Once or twice. Did anyone ever tell you you're completely annoying—and completely charming?"

He smiled and shrugged. "Once or twice."

For a second, it looked like they were about to kiss. But then Caden broke the spell with, "If I get you to laugh, you have to do anything I want. If I don't, I'll do anything you want. Deal?"

"No way!" Kandy said, thwacking him with the pillow.

"I thought you said there was not a chance in hell you'd so much as snicker at anything I did, so what are you worried about?" Caden asked, grabbing the pillow and tossing it aside.

Now Kandy had nothing for protection, so she threw up her hands instead. "You're on."

First Caden went with a joke along the lines of "A guy, a moose, two chicks with mustaches, and a priest walk into a bar." Kandy didn't even crack a smile.

Next he did his monkey impression—which of course included monkey masturbation—and it sent the extras into hysterics. Unfortunately for Caden, Kandy just sat there like a statue.

"And we've already established this doesn't work," Caden said, running through the gamut of gross noises with his little contraption.

"Yes, we have," Kandy said with a total straight face.

"Well, then, I'm just going to have to resort to tickle torture," he said, jumping on top of her and tickling her ribs mercilessly. Kandy held it together for all of about thirty seconds, and then the laughter started pealing out of her.

And it sounded just like a tinkling little bell.

"K.C.?" I gasped. Thinking back, her voice *had* sounded kind of familiar. But it had taken her unique laugh to knock what should've been readily apparent into my apparently very thick skull.

Shamus gave me a dirty look and shushed me. "No reacting to the action, remember?"

"Sorry," I whispered back, still staring at my friend in shock.

K.C. pushed Caden aside, sat up, and locked eyes with me. "Can we take a little break, Mr. McDonohue?"

Shamus glanced at his watch. "Sure. In fact, let's stop for lunch and meet back here in an hour."

Before the words were even fully out of his mouth, Mrs. Kane swooped over to K.C./Kandy. "Are you hungry, baby? I'll go get you some salad. Are you cold? Do you need a sweater? Did that boy hurt you?"

I shook my head at the pathetic scene and headed out of the house with Shamus and Zander. A second later, my used-to-be friend ran out after us, yelling. "Can we talk?"

My dad, Z, and I all turned around and answered simultaneously.

"Of course," Shamus said, a look of fatherly concern spreading across his face.

Zander's jaw nearly hit the ground. "No prob."

I shook my head. "I think I've already heard enough."

"Sorry, Mr. McDonohue. Alexander," she said, nodding toward each of them. "I meant Trace."

Alexander!?! As mad as I was that K.C./Kandy had totally played me, it was still hard to suppress the snickers. There was Z, probably thinking Kandy wanted him, and she hadn't even considered him long enough to learn his name properly. At least something was going right with this day.

K.C./Kandy and I were toe-to-toe by this point, neither of us saying a word. Shamus and Zander could've been watching a Ping-Pong match from the looks of them, heads bouncing from her, back to me, and then back to her. Eventually, Shamus broke the uncomfortable silence. "Well, then, I guess we'll see you back up at the house, Trace."

As soon as the guys were out of listening range, I took the lead. "Why didn't you just tell me who you were?" I felt surprisingly close to crying.

K.C./Kandy grabbed my hands in hers. "Because you already know who I am. The girl who's a feminist, who's dying to go to college to become a psychologist, the one who's a really good friend— that's really me."

"How am I supposed to believe that? I mean, you didn't even tell me the truth about your name."

"Trace, my initials are K and C, for Kandace Clara," she explained. "I've always thought Kandy Kane sounded more like a porn star and Clara is way too *Little Women* for my tastes, so I've been K.C. for as long as I can remember to my friends. Kandy is just for work, you know?"

I shook my head, still reeling. "I think you can still admit you left out a whopper of a fact. And there I was, telling you my deepest, darkest secrets and blabbing on and on about how I felt about

Kandy . . ." I lowered my voice. "Not to mention Caden. You must think I'm a complete idiot."

K.C. gripped my hands even tighter. "I don't think you're an idiot at all. I think you're an amazing person."

"That's nice," I said, getting more sarcastic by the second. "But I think you're the world's biggest poseur. Weren't you the one who told me honesty was the key to any relationship? That if you really cared about someone, you'd trust them with all of you, not just the parts you wanted them to see? That you should never have to change who you are for anybody?" The more I thought about how she'd hidden the truth from me, the madder I got.

"I wanted to tell you sooner about, you know, this," she said, gesturing to her Kandy getup. "In fact, I came this close a couple of times, but every time I tried, you made some snide remark about hating me—you know, me, Kandy, not me, K.C.—oh, you know what I mean."

I wasn't buying it. Not any of it. K.C. could've told me about her alter ego anytime she wanted—she'd simply chosen not to. "No wonder you wrote 'The Girl Behind the Mask.' It fits you perfectly."

K.C. looked like I'd slapped her. "I wrote 'The Girl Behind the Mask' for you," she said quietly.

Now I was so pissed I could barely contain myself. "Maybe you should try looking in a mirror once in a while, because the only mask I see is on you."

K.C. glared at me. "What about the one you hide behind with Zander and your dad and who knows who else in your life? The one where you pretend to be OK with things when you're not and give in just to keep the peace? If that's not a mask, I don't know what is."

I crossed my arms to keep my heart from racing right out of my body. "You clearly don't know your ass from your elbow."

"Oh, I know where everything goes," she said, completely standing her ground. "For instance, I know this costume I'm wearing goes in the closet at night, and I get to go back to being the real me. And I also know that mask of yours is going to be permanent if you don't watch out."

"Give me a break."

"No, you give me a break," she said. "I deserve it. You liked me before you knew what I did for a living. Why can't we still be friends now that you know I'm famous? Or am I just way too uncool for someone as rockin' as you?"

I stuck my hands on my hips, feeling more self-righteous than ever. "It's not your supreme uncoolness that bothers me. It's that you're clearly missing the most important element of friendship."

"And what's that?" she asked.

"Honesty." Bulls-eye.

"This coming from the girl who waited almost a week to tell her dad how she felt about his star client and never got up the guts to tell her boyfriend she hates country music at all?" K.C. shook her head. "Yeah, you are really one to talk, Tracey Tillingham." Bulls-eye right back.

I was still stuck to the same spot when Caden came out a few minutes later. "Hey, Trace. I'm glad you're here. I wanted to talk to you," he said, slinging his arm around my shoulder.

"Sure," I said, though my heart was so not into flirting right then.

Good thing that's not what he wanted. "You and your boyfriend—you're still together, right?"

I nodded. "Right."

"So you and me—that's not gonna happen, right?"

I nodded again, regretfully. "Right."

"In that case, I was thinking I might ask Kandy out. She's so not what I expected."

"She's definitely not what I expected, either." It certainly wasn't a lie.

"So what do you think I should do?" he asked. "You know, to win her heart and all that knight in shining armor stuff."

A brilliant plan was coming to me. Not to mention evil. "She was just out here crying to me about how she wants people to see who she really is, but the whole Kandy getup is obviously getting in the way."

"I'd love for everyone to see how kick-ass she is, too," Caden said. "With or without the outfit and makeup."

"Well, she actually said the makeup is the worst part—it practically makes her break out in hives. But my dad and her mom won't let her take it off. They say no one would listen to her music or buy her CDs without it."

Caden nodded thoughtfully. "Kind of like my manager told me no one would want to hear me without The Menace Men, especially if I wasn't going to be pulling pranks."

"Looks like you guys were meant to be."

"I think we are," he said. "So what can I do to help Kandy? Does she need me to talk to Shamus or her mom about it?"

I put a finger to my lips, like I was giving away a big secret. "No way. Kandy has talked to both until she's blue in the face, and they're not budging. She says it has to look like an accident. Her whole unmasking, I mean."

Caden caught on to where I was headed before I had to spell out anything more. "So maybe I can make it look like a practical joke. That way, Kandy gets to be seen without her makeup and she won't get in trouble. Only I will, and not that much since they expect crap like that from me."

I nodded. "I'm sure she'd be forever grateful."

Caden started whooping. "Woo hoo! This is going to be awesome—I get the girl to fall in love with me and slick her down with oil in front of the world at the same time. I love that!"

"Oil?" I asked, getting the sinking feeling that maybe I'd taken things a step too far.

"Yeah, tomorrow afternoon at the Clubbing with Kandy party. I'm going to rig a bucket of Mazola above the dance floor and have it fall on her when we're underneath it. I'll hand her a towel, she'll wipe her face, and voilà! That'll definitely get her waterproof makeup off, and maybe even unglue that damn pink wig from her head."

"Do you really think that's such a good idea?" I asked, wishing I could just take it back.

"Good? I think it's great!" Caden said, kissing my cheek and bounding off.

By the time I got back up to the house, Zander and Shamus were already heading back down to the set.

"Everything OK, Trace?" Shamus wanted to know.

"Yeah, sure, fine," I said, my mind a jumble of stuff I couldn't begin to figure out at the moment. "I'm just going to grab a bite to eat, hang out here for a while."

"You want me to keep you company?" Zander asked.

"No, that's OK," I said. "You go get all the experience you can. I'll be fine."

"You sure?"

"Yup."

I wasn't hungry after everything that had happened, so instead of grabbing lunch, I restarted my search for my messenger bag. My mind was mocking me the whole time, constantly playing and rewinding the moment K.C.'s laugh had tipped me off to her real identity and then moving on to our "discussion" where she had the gall to say *I* was the one hiding behind a mask. It was like watching an art house movie flick with subtitles, and even those were in a different language. In other words, infuriating and entirely incomprehensible.

After digging through my luggage and underneath my bed and tearing apart Zander's room and the home theater, I had a brainstorm. Walking out into the garage, I checked the recycle bins where I'd dumped all the broken-down boxes and newspapers from when "that girl" (I didn't want to even *think* her name anymore) and I had unpacked the kitchen. And there sat my messenger bag, smushed in between piles of cardboard. I must've picked it up by mistake when I was cleaning the other day.

Fishing my bag out of the bin and my cell out of the bottom of the bag, I immediately powered up my phone. I desperately wanted to call my mom and get her perspective on the whole debacle. But before I could get around to dialing, my phone starting beeping like crazy. I had seven messages, all from Bebe. She must've been out of her mind, wondering how things were going with my dad, because every voice mail sounded more urgent than the last. Her messages ranged from "Trace, it's me. Call me," to "Trace, I still haven't heard from you, and I'm dying to know what's going on," to "Nothing to worry about, but I really have to talk to you as soon as possible." Feeling bad that my mom obviously thought I'd thrown her over for my father, I immediately dialed home. The answering machine picked up after five rings. I left a message and tried her cell. Same thing. Oh, well, I thought. At least she'd know I'd tried and hadn't dumped her for Shamus, after all.

Next, I dialed up Brina. Two seconds later, this is what I heard: *Pant, pant.* A low, manly chuckle. A high-pitched giggle.

"Am I interrupting something?" I yelled into the phone. Lest I'd forgotten about Brina's quest during our last week before heading off to college, the noises on the other end of the line quickly reminded me.

"Just the orgasmic conclusion to another stunning round of Naked Twister," Brina vamped.

I sighed, realizing my mistake a second too late. Talking to Brina right now was most definitely not going to cheer me up. "I should probably call you back later."

Another giggle. "Actually, we should really talk now, 'cause we'll for sure have moved on to something even more dirty later. Right, Sully?"

"Right, Bree," Sully's voice was a low rumble in the background.

"Bree?" Since when did Brina let anyone on God's green earth call her Bree? The last time her mother mouthed it by accident, Brina went off like a rabid dog, screaming that all people named Bree were morbidly obese and ate paste on street corners while mumbling to themselves about alien abductions. "How's that Elmer's glue tasting these days?"

Brina laughed off my jab. "You're so funny, Trace. And I'd really be missing your sense of humor if I hadn't been so busy these past few days. But as it is, I haven't even had time to catch my breath since you've been gone."

Pun intended, I'm sure. "So now that I've got a really graphic picture of what you've been doing burned into my mind, wanna hear what's going on out here?"

"Sure."

"I met a new friend, but she turned out to be nothing like I thought she was."

"She turned out to be nowhere as cool as me, is that the problem?" Brina asked, still clearly distracted.

"No, the problem is she turned out to be Kandy Kane," I said, cheering up just a smidge at how dramatic and "Hollywood" it sounded—something that would usually be way more likely to come out of Brina's mouth than mine. "My dad's executive something-or-other for her new reality show. It's shooting right here, on his property."

"No . . . freaking . . . way!" Brina screamed. I'd finally gotten her full attention.

"Way."

"So what's she like?"

"Well, at first I thought she was smart and funny and cool," I said.

"And what changed your mind? Did she make you, like, fetch her lattes and stuff?"

Just the opposite, I thought. I didn't say it, though, because it made me seem kind of petty. Not to mention delusional. "No," I said. "She . . . well, it's just that she didn't tell me who she was. I found out by accident. It was like a total slap in the face."

All the gross noises had completely stopped by now. "How could you possibly not know it was Kandy? She has a pretty distinctive look, to say the least."

I sighed, knowing how crazy it sounded. "She didn't have her face made up or her wig on, and she was wearing normal clothes. In fact, she was wearing glasses and reading about feminism. How was I supposed to know?"

"The horrible case of acne didn't tip you off, either?"

"Brina, the magazines are wrong. Her face is as clear as a baby's. There's not a zit on her."

"Huh. Well, that sucks." It sounded like Brina might've been working on something like that herself. "Did you by any chance mention to her how much you despised Kandy? I mean, before you found out who she really was?"

"I might've dropped it into conversation a few times," I admitted. Really, when you looked at it from that point of view, I hadn't given her much of an opportunity to spill the beans.

"So there's your answer as to why she didn't tell you sooner," Brina said, wrapping up the situation neatly. "Now let's move on to why it matters who she is if you like her? And anyway, isn't it kind of a bonus that she's famous? Like, maybe you'll get to meet some stars and stuff."

"Yeah," I mumbled. Everything Brina was saying was right. So why was it making me so mad? "Like Caden Collins."

"Ooooooh, he's a hottie! Give him a kiss for me . . . or maybe even something better, OK?"

Just then, my low-battery light started blinking, warning me it was going to shut down my phone immediately. I hoped I'd brought my charger along, but I had the sneaking suspicion it was still sitting in my bedroom at home. "My phone's dying, Brina. I'll call you when I get back and we'll go out before we both take off for school, OK?"

"Sure, that'd be great," she answered. The smacking, wet, slurpy noises had totally started up again. I wouldn't have been surprised if drool started oozing out of the phone any second now. "I'll see what Sully's schedule looks like this weekend and get back to you."

I wasn't holding my breath that I'd even get penciled in. Or remain a wisp of a thought in Brina's head for more than a second after she hung up.

CHAPTER
12

I tossed and turned all night—no z's were caught, counting sheep didn't work for crap, and my mind simply would not shut off—so at some point right before dawn, I just gave up. Shuffling out into the kitchen, I rubbed my beet red eyes and grabbed a mug from the cabinet K.C. and I had had so much fun arranging together a few days earlier. No matter what the tabloids said about her being a diva, I had to admit she was nothing of the sort. She'd rolled up her sleeves to help me and didn't complain once. In fact, she actually seemed to enjoy it.

I quickly pushed the annoyingly nice thought about K.C. out of my head and concentrated on the multistep process of making myself a latte instead. Firing up Shamus's espresso maker, I dumped the last little bit of milk into a measuring cup and heated it with the bubble-blower thing on the machine, barrista style. Once it was nice and foamy, and I poured it over the coffee I'd just deposited into my cup.

And then another Kandy-sweetened thought had the gall to sneak into my head unbidden: It had certainly been nicer—and easier—having my very non-diva-y friend wake me with a Starbucks latte than making one myself. See? This had been my problem all night. I just didn't understand how someone as real as K.C. could masquerade as someone as unreal as Kandy.

"Whoa, I cannot believe my eyes," Shamus said, padding into the kitchen pouring himself a cup of black coffee. "My daughter, up this early?"

"Maybe I was just too excited about the Clubbing with Kandy thing this afternoon to sleep."

"I kind of doubt that, honey," he said, sitting down across from me and placing his hand over mine. "You want to talk about it?"

I sighed and swirled my drink around in the mug. "I wouldn't even know where to begin, Shamus. But thanks for asking."

"No problem," he said. "I hope someday you'll trust me enough to tell me your secrets."

"Oh, I trust you enough already. It's just that I kind of don't trust myself right now."

Shamus took a slow sip of coffee. "I think you should. You're smart, you've got your head on straight. You'll figure out what's right."

"Yeah, I guess I will."

I killed the next couple of hours looking for my charger—which I never found, leaving me with a thoroughly useless phone until I got back to Winnetka since Zander and my dad both had the kind you put in the cradle—flipping through magazines, and watching cartoons with Zander. When it was finally time to head down to the beach house, I was right in step with the guys.

"You want to help Z do an equipment check this morning?" Shamus asked.

"Nah, I've got a few other things to take care of first." Like, making up with my friend K.C. And calling off the evil plot I'd convinced her soon-to-be boyfriend was in her best interest. "I'll catch you guys in a bit, OK?"

As they got busy with work, I sauntered over to where K.C. was sitting. She was all decked out as Kandy, reading the same book as the first day we met. It was a weird dichotomy, seeing the pink makeup stars jutting out from behind her glasses.

"Hey," I said.

"Hey, yourself," she answered, her face a total blank slate. I'm sure if I could've read it, there would've been something like *Screw you* scrawled in big, bold letters, so I guessed I should probably be happy she was keeping me in the dark about her feelings.

Only I wasn't. Face-to-face with my nemesis-turned-friend-turned-nemesis-again, I was finally forced to admit to myself what both Brina and my brain had been trying to tell me all last night and today: It really *shouldn't* matter who K.C. was if I liked her. And I really *hadn't* made it very easy for her to tell me about her alter ego. "I was kind of thinking . . ." I started, trailing off before I even came close to the apology I was considering offering.

"That's something new," she said, snapping the book shut.

I crouched down and touched her arm. Now was as good a time as any to come clean. "I kind of just wanted to tell you I think I might've made a mistake," I said, unable to meet her eyes and staring at the chipped polish on my toes instead. The uncomfortable silence that met my ambiguous request for forgiveness finally made me stop examining my nails for long enough to see how it had gone over.

Just as I'd hoped, K.C.'s frown had softened. "Really?"

"Really," I said. "Although I still don't agree with you not telling me who you were from the start."

"Trace, I know it doesn't make much sense, figuring out how the K.C. you know would allow herself to be Kandy, too," she said.

"But sometimes life calls for big compromises, and this was one of them. I'm still the same person underneath it all."

"I know. My dad explained about it being his idea. And it's really not so bad, when you think of it how he does—you know, that this way Kandy can be a superhero to her fans. So what do you say? Want to give our friendship another shot?"

"Yeah, I do," she said, the beginnings of a smile working its way around the corners of her mouth. "But I have to warn you—hanging with Kandy is not going to be nearly as much fun as kicking back with K.C."

"Come on," I said. "I'm sure things won't be that different."

"Wanna bet?" she said, grabbing my hand and leading me outside the house to where lunch was set up for the cast and crew. "Watch this."

Everyone whispered and stepped aside as we walked by—a little Moses parting the Red Sea action. "What did I tell you? It's like I'm a leper or something."

"Maybe they're just making way for your boobs," I said, clapping a hand over my mouth a second too late. It wasn't exactly great timing, my sarcastic sense of humor making an unscheduled appearance just as we were on our way to maybe getting along again.

But instead of being pissed off, K.C. burst into hysterics. "Oh, I know, they look so ridiculous like this, don't they? Thank God I didn't let my agent talk me into getting those implants—"

Should I ask? Should I not? I wrestled around with the question for only a second before I gave in to my relentless curiosity. "You mean they're real?"

"Well, sure they are. I mean, I can understand your confusion. They do look pretty gravity-defying in my videos."

"They're real," I said again, trying to convince myself. I thought back to a couple of days ago, when my friend was just plain K.C.

and her boobs were just normal big, not under-her-chin-and-never-moving humongous.

"Cross my heart," K.C. said, taking a finger and making an invisible little X over her right one. "I'll let you in on a little secret. It's all about the duct tape."

"Can duct tape do that to me?" I was guessing you could use an entire roll and never get those kind of results.

"Absolutely." Veering away from the food table and the parted Red Sea of extras and crew, K.C. changed directions and started dragging me back toward the makeup trailer.

"I was totally just kidding," I said, trying to turn her back around.

"And I totally wasn't," she said, grinning while she continued to pull me along.

"Please no." I was practically digging my heels into the gravel by now, though that didn't stop her for a second. All I could think was, how embarrassing was it going to be when she realized no amount of duct tape, or underwire, or superglue, or whatever other miracle potion they'd discovered would give me any cleavage at all?

"Too late. We're already here," K.C. said, opening the trailer door and pushing me inside. "Yoo hoo, Mala! We could use your expertise for a second."

Mala took my hands in hers and stood back, assessing me. Then she nodded and let go. "It's like I thought. She's beautiful just the way she is."

K.C. let that tinkly little laugh loose again. "I'm not blind, Mala," she said. "I just wanted you to show her how duct tape can work magic on even the smallest chest."

My cheeks heated up to a hot-day-even-in-hell temperature. Noticing my mortification, K.C. gave me a quick little squeeze and added, "Believe me, I envy you. I've always wished nature hadn't been quite so generous with me. Little ones look so much better in clothes."

"I highly doubt you could find any man alive that agrees with you, but thanks," I told her as Mala retrieved her bag of tricks. Then she gently reached her hands under my shirt and voila! One minute and a strip of gray sticky stuff later, I was the proud owner of boobage for the first time in my life.

I stared down at myself, amazed. My transformation wasn't the most comfortable thing in the world, but it sure looked good. What was peeking over the neckline of my white tank top might even be considered on the large side in say, Munchkinland or Pygmyville. I couldn't wait to see Zander's reaction.

"Wow." One syllable was about all I could manage at that point.

"Told ya," K.C. said, holding the trailer door open for me. "Thanks a ton, Mala. I'm sure I'll see you later."

"You got it, kiddo."

I was tentatively touching my newest additions as we walked back toward the food table. "Seriously, these are one of the best presents I've ever gotten." I felt a lot like a little girl who'd raided my mom's lingerie drawer and stuffed a bra full of Kleenexes to see what I might look like as a grown-up woman. "Oops, I mean two of the best presents I've ever gotten."

"So does this mean we're officially friends again?" K.C. asked, staring at me shyly.

I nodded. "I'm sorry I freaked on you like that. I just really, really hate feeling like I'm the last one to know something."

"Well, if it makes you feel any better, I'm sorry I didn't tell you up front. It's not usually my policy," she said. "But we were getting along so well and you kept making evil comments about Kandy and I just didn't know what else to do."

"I guess I should know by now not to judge a book by its cover."

"I would've told you eventually, Trace. I swear."

"I know. So why don't we just make a pact to be totally, one hundred percent honest with each other from now on and leave it at that, OK?"

"Absolutely," she said, grabbing my little finger in hers for a pinkie swear. "You want me to dress you for the party now?"

I shook my head so hard I could practically hear my brain slapping against my eardrums. "Nope. I mean, you know, my stage fright and all that. I'm just going to watch from the sidelines with Shamus."

"No, you're not," she said, dragging me back toward the house and not stopping until we got to her closet. The big walk-in looked like it had schizophrenia or something—one side was calmly holding neatly hung jeans and T-shirts while the other could barely contain the wild, colorful zoo of outrageous dresses and catsuits. "Now let me see. What kind of outfit says *Of course you should know who I am* without trying too hard?"

"Please tell me you're considering something from that side," I said, pointing to the normal, sane clothing.

"For your television debut? With Caden Collins and me? I don't think so," she said, whipping out the lowest-cut black leather pants imaginable and what basically looked like a leather bra to go along with it. There was no way I could wear any underwear with either.

I ran my fingers across the buttery material. "Try again, K.C. I usually go for more of a casual look. Not to mention covered up."

"Don't be a party pooper. Don't you remember playing dress-up when you were a kid? This is the same thing, only more fun."

I semireluctantly let K.C. work her magic on me. Apparently, she'd learned a lot from hanging out with Mala, because the next thing I knew, my hair was tumbling over my shoulders in shiny, perfect curls, thanks to some miracle hair product of hers, and my face was sparkling with more makeup than I'd ever applied in my entire life, collectively. To top it all off, my body looked positively mad-sick thanks to the used-to-be cow barely covering it.

Kandy spun me around to face the full-length mirror. "So what do you think?"

My jaw fell all the way to the floor. "That you're a miracle worker." It wasn't so much that I thought I looked good—I mean, I did look good, and maybe even great—as it was that I looked like an entirely different person. One at least five years older than the real me and twenty bajillion times more glamorous.

"OK, so don't let me down. I want to see you dancing like a maniac with that boyfriend of yours at the club. I know I'll be with mine."

I drew in a deep breath. "You and Caden? You're together now?" At least that meant I could stop fantasizing about him once and for all.

"Maybe. We hung out all night last night, working on our song and talking. He's really amazing, underneath all the fart jokes."

"I totally agree," I said. "And I'm totally happy for you."

"Yeah, me, too. Look, my limo is here. I'll see you there, OK?"

"Count on it. And thanks for everything."

I was practically hyperventilating by the time I got back to the set. I had to find Caden, and quick, before my revenge plot from yesterday totally blew their budding romance.

And before it busted up my on-again friendship with K.C., once she found out it was my idea.

And before it ruined my dad's big break, once his star was revealed as the normal girl she was and not some superhero in crazy makeup.

Crap. Where was he? I ran frantically from room to room, but everyone was already piling onto the tour buses taking everyone to the club. I ran up the stairs of the first one. "Is Caden in here?"

"Are you kidding?" one of the extras answered. "He doesn't ride with us peons. He has his own wheels."

I quickly hopped off that bus and onto the other, just to make sure. It was full of the crew guys, plus my dad and Zander. No Caden, though. The extras must've been right.

"We were beginning to think you'd gone AWOL on us," Shamus said. "Nice look, by the way. I take it you changed your mind about being an extra at the club today."

I wrapped my arms around my very exposed midriff and sat down next to Zander. "I guess I did."

"God, you look amazing," Z said, eyeing me up and down. "Did you do something different to your hair?"

"Not really," I said, wondering how he could possibly confuse my new duct tape cleavage with maneage.

"Well, whatever it is, you're prettier than ever," he said.

I went to protest—who, me, pretty?—when he touched his fingers to my lips. "Just say thanks, remember?" he murmured.

And I would've, but he was too busy kissing me. It felt about as good as it ever had, and suddenly talking to Caden didn't seem as imperative as it had a minute ago. I'd get to him before anything bad happened at the club.

The place was already dark, loud, and foamy by the time we got there. Really, it was hard to tell who was who underneath all those suds.

"Shamus, where's Caden? I need to tell him something."

Zander shot me a look and pulled me closer. "How about you just stick with me this afternoon?"

"I plan on it," I told him. "I just have to do this one thing first."

"Caden actually just called to say he's running late," Shamus told me. "I'll tell him you're looking for him when he gets here."

I reluctantly gave up on my mission for a moment, hoping I'd soon be in touch with Caden—knowing that it was out of my hands—and started rocking out to Gwen Stefani's "Hollaback Girl." Though I'm not normally much of a dancer, something about the combination of the foam and the insane getup I was wearing made it easy to cut loose, to stop worrying about what anyone might think of me and just have fun. Every once in a while, I would crane my neck around to look for Caden, but I never quite spotted him.

After a set of high-energy songs, the DJ said, "We're going to slow things down a little now. This next one goes out to our very own Miss Kandy Kane, from her guy, Caden."

A big *Awwwwwwww*, went up in the crowd, and everyone parted to let Caden through.

I grabbed his shirt as he passed by me. "Don't do it," I yelled in his ear.

He shook his head and smiled at me. "Trace, everything's cool. Don't worry. It's going to go off just like we planned."

"Kandy really didn't say that stuff about wanting to be un-masked. I made it all up because I was mad at her. Seriously."

"Don't worry, I'll deal with your dad if he gets upset. I just want Kandy to be happy."

Caden finally broke loose from my death grip and headed over to where K.C. was waiting for him. She broke into a big grin and fell into his arms.

Shit. Now what was I going to do?

As Caden and Kandy's version of "Do Over" blared through the speaker, everyone started slow dancing. Each time Zander and I shuffled round and round, I pushed us closer to the center of the room where Kandy and Caden were enjoying their little coming-out dance.

"I thought you didn't want to be on camera," Zander said once we were practically on top of the happy new couple.

"I guess I changed my mind," I said, catching a glimpse of a bucket dangling high above our heads in the rafters.

"You are a total mystery sometimes, you know that, Trace?" he said. "Beautiful, but mysterious."

It looked like I was going to have to stay that way for a moment. Because just as Zander was moving in to kiss me, I saw the bucket overturn and oil start tumbling from the ceiling. So I did what any good friend—or secret service agent—would do. I made a mad rush at K.C., tackled her to the ground, and used myself as a human oil shield.

A split second later, gobs of goopy yellow slop came splashing down all over me, and lights flashed as a million and one cameras got a shot of me lying on top of K.C., all slicked up in my leather.

"I'll explain later," I said, looking down at her surprised face.

"Thanks for saving me from the vat of Crisco," K.C. said. "You're a true friend, Tracey Tillingham. Not like that loser I thought I wanted to date."

"It's not his fault," I told her. "I can explain."

"No explanations need," she said. "It's all perfectly clear. So could you get off me now, Earl? You're getting a little heavy."

As I flung my body off of K.C. so as not to get any oil on her, Mrs. Kane came charging out of nowhere, screeching, "If you hurt one bone in her body, I swear my lawyer will be contacting you!"

K.C. got up, brushed the few oil splotches that had escaped off of me and onto her, and looked at Caden with disgust. "I should've known I couldn't trust you. You're nothing but a big jerk with an immature sense of humor."

"Trace, tell her about the plan," Caden said, glaring at me.

"Don't you try to put the blame on someone else," K.C. spat. "This stupid prank has Caden Collins written all over it."

"Kandy, I can explain everything." He was practically begging her to listen.

"I don't need to hear another word from you. Just leave me alone. You're dead to me."

CHAPTER

13

No one said much of anything on the bus. And once we were back home, my first order of business was to take a steaming hot shower and wash my hair a few thousand times. But there was no escaping the consequences of my actions after that. I'd just gotten dressed and was toweling off my hair when Shamus asked to see me alone in his office.

"What in hell was that all about?" Shamus demanded.

I tried my best to explain the situation, and how the whole thing had snowballed, and how I never meant to hurt anybody, but all of it sounded like so much flimsy bullshit.

"Trace, let me put it to you this way. My career is on the line here, Mrs. Kane is talking lawsuits, and my two star clients were just about to hook up and now they're not even talking to each other."

"Three strikes. So I guess this means I'm out, huh?" I said, swiping at tears with the back of my hand.

Shamus nodded. "Well, yeah—although not for the reasons you might think. Your mom called me tonight. It seems she's been trying to get in touch with you for days. She needs you home ASAP."

My heart started racing faster than it already was. "Is everything OK?"

"Everything's fine."

I couldn't think of a single reason short of terminal illness that would make my mom ask me to come home early from my first ever visit with my dad. "Are you sure no one's dying?"

All the frustration finally seemed to fade from Shamus's body. "Quite the opposite," he said, pulling me in for a halfhearted hug.

"What's that supposed to mean?" I asked into his shoulder.

"I'll have to let your mom explain it to you."

I pulled back from the embrace and gazed up into my dad's eyes. "But how can I leave now? I mean, we haven't even had our big bonding moment yet. You know, the heart-to-heart that's gonna take us from physically related to spiritually connected?"

Shamus chuckled. "Trace, do you think Rome was built in a day? We have a whole lifetime ahead of us to bond. This week was just a beginning. It was never meant to be the be-all and end-all."

"It wasn't?" I asked, still sniffling. I guess I'd always thought it was make or break—either he'd like me or decide I wasn't worth the hassle based on this one visit.

"Not even close."

"That's good to know. And I'm really sorry I messed everything up, Shamus."

"I know," he said, pulling me into a real bear hug this time. "I know."

Back in my PB Teen room, I dialed Bebe on Shamus's landline and started randomly throwing things into my suitcase. After listening to what my mom had to say, I discovered it truly *was* an emergency.

"You're getting married?" I yelled when she finished with her story.

"Yeah," Bebe replied, clearing her throat and sounding more awake. "No surprise there."

"Married?" I felt like I was doing a bad imitation of Long

Duck Dong in that old John Hughes movie *Sixteen Candles*. "This Saturday?"

"That's the idea," she said. She made it sound less momentous than if the captain of the football team had invited her to the prom.

For the life of me, I couldn't wrap my brain around what Bebe was saying. "That's . . . that's . . ."

"Only two days away?" Bebe said, finishing the sentence for me.

"I was going to say crazy."

Bebe giggled. "Crazy is right. We've been totally insane this week making all the arrangements, but I think we're actually going to pull it off."

"You're getting married on Saturday," I said yet again, without the question mark at the end this time. I figured maybe if I stated it like a fact, I'd start to believe it myself.

"Trace, for the millionth time, after a lot of serious thought, Mr. Steve and I decided to move up the date of our wedding considerably at the request of his family. And since everyone was already going to be here for the family reunion, it's happening this Saturday."

"And all I'm saying is, why they'd want to make it look like a shotgun wedding is beyond me."

Bebe cleared her throat. "About that," she said slowly, like I was just coming out of a coma and she didn't want to send me back down into the depths of Oz. "It kind of is."

I sucked in a huge gulp of air. "Don't tell me you're pregnant."

Silence. Silence. Silence. Then, "Yup. Your baby brother or sister is due in the beginning of May."

While I always dreamed of having a sibling, this wasn't exactly the scenario I'd had in mind. I had actually been hoping for something more along the lines of a kid a couple of years younger than me that I could've bossed around while playing Barbies when I was five, not someone who was arriving just as I was leaving the nest.

"Mom!" I said, shocked and appalled even though Bebe was clearly over the age of consent. "How could you? Didn't you learn anything after the last time?"

"Sure," she said, as calm and easygoing as ever. "I learned how much I love being a mom and how much I'd love to do it again sometime with someone who was willing to stick around and play daddy."

"Well, at least you've got that going for you, right?"

"Right."

"So I guess this is where I'm supposed to tell you how happy I am for you guys."

"Right again," Bebe said.

"OK, I'm really happy for you guys. And maybe just a teensy bit surprised, too," I said, thinking that was just about the biggest understatement in the world. I mean, not that I'd thought they'd ask permission or anything, but I would've at least liked to have known a baby was even the remotest of possibilities in their lives. I abruptly changed the subject before I had to think any more about it. "So how'd you get the House of Blues on such short notice?"

"Yeah, well, see here's the thing about that—"

I was glad this conversation was happening on the phone and not in person so she couldn't see the depths of my disappointment. "Don't tell me—no House of Blues, no MC Hammer officiating, no crazy eighties band playing till four in the morning." We'd had the coolest, most perfectly-suited-to-my-mom wedding ever planned down to the most minute detail. And it was supposed to happen on New Year's Day of next year, not Labor Day weekend of this one. Though I guess the labor part actually made more sense now that she'd be going through it in nine months.

"Sadly, no," she told me. "More like Winnetka Country Club, a minister from Mr. Steve's Waspy church, and our eighties iPod mix playing at appropriate decibels through the sound system."

"That should be—" Forget it, I thought. There were no words to cover this situation.

"Not as cool you were hoping it would be. That's what you were thinking, right, Trace?"

"You might say that." I tossed a toothbrush into my suitcase and zipped it shut. At least the packing had been easy. As for the conversations I'd been having the past half hour? Not so much.

"I know none of this is exactly how we planned it, but that's just how life is," she said. "Nothing ever happens the way you expect it to, and you've got to be OK with that or get used to feeling very disappointed."

It sounded a lot like what K.C. had said before, about life being full of compromises. I guessed both she and my mom were right. "Well, one thing's for sure. That definitely applies to my visit here."

"You want to talk about it now or save it till you get home?"

A knock at the door provided me with the correct answer. "I believe that would be wait till I get home."

"I'm sure Shamus already told you this, but I got you on a six a.m. flight. I'll meet you at the baggage claim, OK?"

"I thought I had a nonrefundable, no-changes-allowed, Saturday-night-stay-required ticket."

"You did," Bebe said. "It was going to cost us more than we could afford to get you home early, so Mr. Steve threw in his miles for you."

"Well, be sure to thank him for me," I said. "I'll see you tomorrow."

Though I wanted to just crawl into bed, pull the covers over my head, and pretend the whole thing had never happened, it was clear I wasn't going to have the luxury of doing so. I mean, not with all that damn knocking, anyway.

"Come in," I sighed, throwing myself down on the bed and burying my face in the pillow.

"Hey." Was this room rigged for surround sound? I picked my head up to see. Nope, it was two voices greeting me all right.

"You OK?" Shamus asked, perching himself on the edge of my bed.

"I'm fine," I sighed into the pillow. "Maybe a little in shock, but fine."

"Trace, there's one more problem we need to talk to you about."

I couldn't imagine what it was, but from the looks on their faces, I wasn't going to like what I was about to hear. Especially since I seemed to be the third wheel in their we-filled plan. "Hit me."

"I've been on the phone with Zander's parents and the airlines since we got home. It would cost Zander well over a thousand dollars to fly home early," Shamus began.

"Yeah, and remember the pay-my-own-way kick my parents are on?" Z jumped in. "Well, the 'rents said they won't cover the change fees for me. Trace, one thousand bucks is practically all the money I saved this summer. And it's the only spending money I have for the semester."

"So you won't be able to come home with me, or to the wedding. Is that what you're telling me?"

"Yeah. I'm sorry."

"It's OK," I said, not really meaning it, but what else was I supposed to do? Throw my arms around his ankles and beg him to come with me? "No worries. Really, both of you. I'm going to be fine."

"If you say so," Shamus said, kissing the top of my head. "The limo will be waiting in the driveway by four. Call me when you get home so I know you're safe."

"I will."

As soon as Shamus left, Zander turned off the lights and curled up beside me in bed. "That was nice of you, saving Kandy from Caden's stupid prank tonight," he said. "Especially knowing the way you feel about her."

"I actually got to know her a bit while I was here," I told him. "And I like her, and Caden, too. It's hard to explain, but the oil thing was just a big misunderstanding."

"Well, there was no misunderstanding about how Kandy feels about Caden now. He's never getting another chance with her."

"I still hope things work out for them."

We were both silent for a minute. And I was finally relaxing when Zander had to go and get my adrenalin pumping overtime again. "Hey, Trace?" he whispered. "I hope things work out for us, too. I mean, what do you think is gonna happen to us at school?"

I put a finger to his lips, just like he'd done to me earlier on the bus. "Shhhh. We'll have plenty of time to talk about things on the drive out east."

I didn't give him a chance to say anything more because I was too afraid of what the outcome of our conversation might be. So instead, I decided to show him what a good girlfriend I was.

And all I know is, I didn't hear any complaints.

CHAPTER

14

"No way." I abruptly stopped rolling my suitcase toward the stairs and gave both Bebe and the sea foam green dress draped over the living room couch a wide-eyed stare. "Are you punking me? Where's the hidden camera?"

Bebe plopped herself down next to the hideous thing. A butt-load of taffeta flew up in the air and then fluttered back down in crisp-sounding layers. "I know, I know, it's not really your style. But I had to delegate some stuff or this wedding was never going to happen."

"So who's responsible for this crime against good taste?" I asked, my eyes still refusing to pop back into their sockets. "Wait, don't tell me. It's Grandma, right?"

Bebe's mouth curved up in a huge smile even as she shushed me. "Good guess, but no," she whispered. "It was actually Steve's cousin Melinda."

"The freakishly tall former volleyball captain?"

Bebe nodded.

"Well, that explains the dress, but not the whispering," I said in a totally exaggerated whisper. "Why are we being so quiet?"

Bebe started talking in a normal, if low, tone again. "Your

grandparents are here, so I didn't want you to say anything incriminating."

"Where here? I don't see Mr. and Mrs. Fo Shizzle Bedizzle anywhere." Whenever I start getting down about my immediate family being so completely not normal, all I have to do is conjure up my grandparents and suddenly Bebe, Mr. Steve, Shamus, and I seem as baseball, hot dogs, and apple pie as the Brady Bunch. Don't get me wrong—I love Grandma and Grandpa, it's just that they are seriously deranged. Like, last year they tried to learn to talk street and break-dance. Needless to say, it wasn't like anyone was going to mistake them as being from the hood anytime soon. Or possibly even from Earth.

"That's another thing I wanted to talk to you about," Bebe said. The slight grimace on her face clued me in to the fact that whatever bomb she was about to drop wasn't going to be pleasant. Or who knows, maybe it was just the morning sickness taking its toll on her.

"Oh, no, here we go again."

Bebe was having a tough time meeting my eyes by this point. "See, it's like this. Grandma's camping out in your room, and Grandpa took over the guest room."

This whole scene was getting weirder by the minute. I gave Bebe the old palms up—like, *Huh? Whatchootalkinbout?* "Why can't they both shack up in the guest room like they always do?"

Bebe tried to stifle a giggle. "I know I should be taking this more seriously, but it seems they're having a little tiff. Grandma says she can't tolerate Grandpa's incessant burping anymore, and Grandpa says he won't listen to her obnoxious snoring a single night longer. Basically, they're refusing to sleep together."

I slapped my forehead. "So that means I'm either bunking with Grandma and being kept awake by all the noise, or sacking out on the couch and getting no sleep because it's so uncomfortable."

Bebe nodded. "I guess so."

"College is looking better and better every day," I said, a twinge of anxiety plucking at my nerves. Turning my attention back to the present instead of dwelling on a future that was so full of unknowns I couldn't even begin to grasp the full extent of it, I grabbed a hunk of gross shiny fabric and shook it at Bebe. It sounded like an entire herd of third-graders walking down the hall in nylon track pants. "Seriously, though, couldn't you at least have given Mr. Steve's cousin Melinda some parameters? Like, maybe nothing a Disney character would wear in the triumph-over-the-evil-creature-and-get-a-sloppy-kiss-from-the-prince scene?"

Bebe ran her fingers along the scooped neckline and laughed. "I did. I said something about black and simple, but Melinda wouldn't hear of it. 'Oh, no,' she told me. 'Black is for funerals.'"

"Then you should've told her sea foam is for helpless princesses."

"The sad part is, she probably would've thought that was a good thing," Bebe said. "Cotillion girl that she is. And anyway, only the maid of honor gets to wear sea foam. The rest of bridesmaids got carnation pink, turquoise, and lemon yellow."

I rolled my eyes and sighed. "We're going to look like someone puked up a bag of tropical fruit Skittles."

That made Bebe laugh out loud. "You certainly have a vivid imagination."

"And you're certainly taking this all very well." The Bebe I knew and loved normally would've gone kicking and screaming from here to hell about having her raucous and super-cool wedding plans replaced by these random and sketchy ones. "What gives?"

Bebe shrugged and smiled. "Steve and I are terrifically, magically, wonderfully in love. We're having a baby together. Life is good. The wedding's just a formality."

"Yeah, a formal formality that isn't you." I hated to be the one to break it to her, but what could I say? I was her daughter and it was my job to tell it like it is.

"Don't you get it, Trace? Anywhere Steve and I are together, we have our best friend by our side. We're home and we're happy and there's good love all around, to paraphrase Billy Joel."

"Even at a stuck-up country club in a seasick-colored dress?"

Bebe nodded. "Even there."

Someday, maybe someday, I'd feel that way about someone. As for now, it didn't seem to be in my operating instructions. I mean, physically, Zander and I had been in the same place for the past week and it ended up feeling less like home and more like separate apartments. On separate planets.

Speaking of which, I wanted to check if my boyfriend had by any chance e-mailed me to say how much he missed me, or how much he regretted staying on at *Kandy's Room* instead of hopping my flight, no matter how much it was going to cost him and how badly he'd have to starve at school. "Since grandma kicked me out of my own room, can I use your computer, Bebe?"

A look of disappointment crept across her face. "Sure. But I was kind of hoping you would give me all the scoop about Shamus and Zander and your trip first."

"I will, I promise. Just later. I have a lot of other stuff to do, like finishing packing for school and loading up the Bug, before I can get into all that."

Grimace times two.

"Weren't you the one who always warned me about my face getting stuck in an expression similar to the one you're making right now?" I teased Bebe before realizing we might have another issue to deal with. "You *are* still driving me and Zander out east, aren't you?"

"Actually, it was Grandma who liked to tell you your face was going to get stuck like that. And the answer to your question is, with everything else going on, I kind of had to arrange alternate transportation for you guys . . ." Bebe said, trailing off.

"Not this again. I can only imagine what horror awaits me." I had kind of glossed over in my mind the fact that a pregnant Bebe might not be up for driving halfway across the country the day after she got married. But now that she mentioned it, it kind of made sense.

"That depends on your definition of horror. Does the Country Squire station wagon, belches, and snores sound particularly scary to you?"

"Ye-es," I said slowly, hoping this was some kind of a weird dream I'd wake up from at any minute. When I realized it wasn't, I also realized I was just going to have to suck it up, for my mom's sake. "But you know what? Anything for you. And my new baby sister or brother."

"I'm sorry to throw all of this at you at once, hon."

"I can handle it," I said. "I'm a college girl now, right?"

I gave my mom a quick kiss and headed for the kitchen, where I logged on to my e-mail account. I was greeted with spam, spam, spam, and more spam. The names Zander and Shamus were nowhere to be found. Neither was Brina or anyone else I actually knew—after five days away, how pathetic can you get.

I deleted until my fingers were raw, then noticed I actually *had* received a single personal message. At least one was better than none. The note was from Caitlin, a girl I'd met when visiting Fairfield. Her message was enthusiastic yet cryptic.

Subject: Will you still talk to me?

Trace:

I won't even bore you with the details of my summer, because obviously yours was much more exciting. As your senior buddy, I'll be waiting for you at your dorm room on Monday to help you move in. We'll talk then—if you're still willing to associate with unfamous people, that is. ;)

Caitlin

I wasn't sure what she meant by me having an exciting summer or agreeing to hang out with unfamous people—though I had a general idea I wasn't going to like whatever it was. I quickly fired up my IM and shot a note off to K.C. I had to find out what was going on—and also had to try and patch things up between her and Caden.

> **runrgrl:** U still mad about yesterday?
>
> **mintyfresh:** Not mad, just done with him.
>
> **runrgrl:** It wasn't his fault. It was mine.
>
> **mintyfresh:** Don't believe that for a second. Have U seen our pix?
>
> **runrgrl:** Pix?

I waited impatiently for a response, gnawing off one fingernail after another. Finally, a chime signaled the end of my digit-biting torture.

> **mintyfresh:** We're all over the news. U more so than me, of course. U OK?

I immediately went into panic-attack mode. I'd been convinced Shamus would be able to keep the footage from yesterday afternoon's debacle under wraps. Or even if he couldn't, that somehow I'd be spared from the story. I mean, who cared about me? I was just some nameless, faceless eighteen-year-old girl, not a one of *them*. My nails were becoming nubs by this point.

> **runrgrl:** Haven't caught it yet. Didn't even know I was famous until a minute ago. Why showing more of me than U?

> **mintyfresh:** How do I put this delicately? U. On top of me. Covered in oil. Low-cut leather pants. Butt cleavage showing.

Droplets of sweat popped out on my brow and above my lip. She had to be kidding. That's all there was to it. I refused to believe I'd committed social suicide by getting caught draped all over MTV's hottest act—with major plumber's crack in those low-slung leather pants, no less—right before I was about to head off for college and needed to make all new friends. Nice work, Trace, I thought.

> **runrgrl:** LOL. But not really. You're joking, right?

K.C. suddenly signed off without giving me the answer I desperately needed to hear. I could almost picture the scene, with her mom ready to give her another lecture and K.C. having to hop immediately or have her Sidekick taken away. I was just going to have to do my own detective work. So I Googled "Kandy Kane Caden Collins foam dance" and about a bajillion and one results popped up. I clicked on the *Daily Post*'s gossip page and screamed. "AHHHHHHHHHHHHHHHHHHHHHHHHHHHH!"

Bebe, Mr. Steve, and my Grandpa all came stampeding into the kitchen.

Mr. Steve was the first to arrive. "What happened?"

Bebe skidding in a close second. "Are you all right?"

Silence. *Bu-u-rp.* There was Grandpa, rounding out the mix. "Tracey Rosalita Tillingham! Who is that ridiculous-looking girl you're lying on top of in that picture on the computer? Why are you wet? And is that your stark white little heinie hanging out of the top of your pants?"

My only consolation was that he hadn't said *big fat ass*—and that was probably only because my butt had been significantly whittled down during my marathon training. With nowhere to run and no elaborate lies to fall back on, I buried my head in my hands and nodded.

"Oh, Trace," my mom said, rubbing my back in soothing strokes. "We do have a lot to talk about, don't we?"

I nodded again. If it was possible to die of embarrassment, surely my life would be mercifully over in a matter of mere minutes.

" 'What's Cooking with Kandy Kane?' " Mr. Steve read over my shoulder. " 'It seems our sweet little Kandy has gotten herself into a quite a mess. At a dance party celebrating the impending release of her new reality show, Ms. Kane came out publicly with new bad-boy boyfriend Caden Collins, then got into a little girl-on-girl oil-wrestling action right in front of him with a woman known only as Earl. How will Kandy's young fan base—never mind their moms—react to her sudden Lindsay Lohan–like behavior? And what will be the next ingredient in Kandy's recipe for career disaster? Stay tuned, we'll be following this story closely.' "

"What do you have to say for yourself, young lady?" Grandpa demanded.

I tried to think of an appropriate answer. *No, Grandpa, I don't swing both ways,* didn't seem like the right response. Finally I settled on, "It's not how it looks. I was just saving my friend from a guy who was trying to prank her."

Grandpa looked seriously concerned, like maybe he'd left his tea water boiling back in New Jersey three days ago. "Looks like you were the one trying to "prank" her. And if that's what you kids are calling it these days, I'd better inform my Slanguage teacher at the senior center."

"Over my dead body," Grandma yelled from the other room.

"Huh?" Bebe, Mr. Steve, and I all said at the same time.

Grandpa made a face and ignored her. "Ball, bang, bash, bosh— those were the words she taught us for those kinds of shenanigans. Never mentioned pranking, though. Maybe we've only been taught the words starting with B so far?" my grandfather mused.

I couldn't believe what he was implying. I wanted to take a bar of soap and wash his brain out with it a couple hundred times. "Grandpa, I was not trying to get busy with Kandy!"

If he heard my protest, he didn't show any indication of it. He just kept on mulling over his Slanguage instructor's apparent disappointing omission. "Nope, she must've at least hit the Ks, because I remember something about knocking the—was it *shoes?*"

"Please stop it," I begged, not wanting to hear any more euphemisms for sex coming out of his mouth. "I was simply trying to help out a friend."

"Dad, why don't you give Trace and me some time alone?" Bebe said, pushing my grandpa along with Mr. Steve out of the kitchen. "Go watch a ball game or something."

"Yeah, aren't the Cubs playing today?" I added, hoping it would provide some incentive for them to vacate the premises. I needed to talk to my mom, and fast. Bebe would know what to do about the mess I was in. She'd had so many embarrassing screwups to contend with in her life, she almost qualified as an expert witness by now.

"We'll be chilling in the other room if you need us," Mr. Steve said, taking a seat on the couch with the clicker in hand.

"That's marinating, Steve," my grandpa informed him, getting comfy on the leather reclining chair. "Chill is so five minutes ago."

"Thanks for the 411," Mr. Steve said.

"Crap, Steve-o. 411 is, like, five *years* ago," Grandpa chided him.

Mr. Steve shoved a handful of chips in his mouth and munched away, I'm sure in an attempt to avoid getting corrected by my grandpa again.

With the guys conveniently out of our way, Bebe opened the refrigerator and handed me a Red Bull. In her expectant state, she stuck with bottled water. "OK. Out with it."

I popped the top, took a big swig, went into sugar shock, and spilled my guts all in fast succession. What had taken me an entire summer to build up in my mind and then only five days to screw up in person was thrown up for scrutiny all in a matter of minutes. For the most part, Bebe stayed silent, sticking with nodding and *mmm-hmm*-ing and the occasional giggle instead.

"So, what do you think I should do?" I asked breathlessly when I was done with my verbal vomiting. "How can I fix things?"

"That depends on which part you want to work on fixing first," she said gently. "What's bothering you the most right now?"

That was an easy one. "Shamus. I feel like I let him down, and also like I still don't know him as well as I should by now."

Bebe looked surprised. "You're more concerned about your dad than the fact that your bottom is being displayed all over the world as we speak?"

I knew it sounded weird, but it was the truth. "Bad as that is, at least I have a plan for how to get over the horrific booty flash," I said. In reality, my plan consisted of complete and utter denial. How could people identify me just from my butt? It wasn't as if I had a mole the shape of Texas that was going to give me away. Like, when I got out of the shower in my dorm, people wouldn't suddenly run screaming, *Oh, my God! There's the chick who hopped on top of Kandy Kane—look, I can see where Waco and Lubbock would be on her ass!*

"And you don't have a plan when it comes to Shamus, I take it?"

"None at all," I said, picking at an old tomato-sauce stain on the place mat in front of me. "Other than beg forgiveness again. And then pelt him with questions about whether he likes mushrooms on his pizza and other important stuff like that."

Bebe patted my hand. "You know something, kiddo? Getting to know someone on a really deep level isn't an overnight thing. And you don't have to try so hard. Just let it happen."

"That's it?" I asked incredulously. "That's all you have to offer me after what I've been through?"

Bebe took a quick chug of her water. "Oh, I have plenty more where that came from. But if you didn't like my top piece of advice, what makes you think you're going to appreciate number fifty-one and six hundred and eighty-two?"

"It's just that I was kind of expecting something more along the lines of *Make up a hundred-page list of interview questions, buy a ticket to California for next weekend, and then fly out there and lock your dad in a room until you know everything about him*, as opposed to the wimpy wait-it-out technique you're suggesting."

"Sometimes the supposedly wimpiest way is the hardest one of all."

I rolled my eyes. "Now you sound like a bad fortune cookie."

"Or a wise older woman," she said, shrugging. "Depends on which way you look at it, Trace. So answer me this. What was the best thing about being with Shamus this week?"

I stared around the room trying to think of a good answer. The best I could come up with was, "That I finally got to be with my dad."

"What else?" Bebe was staring at me so intently I felt like she was taking an X-ray of my thoughts. I didn't appreciate her prodding around my psyche like an overzealous dentist searching for nonexistent cavities, so I watched the second hand tick around the kitchen clock and bided my time. When a minute finally clicked by, I gave her the perfect answer. "That he made a special room for me in his house, just the way I wanted it."

"If he already made room for you in his house," she said, "what makes you think he won't continue to make room for you in his heart?"

I sighed. "I know you're right. It's just that I feel like we've wasted so much time already. I don't want to waste any more."

"Building a relationship with someone who's important to you is never a waste of time. So why don't you just sit back and enjoy it instead?"

I knew it wasn't like we were actually going to solve anything right then, so I changed the subject. "Don't you want to hear about my plan to fool the masses into believing it wasn't my butt they saw on TV?"

"I have a feeling I'm going to find out soon enough," Bebe said, pushing back the chair and going to join her homey in the den. "So surprise me."

I headed back to the computer and clicked a few more links from my Google search. All had the same horrific pictures of my rear end with the block bar fuzzing out the nakedest parts, the same barbs being thrown at Kandy regarding her judgment or lack thereof, and the same intimations that she and I had something going. Though it was all supremely mortifying—just as much so as it had been when I first made the discovery—I'd decided by this point that I had several things going for me:

1) I had not run across any pictures of my face thus far. They just zoomed in on my bottom and Kandy's top. Thank God for horn-dog editors.

2) I certainly didn't look like the girl in those pictures every day, anyway—pseudo-dominatrix outfit, heels tall as the Sears Tower, do worthy of *Your Prom* magazine—so I didn't quite see how anyone could possibly recognize me once I had my normal uniform of baseball cap, Levi's, T-shirt, and Chuckie Ts on.

3) The papers so far had only identified me as Earl since that's what K.C. had called me during the oil debacle. I didn't think there were a lot of people in this world who would put two and two together to link my nickname from the unfortunate Mixed-Up Creamery incident with my rear end and make it equal me.

With all that in mind, I decided I was basically in the clear. If anyone ever asked me—and I kind of doubted that would happen—I'd give them such a strong out-and-out no that they'd never ask again. I finally exhaled for the first time since I'd learned of my predicament. Things were going to be fine.

That calm, collected feeling lasted all of about five minutes, until my cell rang. "Hey, Earl," an unfamiliar male voice said on the other line.

"Who's this?"

"It's your former boss, calling to say hi to his super-famous coworker."

"What are you talking about, Sanford?" I did *not* like where this conversation was headed.

"Is that really you with Kandy Kane, Trace? I mean, I never knew you had such a nice ass."

"Thanks," I said. "I think."

Things were not going according to plan.

The second I hung up, my phone rang again and Brina was screaming on the other end, "No fair! You're getting way more camera time than I ever did on *TRL!*"

I held the phone away from my ear as she went nuts, then slowly brought it back to my face as her tirade wound down. "Please tell me you didn't just say I was on television."

"Trace, you're everywhere."

I tried to stem the rising tide of panic welling up inside me. "Brina, it's just my butt with a black bar across it, correct? So only you know it's me, right?"

Brina cleared her throat. "Trace, it's all of you, especially your face. And it looks kind of greasy, to tell you the truth. Have you tried Proactiv? It really works, I swear."

"Oh, no," I said, pinching my temples in a desperate attempt to stave off the migraine headache that was threatening to appear and stop any tears that even thought about escaping from my eyes. This was no time to get hysterical. I needed an entirely new plan—one way more complex than the simple denial option I'd previously decided to go with.

"Oh, yes," Brina told me. "And if you don't mind my asking, where'd you get those boobs? Are they permanent?"

I had forgotten about the duct tape trick. For the millionth time that day, my hands flew to my chest and peeled my shirt—which was annoyingly attracted to the remnants of leftover gray sticky stuff stranded on my rib cage—away from my body. "They were an optical illusion."

"I didn't *think* you could have and recover from plastic surgery that quickly," she mused almost to herself, clearly having spent too much time on the concept already.

"Oh, Brina, what am I going to do?" I wailed.

"Do?" she asked, sounding like she thought I'd left my brain back in LA. "Revel in it. Be the most famous girl on campus. Try to turn your fifteen minutes into a whole freshman year of fame."

I shook my head. Brina was obviously thinking about what her reaction would've been to this situation and not factoring me into the picture at all. "You know me well enough by now to know that's the last thing I want. I'd rather die than have everyone on campus find out about yesterday."

"Right," Brina said. I could almost hear her nodding, the dusty remnants of long-forgotten stuff rattling around in her brain. "Well, then, I have an idea, but you're not gonna like it."

"Try me." I was ready to wear a prosthetic nose, arm flab, and cankles if it meant my little secret would stay one, at least until I had time to make friends and get settled in on campus.

"It's pretty extreme," she said, dragging out the already torturous process.

"Will you just tell me and get it over with?"

"I've got a better idea. I'll pick you up in fifteen minutes. You are back home, aren't you?"

"Yeah."

"Great, we are going to have a rockin' time together."

"You mean you don't have plans with Sully tonight? And we're gonna get to hang out all alone, just the like old days?"

Brina laughed. "Now I never said that. We're going to hang for a while and get you all fixed up and *then* I'm going out with Sully."

"So we're not going to have the final night out the way we always planned? The one where we revisit all the places we used to go and cry about how much we're going to miss each other this year?" We'd talked about it for-ever. Ever since we'd bonded in third grade over our shared hatred of the Care Bears, we'd dreaded the day we'd be separated. We'd even decided to have an elaborate ceremony the night before we both left for college and plotted out each and every landmark in town we'd visit to commemorate our friendship. And now she was trashing it without a backward glance.

"Come on, Trace. Now that you've got a dad in LA, I bet we see each just as much as ever."

"I highly doubt that."

"With Kandy and all that excitement going on? I'd be out there every weekend if I were you."

"Yeah, but I'm me," I said, as if that explained everything. The truth was, my answer probably confused me even more than her.

CHAPTER
15

After my completely disturbing conversations, I paced the living room floor, practically wearing a hole in the carpet from going back and forth, back and forth. I knew none of this ridiculous predicament I'd gotten myself into meant my life was over—not really, anyway—but I still wanted my old life back just the same. The one where I could pretend my dad and I were going to stuff an entire lifetime of catching up into one week, where Brina and I were joined together at the hip and not divided by boyfriends or headed to opposite ends of the country, and, most important, the one where my backside wasn't being prominently broadcast all over the Internet.

As soon as I saw the Maldonatis's sensible sedan pull around the corner, I was outside in a flash. "So what's it gonna be?" I asked Brina once we were wandering the aisles of Walgreens.

"Like I was saying before, Trace, I think the situation calls for something drastic," she said, picking up and then quickly putting back one box of Feria after another. "I know how you are about your hair, but . . ."

I reached up and smoothed my long curls. I'd survived a lifetime of bad hairdos and unfortunate Sun-In incidents before I'd finally figured out long and wild and natural was my best look. The fact that Brina wanted to take that away from me now was enough to kill me. "Don't even think about it. You know it's taken me this long just to get it to look semicute on a regular basis."

"Fine," she said, putting a particularly scary shade of amethyst back on the shelf. "I'd love to see you take the other way out anyhow. Play it up and stretch it out, I always say."

I closed my eyes and shook my head, trying to sort out which would be worse: having every person who met me at Fairfield already feel they knew me intimately or a yearlong string of bad hair days. "So those are my only choices? Trying to hide who I am by dying my hair some freaky color or announcing my connection to Kandy Kane to the entire campus through a megaphone the minute I get there?"

Brina held one of those weird little fake hair samples up and compared it to the real stuff on my head. "Is that all you think I'm suggesting? That we color your hair?"

I nodded.

"That's grade-school stuff, honey. Don't you think a bunch of smart college kids will see right through that?" she said, pulling a pair of scissors off the display rack and adding it to her ever growing bag of appearance-changing tricks.

I backed away from her and the intended weapons of mass hair destruction. "There is no way you're taking those to my head."

"Why not?"

Was she insane? "What makes you think you can make it look decent when a slew of well-trained stylists couldn't do that my whole life?" I crossed my arms and tapped my foot while I waited for her to think up some brilliant answer.

Per usual, she didn't disappoint me. "Who gave all her Barbies a perfect Pixie?"

I felt like alien spaceships had landed in my eyes, they'd gotten so big by now. "Brina, your Barbies all ended up looking like Courtney Love on a bender!"

Brina waved away my concerns. "That's only because they were always naked. Their hair looked awesome, remember?"

"No."

"Trace, would I steer you wrong?"

I gave her my famous eyebrows. What kind of a question was that? We'd been friends for nearly a decade—of course she'd steered me wrong. "Let me see. There was the palazzo pants debacle, the Sadie Hawkins dance embarrassment, the *Just climb over that fence, nothing bad will happen* catastrophe when the whole class was treated to an unobstructed view of my underwear—"

Brina clapped her hand over my mouth. "No more arguing. You're just going to have to trust me on this one."

Brina paid for the arsenal of hair stuff and we headed back to her place. At the Maldonatis's, we stampeded up to Brina's room with a stolen bottle of wine. It totally reminded me of the scene last Thanksgiving when Brina, Bebe, and I, plus Sully and Brina's brother Brad were seeking refuge from Uncle Mario's farts and the old-lady bitchfight in the kitchen. This time, though, seemed like maybe it wasn't going to be as much fun.

Brina poured us both a small glass, handed me one, then held hers up in a toast. "Here's to an awesome freshman year and hoping our relationship comes out of it stronger and better than ever."

I clinked her glass and took a sip. The weird combination of the gross flavor, burning sensation in my esophagus, and Brina's sweet words all mixed together into a potent sentimental cocktail. "Oh, Brina. You don't ever have to worry about us. We'll always be best friends, right?"

She eyed me carefully. "Sure. But I was actually referring to me and Sully and you and Zander."

I picked at a fuzzball on her carpet. "Oh. Yeah. That." With all the craziness, I'd kind of put Zander out of my mind. The question that had been bouncing around my head all summer—the whole *Does he or doesn't he love me*, *Will he or won't he stay with me*—had sort of faded in importance next to everything else going on in my life. Now she'd put it right back into the amazing mess called my brain and my heart started fluttering around again, a nervous firefly looking for a way out of its jar with the holes punched into the lid.

"Surrender. Have faith. Believe," she said, giving me an abbreviated self-help lesson.

I exhaled slowly and tried to absorb an entire planet of good vibes. Everything was going to turn out great, right? Right? The question rang in my ears until the last echo was gone. I figured the universe must've gone on break, because I didn't even get an answering machine. "Let's do this thing."

Brina dragged me into the bathroom, sat me down on the toilet, and draped a pristine white towel over my shoulders. I tugged at it, trying to quell the rising tide of panic threatening to turn me into some sort of a toxic-waste spill on the tile floor below. "What color did you end up choosing?"

Brina plucked the box out of the plastic bag emblazoned with the highly uncreative blue and red Walgreens logo. "I almost went with Flaming Red," she said. "But in the end, I thought simple and striking was the best. So here you go."

I caught the box she threw to me. "You have got to be kidding me," I said, my jaw ready to hit the floor. I had been thinking more along the lines of adding, say, coppery highlights to my hair, not being transformed into a ghoul fit only to roam the streets at night looking for necks to bite. "Isn't this a bit extreme?"

Brina was losing her patience by this point. "Trace, you said you wanted me to help you fix your little problem with fame that I don't even think is a problem. And what you're failing to recognize is that I've got my own problems, like only having an hour left to get ready for my final night alone with Sully before I head off to college. So what's it gonna be? Black Leather hair and a choppy modern do or living with the knowledge that the entire world has seen parts of you that you wish had been left undercover?"

Nice speech, I thought, throwing my arms up in the air. "My future's in your hands," I said in a squeaky, terror-fueled voice. "Don't mess it up."

"Never fear," she said, a gleam in her eye clueing me in to the fact that she was enjoying our afternoon of female bonding way more than I was. "The official hairdresser to Barbies everywhere is on the case."

Brina unceremoniously glopped a whole bottle of slimy gel on my head, mushed it around, put a shower cap over the whole mess, and tossed a magazine in my general direction. "This should hold you," she said, heading out of the bathroom.

"You're leaving me here all alone?" I called after her. I would've preferred some hand-holding and soothing phrases to the impersonal words in the *Entertainment Weekly* she'd just handed me.

"Dude, I've got to get ready," she said, annoyance oozing out of every pore. "Don't you get it? This is *it*. My last chance. Tomorrow night we'll be at Bebe's wedding with you, and then—*whoosh!* I'm outta here. I need to make sure tonight is completely perfect so it'll hold Sully until Columbus Day."

My eyes, which had been greedily taking in shots of a shirtless Orlando Bloom on the beach, suddenly aimed themselves straight at Brina. "Don't you at least want to give it until Thanksgiving? Get yourself used to being on campus and your new friends and all that?"

"I've already gotten used to having Sully as my boyfriend," she said. "And I don't want any junior miss cheerleader taking it all away. Therefore, I'll be making random and frequent appearances designed to keep this thing together."

I thought about my conversation with Bebe earlier. "Should a relationship really be such hard work?" I asked. And I didn't mean it as a rhetorical question, either. I really wanted to know: Were all relationships so full of scary stuff, or were we going about it in all the wrong way?

"If it's worth it, yeah," she said with total conviction and disappeared into her room.

Brina and Sully seemed so perfect together, I guessed she was probably right. I just wished having a boyfriend wasn't so damn exhausting.

I got so engrossed in an awesome article about the *OC* gang, I almost missed a totally glammed up Brina making her grand reentrance into the bathroom. In her Free People floral skirt, pink halter, and sky-high black espadrilles, Brina looked about as hot as she ever had. She cleared her throat, definitely waiting for me to shower her with compliments.

Of course, I took it in the opposite direction. "Nice try," I said, reveling in how much fun it has always been to yank her chain. But no sooner had the words come out of my mouth than I wanted to suck them back in. What was I thinking, heckling her when she was in charge of cutting my hair?

"You're lucky I'm in such a good mood," she said, opening and closing the scissors menacingly.

After rinsing the glop out of my hair, Brina got right to work on the snip, snip, snipping part of the process. I tried not to look at the humongous piles of black (!) hair falling to the floor. Luckily, I wasn't allowed to turn around and face the mirror, or I might've panicked and run screaming away sporting one of those horrible asymmetrical retro eighties dos.

Every time I thought Brina was just about done, she'd stand back, survey her work, and cut some more. I tried not to think that maybe the reason was because she couldn't get the damn thing even. It occurred to me what was probably happening was that one side was shorter than the other, so she'd go to fix the opposite side, only to notice she'd gone a little too far and needed to trim the side she originally intended to match, and so on and so on in a never-ending cycle. I was convinced she was going to go right on cutting until there was nothing left on my head but a few sad tufts and I'd end up looking like someone's lawn after their dog had peed all over it and left a million telltale burnt-out spots in the grass.

Finally, Brina stopped cutting and started grinning. "Perfect."

I reached up to touch my head. It felt miles lighter than before, like it might float away at any moment if I wasn't careful. "Do I look OK?"

The grin turned to horror. "Shit, no. Tell me this isn't happening."

I grabbed for my head again, trying to discern whether I actually had any of those dog-pee spots I'd imagined moments earlier. "What? What?"

"This!" she said, holding up what used to be her mother's white towel. It had suddenly turned into the hundred-and-second Dalmatian. It was all splotched with Black Leather Feria. "My mom's gonna kill me! She cannot, under any circumstances, find this before I leave."

"Should we hide the evidence?" I still hadn't gotten up the courage to look at myself in the mirror yet, and kind of liked that there was another crisis going on so I could avoid the inevitable for even a tiny bit longer.

"More like you're taking it with you," Brina told me. "Now stuff that under your shirt and let me blow-dry your cool new do."

It was all over in a matter of minutes. Brina added a slash of red lipstick, glittery eye shadow, smudgy black eyeliner, and gobs of mascara to my face, took a BedHead hair stick and rubbed it all over until it felt like spikes were sticking straight out of my head, then spun me around to see the final product.

"Tah-dah!" she exclaimed.

I stared and stared at the stranger looking back at me in the mirror, then stared some more. I was completely speechless.

"So what do you think?" Brina asked. I hadn't seen her glow like this since the local paper ran the story about how her love affair with Sully had started with all those romantic slp notes.

I opened my mouth and tried to speak. Still nothing came out.

"It's amazing, right? You're like a totally new girl. No one will ever recognize you now."

As I stood gaping at my reflection, all I could think was: Well, that goes twice for me.

CHAPTER
16

"Trace, all you need to do is walk down the aisle with Steve's nephew," Bebe repeated yet again. "And smile. That's it. It's not brain surgery."

I knew I was supposed to be the one calming my mom down—it was her wedding day, after all—but between the sea foam dress and the drastic measures I'd taken with my appearance, I just wasn't feeling all that confident. "Bebe, after how Grandma and Grandpa reacted to my hair, I'm afraid Mr. Steve's family might shoot me on the spot for messing up your otherwise picture-perfect wedding."

The main gist of the conversation I was referring to had gone something like this.

Grandma: Trace kind of looks like Snow White now with her sassy black hairdo, doesn't she?

Grandpa (*grumbling*): Only if the prince had decided not to kiss her and left her rotting in the glass coffin instead because he was afraid she might be a vampire.

Grandma (*getting angry*): You know what I think? Our little Snowy here didn't want that damn kiss because the prince was a total windbag, so she turned her head and played dead in lieu of locking lips with a gassy old guy.

Grandpa (*insulted*): Now wait a minute here. If the prince

burped in Miss White's presence, it was only because she was snoring so loud he thought she wouldn't notice.

Bebe (*trying to keep those two from throwing punches*): Break it up, break it up.

Grandpa (*storming upstairs*): If you need me, Belinda, I'll be in my room.

Grandma (*following close behind*): And I'll be in mine!

Me (*quietly*): Technically, I think that's still my room, Grandma.

Grandma (*completely annoyed*): OK then, I'll be in your room!

Me (*under my breath*): Great. Can you pack my stuff for college while you're in there?

After an initial reception like that, was it any wonder I was worried about what people unrelated to me might think about my new look? The only upside of the situation I could see was that I'd definitely met my goal. No one would ever mistake me as Kandy's gal pal Earl now. I was about a million miles from the underdressed golden girl I'd been a couple of days ago—according to my grandparents, I now looked like the decomposing, bloodsucking evil spirit of Snow White. And the worst part about it was, after taking another hard look at myself, I was afraid they might be right. I didn't even want to get out of bed, much less have everyone looking at me in a church.

"I feel so ugly," I said.

Bebe lifted my chin and forced me to meet her eyes. "I think you look beautiful," she said. "Tragic and beautiful and fragile and strong. The perfect combination for any heroine in my book."

I sniffed back a tear and tried to put on a happy face. "So does this mean I'll be starring in your next novel?"

Bebe nodded. "Definitely. I'll write about an incredible young woman who thinks she has to hide her true self. And then one day she'll finally realize she's perfect just the way she is and find the love and acceptance she's been searching for all along."

I knew where this was headed: straight into Moral of the Story Land. "And in your book, will all that have been right in front of her face the whole time?"

"You know me too well, don't you?" she said, fussing with the ridiculous layers of my dress.

"I do," I said as the strains of the brass quartet filtered through the walls of the dressing room we were holed up in. The simple, timeless tune brought a huge lump to my throat. D-day was here. Everything was changing; there would be no turning back, no freeze-framing, no instant replays. This was real life, in real time, happening here and now. I sincerely hoped we were all ready for it. "I'm really glad you're happy, Bebe."

Now it was my mom's turn to get all misty. "You will be again, too, honey. Sooner than you think. Now let's get going."

I knew she deserved my support, so I sucked it up and started walking with my shoulders thrown back and a smile plastered to my face. And when I got to the front of the church, I stood proud and defiant as everyone turned to watch my mom glide by in her super-virginal white gown. Which was kind of a joke, with my mom having her grown daughter as maid of honor and who knows who growing inside her as we speak.

But when Grandpa delivered Bebe to Mr. Steve and they clasped hands and gazed at each other, all smiles and tears rolled into one, it was clear everything was just as it should be. It was the fairy tale ending Bebe had been writing about for so long but never experienced until now.

The fact that a key role was being played by Snow White's vampire twin was just par for the course in our family.

*　*　*

As the day went on, things continued looking up. The reception at the country club turned out to be nowhere near as cheesy as I expected. Granted, it wasn't the House of Blues and not even slightly edgy, but it had numerous other things going for it—like the fact that everyone seemed to be having a great time.

Even me. Between Brina and Sully, Grandpa (who stayed as far away from Grandma as possible) and my new stepdad—how weird, my former guidance counselor was now sort of semirelated to me—I never left the dance floor. The eighties dance tunes I'd complained about having to listen to while I was growing up now seemed retro enough to qualify as cool, so I just totally went for it, never worrying about whether I might look stupid. The end result was a sweaty, goofy, and remarkably happy daughter of the bride—something I would have thought I'd be pretty much incapable of after the events of the past week.

And then everyone had to go and ruin my fantabulous time by slow dancing. As soon as I heard the first ballad weeping out of the speakers, I knew I was a goner. I plunked myself down at the head table, watching the happy couples swoosh by while simultaneously watching my formerly sweaty, goofy, remarkably happy mood morph into a soggy, humorless, miserable one. Dramatic much, I know, but that's how I felt.

First I lived through "Open Arms" (by Journey, whose lead singer shares the same name as my mom's new husband in a weird but perfect coincidence). Then came "Endless Love," and it was. Endless, that is. As an encore, they played "Up Where We Belong." Mr. Steve topped off the whole ooey, gooey lovefest by scooping Bebe up in his arms and carrying her off the floor a la Richard Gere and Debra Winger in that old movie *An Officer and a Gentleman*. Another Bebe classic favorite, of course, that we used to watch mainly when one of us was feeling particularly pessimistic about the opposite sex.

Sigh. Normally I would've been pretty cynical about the possibility of someone being literally swept off her feet, but now that I'd witnessed it, I was a true believer. And while I was thrilled for Bebe, it made me feel even sorrier for myself than ever. Because a light had suddenly gone on in my head, and I didn't like the fact it kept illuminating: To get swept away, you have to be willing to go with the flow. It had taken Bebe thirty-seven years to take that scary leap; as for me, I was pretty much convinced I'd spend the rest of my days kicking and screaming against the tide. You know, living alone, constantly talking to my fifty cats, and actually believing they gave a crap about what I had to say.

By the time Bebe and Steve returned to the reception hall and took their seats beside me, I was well into in the depths of gloom about having to spend the rest of my life unlovable and unloved except by felines. Which was probably the reason I reacted so negatively to all the glass clinking. I had no one except my fifty fictitious furballs to kiss, and probably never would again, seeing as Zander had seemed so enthralled with Cali he could conceivably decide to stay there forever. So while everyone else was busy smooching, I was seriously considering the possibility of burying my spiky black head in the toilet and flushing. Sewer life couldn't be anywhere near as bad as being stuck all alone in Makeoutville. So I'd have a few giant rats and alligators to deal with . . . big deal. Me and my kitty posse could handle it.

"Did I happen to mention that as maid of honor you might be expected to give a toast?" Bebe asked when she was done kissing her new husband.

"God, no! You know how bad I am in front of a crowd!" I hissed.

"I'm sorry, Trace. I forgot in all the hoopla. Maybe no one will remember to ask you to give one."

What was I supposed to say to that? I went with nothing.

"Trace, are you feeling OK?" Bebe asked. I guessed she'd noticed my horrified expression. Maybe I'd even been muttering a thing or two about heading to the ladies' room and joining the rat and alligator infested underworld.

"Yeah, fine. Just a little . . . you know . . . like . . ." I couldn't quite come up with a word that captured ugly, jealous, scared, and envious all at the same time. Ugjeascarvious, maybe? Before I had a chance to try that one out on her, the glass clinking started again. I sighed and closed my eyes.

When I opened them back up, Mr. Steve's brother, who had served as the best man, was standing up and waiting for silence. Eventually, everyone quieted down and Mr. Boring Banker launched into a well-meaning but completely snooze-inducing speech. I swear, he could've marketed it as the latest insomnia remedy and become a zillionaire in a matter of minutes. My eyelids immediately fell to half-mast as I totally zoned out—I probably heard only a few words of every other sentence. Like, blah blah, best brother anyone could ever ask for. Blah blah blah, lucky guy. Blah-beddy blah-beddy bloo, great couple, happy life together. Blah blah blah, Trace?

My eyelids flew from half-mast to there's-no-way-they-can-get-any-wider when I heard my name. What Trace? Why Trace? He couldn't possibly mean *me* Trace. I looked around the room. Everyone was looking back at me expectantly. Finally, Bebe nudged me. "Go ahead. Just say something quick and it'll all be over."

I stood up, my legs shaking uncontrollably. I wasn't surprised. Whenever the spotlight lands on me, I get so unnerved I practically faint dead before I can speak a word. This simple fact has always made oral reports, being in the school play, and celebrating my birthday complete torture. Really, I get so unglued I start to think pieces of me are going to start flying off in different directions, and I just know there's no way in hell I'll ever be able to stick myself back together again. So the bottom line is this: Me plus any sort of a performance equals imminent disaster. It's about as far from a win-win situation as you can get. More like lose-lose—the audience loses their patience with me as I lose control of my body parts.

"Uhhhhhh," I started my sure-to-be-crappy speech. Relax, I told myself. This time will be different. All you have to do is think. The word raced around in my brain, searching for intelligent life, but came back empty-headed. I mean, handed. Think, I urged myself again. Still nothing but echoes bouncing off the dark recesses of my skull. *THINK,* I finally screamed at myself.

"Think," I said out loud, the silent mantra slipping out of my mouth unintentionally. I stared out into the sea of confused faces, cleared my throat, and tried again. "What I meant was, just think. Less than a year ago, my mom and my guidance counselor hadn't even met. But thanks to my pathetic grasp of trigonometry and Bebe's even more pathetic sense of direction, here they are today, in love, married. . . ."

Little bursts of applause broke out here and there. My audience was grinning at my now almost brilliant speech. People started tapping their glasses with their spoons again, Bebe and Mr. Steve kissed, and I didn't even hate all the clinkers this time. I mean, I was totally on a roll and it felt great. I raised my voice, speaking as confidently as I ever had in my life, and zoomed toward what was sure to be a killer closing.

"In love, married . . . and expecting my baby brother or sister in the spring! Isn't that just so amazing?"

Instead of being greeted by thunderous applause, there was

dead, cold silence. I kind of sensed something had gone awry, so I looked over at Bebe. She shrugged—she wasn't sad or mad, just maybe a little, I don't know . . . *embarrassed,* possibly? I shot a glance at Mr. Steve. He was trying not to laugh. Farther on down the row, though, his family looked like their heads were going to explode.

"Yeah, ummm, just kidding about that last part. . . ." I said quickly, trying to cover up my major faux pas. Clearly, there hadn't been any big announcement before I opened my even bigger mouth. But I'd just figured everyone had to know. Why else would there have been such a damn rush to put this thing on in a week's time? Were these people completely dense?

I decided to give myself the hook before I screwed anything else up. "Please, everyone raise your glasses in toast to Bebe and Steve. Long may they live, long may they love, and may the years ahead be fertile."

A few stray giggles lit up the room, followed by a buzz of whispers.

"I mean, full of everything the love they make together brings," I said, still tripping over my tongue.

Louder laughter this time.

"Oh, my God, you know what I mean." My triumph over stage fright had slipped through my fingers once again, and while everyone sipped their champagne, a blush that threatened to turn my Black Leather do into a Flaming Red one engulfed my entire skull.

"Sorry," I mumbled to Bebe.

"You did great," she whispered back. "No big deal. Everyone was going to find out soon enough, anyway. I'm about to pop. Sucking in my stomach is going to work for about a week more and that's it."

"I really didn't mean to ruin your big day," I said, staring down at the wedding cake the waitress had just placed in front of me.

Bebe laid her hand on top of mine. "You couldn't have ruined it if you tried. And you didn't, anyway. I loved what you said. Don't sweat it."

But I was sweating all of a sudden. Buckets of the stuff appeared on my forehead, upper lip, pits, everywhere. Sadly, wet sea foam taffeta resembles something closer to seaweed. It definitely wasn't my best look. "I need some air," I whispered, practically panting in an attempt to get some oxygen in my lungs. "I'll be back in a bit."

I ran from the room and burst through the emergency exit. Moments later, I found myself wandering along a well-groomed path, staring out into the twilight at the golf course and pool and perfectly manicured gardens. The peace and tranquility of the scene calmed me down enough to stop all the sweating and blushing and general mortification, so when I came to a gazebo, I stopped to relax.

Leaning back against the white wooden slats, I loosened the string on the horrifically ugly drawstring pouch I was carrying as part of my tropical Skittles bridesmaid getup and pulled out my cell. I wanted to check in with California, to see what was happening to the other half of my slightly surreal life. Or would that be my pseudo-real world?

First I tried Z but was immediately launched into his voice mail, which he thinks is completely hilarious. His entire message consists of one word: *Beeeeep!* I decided that unless I wanted to turn into a self-fulfilling cat-woman prophesy, it was about time I let loose with a little real emotion.

Hey Z, it's me. I just wanted to tell you that I totally miss you and wish you were here. The wedding was cool, but the slow dances really sucked without you. Can't wait to see you tomorrow.

Feeling magnanimous, I decided to check in with Shamus as well. Voice mail again.

Shamus, sorry for any trouble I caused you, hope everything is cleared up by the time you get this. I'd really love to get back together soon when you have more time to hang out. I think we probably have a lot more in common than we've found out yet. Like Led Zep—you must like them, right? Well, I do, too. Bye. Oh, it's Trace if you didn't already know that.

I clicked end before I had a chance to regret putting myself out there and erased the whole damn thing. The main points I'd wanted to make were in there, stuttery, stumbly, brain-dump method aside. He'd get my gist, and that's all that mattered.

One last call, and I thought I'd be ready to go back and face the music, so to speak. I punched in K.C.'s digits and got lucky. She answered on the first ring. What she couldn't do was hear me very well. "Trace? Trace, is that you?" she screamed on her end.

"K.C.!" My exclamation bounced around the pool, over to the ninth hole, up to the tennis shack, beyond the rose garden, and then back again to the gazebo. I was pretty sure I'd just broken one of the country club's top ten commandments: Thou shalt not raise your voice on a beautiful, silent night in the manner of a rock-music-listening ruffian. Please keep your tone more accordant to the type of person who would enjoy whispering under the strains of Chopin or Mozart.

"Trace, I'm here with Shamus and Zander and the rest of the crew! We're celebrating the wrap of week one. Can you believe it?"

Not only could I not believe the show was actually going to make it to the air, but I was finding it hard to fathom that my dad, boyfriend, and potential new best friend were out partying without me. It just didn't seem fair.

"Wow, that's really cool," I said, in a voice more accordant to a classical-music-appreciating country club member. Think low, unenthusiastic, and monotone, and you'll get the picture.

If she noticed I was less than amped, she didn't mention it. "Trace, I have something super-important to ask you."

"Shoot," I said, twirling the strings of my bridesmaid/mermaid pouch around my fingers as she pitched her case.

"It's a huge favor, actually," she said. "And promise me you won't say yes unless you are completely comfortable with the idea. Don't compromise yourself for me, OK?"

"K.C., just ask me already. You don't need to butter me up."

I heard her take a deep breath on the other end. "How would you feel if one of the clips in the montage that starts my show was from the club?"

It took a moment to register what she was asking. She couldn't possibly mean a clip that showed my butt hanging out, could she? "You mean before I tackled you? When we were all slow dancing in the spotlight?"

Silence. Then, "Nope, I actually meant after that. Kind of like the ones you were stressing out about yesterday."

Oh, please. She had to be kidding. "The pictures where I look like the Coppertone kid with the dog pulling down her underwear? I don't think so, baby cakes."

"Trace, what if I totally, one hundred percent assured you that your bottom would be totally fuzzed out? Would you agree to it then?"

Maybe, maybe not, I thought. On the one hand, I wanted to help K.C. out. On the other—what, was she crazy? "Why is this so important to you?" I asked, stalling for time.

"All the publicity from it seems to have turned into a good thing after all. Tons of shows are asking me and Caden to come on and sing live—"

Wait just a minute. Did this mean she and Caden were back

together? "What about him being dead to you? Did you guys make up?"

"Not even close," she told me. "But we do make good music together. And if I can't go to college right now, I can at least put out the best songs possible."

"How could showing pictures of me possibly impact any of that?"

K.C. barreled on. "Having the clips of me and Caden first getting along and then fighting—and then you coming in and saving me from him—will make people even more curious about us, boost my ratings, and have our new single flying off the shelves. Are Caden and Kandy together? Are they not? Tune in and see."

Yeah, I understood the marketing strategy. What I didn't get was why K.C. cared so much—I mean, she'd practically told me she'd like to chuck it all away and go to college, and now here she was acting like she adored the spotlight. Another stall for time was clearly in order. "I'm not sure . . ."

"Trace, please? Please, please, please do it for me?"

I reached up, touched my cropped hair. I'd already taken care of disguising myself. The pictures were already out there for everyone to see. What harm could it do, really? And if it would help K.C. out that much . . .

"Maybe," I finally said.

"Really?" K.C. sounded like she was holding her breath.

I decided to drop a small bomb on her. "In return for a couple of favors, I might."

K.C. audibly gasped on the other end. "Anything. You name it."

I started ticking things off on my fingers. "Number one, tell me what happened to the girl I know and love who said she didn't even want to have a TV show. Why the sudden turnaround?"

"Trace, it's like this. There's no way I'm going to be able to become invisible now, go to college, be a normal teenager. So I've decided to ride this wave while I can and make as much money as possible so my mom can't run my life anymore, I can pay for my own education, and do whatever I want once it's over."

That at least explained things better. I moved on to my next request. "Number two, I want you to promise me that you'll never, ever reveal the girl on the TV is me. I chopped my hair off and it's black now, so no one will be able to connect me to you, unless I tell them."

"Cross my heart and hope to die."

That covered a vast amount of territory, I thought, giggling to myself before swooping in for the kill. "Number three, I want you to watch Zander like a hawk while he's out there without me. Any canoodling with any other girls and I want to know about it."

"I really don't think there's anything for you to worry about," K.C. said. "But no problem. I will keep my eyes and ears on him."

"Great, then," I told her. "You've got yourself a deal."

K.C. let out a huge whoop. "I knew I could count on you!"

"That's just me," I said, wondering if I'd just made a humongous error that I'd live to regret. "Always doing things to make other people happy."

After K.C. and I said our good-byes, I made my way back to the reception only to find the whole thing was just about wrapping up. I smiled from the sidelines as I watched the happy couple dance one last time to their wedding song, Rick Astley's "Never Gonna Give You Up," surrounded by family and friends. Everyone had their arms wrapped around each other and were swaying to the music. It reminded me of all those eighties benefit songs Bebe loves so much, where the biggest stars pitch in to help out for a good cause. My closest guess was that this one might be raising funds for clueless late-thirtysomethings addicted to bad music.

When Bebe noticed me hanging out along the fringes of the scene, she—along with the fifty-some-odd people attached to her—swung on over and added me to their ranks. Within seconds, I was front and center, sandwiched in between my mom and Mr. Steve. Both were singing at the top of their lungs, and I wasn't even all that embarrassed. I really must be growing up, I thought, smiling to myself.

"Welcome to the family," I said in Mr. Steve's ear, interrupting his warbling for just a minute.

"Right back at you, Trace," he said. "Thanks so much for sharing your mom with me. It's the greatest gift anyone could ever give me."

"You're welcome," I said, realizing I'd been so wrapped up in my own drama I'd forgotten to purchase a present for those two. Oh, well. I'd read somewhere—probably that damn *Emily Post's Teen Etiquette* book again—I had a whole year before it would be considered late. I was sure that would be enough time to come up with just the right thing.

CHAPTER 17

As people started piling out of the country club and into their cars, Brina tapped me on the shoulder. "Want a ride?"

I stared at the ever present Sully on her arm and shook my head. "I still have to finish packing, and we're taking off first thing in the morning . . ."

Brina grabbed my hand and held on tight. "All the more reason why you have to come with me now. I mean, what about the night we always planned? The one where we visit all the places from our past and cry and vow to be best friends forever, no matter what?"

I stared from Brina to her boyfriend and back. I didn't think there was a chance in the universe she'd be dropping off Sully before me. And having him tag along on our magical memory tour, and us needing to explain everything, and me having to turn away every time those two decided to make out—well, it just didn't sound like that much fun. "I thought you two had other plans. Not to mention the fact you said we didn't have to bother with our big night out since you decided we're going to see each other more than ever now that I have a dad in LA."

Sully cleared his throat. "Seriously, Trace, it's cool. You guys go have fun without me. I've got to get home before curfew, anyway," he said, reminding me once again that no matter how mature he seemed, Brina's main man was still only a soon-to-be high school junior.

"Yeah, and since we've had all summer to perfect the late-night sneaking through the window thing," Brina added with a laugh, "I get the best of both worlds."

"Just let me check and see if it's OK," I said, running over and letting Grandpa, who was supposed to be the one driving me home, in on the scoop. He harrumphed a bit, muttered something about not wanting to sit next to that woman—I assumed he was referring to Grandma—and then finally relented. I patted his arm and trotted back over to my friends. "We're good to go."

The valet delivered the sensible Maldonati sedan to us, Brina took the wheel, and we started cruising. In no time at all, we were dumping Sully rather unceremoniously at his doorstep. "Nice hair, by the way," he called over his shoulder at me. "You look like a rock star."

My smile nearly lit up the car. At least one person thought so.

"Catch you on the rebound," Brina shouted after him as he unlocked the door. He gave her a cute little salute and disappeared inside the already dark house, and we peeled off. A few blocks later, Brina pulled into the grammar school where we'd met, dorky third-graders with matching blue plastic-framed glasses. "You know what I've always loved best about you?" she asked as we raced over to the swing set.

"No, what?"

"That you were always game to try any ridiculous thing I dreamed up," she said. "Like, remember when I dared you to kiss Paulie Romano? Or jump out of that tree over there to test out my homemade parachute idea? Or the time we put Saran wrap over the girls' room toilets so that bitch Sarah Covington would pee all over herself, but the poor art teacher was the one who ended up getting wet instead?"

I laughed. "How come all those stories have a painful ending? Like, with Paulie running away yelling *Cooties!* or with me breaking my arm, or us being sent to the principal's office?"

She shrugged. Each of us grabbed a swing and started pumping maniacally, trying to beat the other. The googly feeling in the pit of my stomach kept telling me to stop, but my legs just kept on going. It was the way things had always been—me wanting to play it safe while Brina pushed us closer and closer to the edge. I guessed that meant we were a pretty good pair, and that as long as we were friends, neither one of us would ever go too far in any one direction.

I gave a little yell as I sailed higher and higher into the air. I was going to become part of the sky pretty soon if I didn't slow down. Brina's swing whooshed by me, faster and higher, as usual. "Come on, you loved all the attention. You never would've done anything even remotely crazy without me."

It was true—I had always been stronger and braver with Brina by my side than I'd ever be alone. "Now you want to know what I liked best about you?" I asked, turning the tables.

"Nope," Brina said on a backward trajectory.

"Too bad, 'cause I'm gonna tell you anyway. I loved that once you got us into trouble, you'd always apologize and tell me how right I was for not wanting to do whatever loony thing we'd gotten caught for, and then say you wished you were more like me."

Whoosh. "My life would definitely be a lot less messy if I was," she said.

Whoosh times two. "And my life would definitely be more exciting if I was more like you," I told her. "You're so not afraid to throw yourself into whatever you want with all your heart, even if that means looking like a fool, or failing, or getting caught, or getting in trouble. I totally admire that in you."

"So maybe we're just two halves of a perfect whole," Brina yelled as she swung by. "And that's why we're going to best friends forever, right?"

"Absolutely. You want to know something else?"

"Sure."

"I just lied. My favorite thing about you is that there's never a dull moment when you're around."

"So true, so true," she said, leaning way back so her hair nearly touched the ground with every downswing.

Our little playground competition had gotten completely over the top by this point—I mean, not literally yet, but it seriously felt like a little more effort might send one of us flying around the bar—and I was kind of freaking out about it. So I tentatively started touching my feet to the ground, trying to slow myself down. What were the teachers at this place thinking, I wondered? A kid could get killed on these contraptions.

"So what about Sully?" I asked.

"What about him?" Brina asked, giggling like the grammar school kids we had been all those years ago.

"What do you like best about him?" I suddenly really, really needed to know the answer. Like, if Brina said the magic word, I'd once and for all understand making a relationship work, even when you're at different schools in different states.

Brina flew by me again and again. "That he's just so . . . so . . . Sully!" she finally answered. It wasn't exactly the revelation I'd been looking for.

I was at a dead stop now. "What's that supposed mean?" I called up after her.

Brina let go of the chains and went flying off into the air just as the swing was at its highest point. Leave it to her to opt for thrills-and-potential-death method over the old use-your-foot-to-stop one. "It means I love everything about him," she said, sticking a perfect-ten landing before heading straight for the monkey bars. "His eyes, his pecs, his thighs, his fingernails, his hands, his biceps, his triceps—"

"What about stuff you can't touch, though? Like his brains? Or personality? Or sense of humor?" I asked, following close behind, laughter covering up the fact that I was dead serious about the question.

"Oh, yeah. Of course. All that stuff, too," she said, climbing up and expertly taking one rung after another. "When I said every-thing, I meant literally everything about him. There's not one thing—I mean, besides his age, and that's only because it would be fun to be in school together longer—that I'd change about him."

"Really?" How could she not want to change anything about the guy? There wasn't one measly thing that bugged her about Sully? I could already think of a handful of things that annoyed me about Zander and I hadn't even been trying to come up with any.

"Really," she said, almost at the last rung. "So, what about you? What do you love best about Zander?"

Following a few bars behind her, I let the question bounce around my mind. Though it stopped to check out all the bones that made up my skull and examine my gray matter and random thoughts, it never quite came back with a satisfying answer.

"Too many things to pick from, huh?" Brina asked sympatheti-cally, done with all the monkeying around and running for the sandbox next.

I dropped to the ground and chased after her. Plunking myself down in the sand, I started scooping up great big handfuls of the stuff and letting it run through my fingers. "That he's just so . . .

so . . . Zander," I finally said, oh-so-quietly taking the easy way out by copying Brina's answer. I by no means sounded as sincere as she had, sotto voce or no sotto voce.

"What's that supposed to mean?" Brina asked, throwing the same question back at me that I'd asked of her just seconds earlier. A smile played around her lips, and I imagined she was hoping for a juicy, slightly off-color answer.

But I was too busy finding the whole conversation vaguely disturbing to be able to think of any nasty revelations. Why was it that Brina could easily come up with one hundred and one body parts she loved on Sully before she even got started on his many fine qualities and attributes, and I was finding it difficult to sputter out one measly adjective about the boyfriend I was so desperate to hang on to and who I was willing to pretend to be perfect and had just asked my friend to spy on in my absence? Even my twisted mind could see how whacked the whole thing was. I dug my toes in the sand and made my confession. "You know what, Brina? I honestly don't know. My mind is a big blank."

Brina stopped patting the castle she was building and stared up at me. "What?"

"Seriously, I have no idea what I love most about Zander these days," I said, letting my body fall back into the soft silt. I stared at the stars lighting up the sky as if I might find the answer spelled out for me there. "It would probably be easier for me to say what I love least about him at this point."

"Well, let's start with what you know, then. What *do* you love least?" Brina asked, interrupting my stream-of-consciousness confession.

The answer was with me in an instant, it was so easy. "The way he's always cracking his knuckles," I said, doing an imitation of his near-constant finger contortions. "Even when his hands are in his pockets. It sounds like fireworks are going off inside his boxers and it drives me insane. And then he wants to touch me with them? Ugh." I visibly shuddered, and it was only half embellished.

Brina threw her head back and laughed. "That's funny. But totally beside the point. Let's get back to the *love best* dilemma."

I exhaled slowly. "I wouldn't say it was a dilemma, exactly. Maybe more of a quandary? Or a slight bump in the road?"

"Beside the point again. The question was, what do you love best about Zander?"

I sighed more deeply this time. For the life of me, I just couldn't come up with some big, meaningful answer. "I guess the fact that he's still my boyfriend," I finally said. "Is that totally lame or what?" I glanced at Brina from out of the corner of my eye, afraid of the expression I might see reflected on her face.

"That, my dear, isn't what I'd call lame," Brina said, suddenly turning into the Dr. Phil of Hubbard Woods playground. "Or a dilemma, or a quandary, or a slight bump in the road. It's what I'd call a big, fat problem."

"C'mon, let's get out of here," I said, grabbing her hand and pulling her to her feet. "We've still got a lot of places to hit before the night is through."

Brina tried to protest, but I wouldn't hear of it. Once we were back in the car, I turned the radio up and sang at the top of my lungs as we drove along, all in an attempt to stave off any continuation of the conversation we'd just started. This night was supposed to be about fun and memories, not shrinking my head.

Soon we'd made it to our next destination: the graveyard we'd snuck off to during eighth period one Friday in seventh grade because Brina decided we hadn't lived yet because we'd never cut class or smoked a cigarette, and it was high time we did both.

"Why is it I'm sensing a theme here?" I said after we'd rehashed all the gory details of the story. "Have you really spent the last ten years trying to get me expelled? Or, worse, arrested?"

"Yeah, and what a decade it was," she sighed, putting her hands behind her head and leaning back against an ancient gravestone.

I crossed my legs like a nursery school kid and picked at random blades of grass, taking what Brina had said to me at the playground and rolling it over in my mind. She couldn't possibly be right, could she? Was my relationship with Zander really in deep trouble?

Brina produced a cigarette from out of thin air and lit it. Taking a puff, she coughed just a little before passing it my way. "For old times' sake," she said. From where I was sitting, it looked like her teeth were glowing.

"No, thanks," I said, pushing her hand away. "Don't you think I learned my lesson the first time?"

When the school narked on us to our parents, Brina had gotten grounded for a month. I wasn't so lucky. Instead, Bebe had sat me down with a pack of Marlboro Reds and told me not to leave the room until I smoked every one. And if I couldn't, that I was never to smoke again. By my second cigarette, I was Earl times three. Her tactic worked—I couldn't stomach the idea of taking a single puff, much less actually finish an entire cigarette, even this many years later. The added benefit of having such a cool mom was that I would most likely avoid a lifetime of ill health and could run a marathon instead of getting winded after jogging half a block.

"Here's another lesson you might want to learn—having a boyfriend just for the sake of having a boyfriend is worse than having no boyfriend at all."

Duh. Like I didn't know that. "Like I don't know that," I told her. "Do you?"

Huh? Zander wasn't that kind of a boyfriend—the kind you

hang on to well after things should've been over just because you were afraid of being alone. Was he? "I do," I insisted.

Brina took another drag, then stamped the cigarette out in the grass. "I think we have time for one more stop on this tour. Cool?"

"Cool."

Soon we were walking along the shore of Lake Michigan, dresses hiked up high, bare feet splashing in the water. This beach had been the scene of a million and one endless summer days when we were kids, and then, as we got older, a million more make-out sessions with our boys du jour and late night talks and other general merriment. We went through as many *remember when* stories as we could think of, all the while searching for sea glass in the moonlight.

When we'd had enough of that, we climbed the lifeguard tower and just sat in silence for a while. It was peaceful, comfortable. And it felt about as close to heaven on earth as you can get, practically being able to touch the stars with someone you love and trust and have the best time in the world with sitting by your side.

"I'm going to give you one more shot at the million-dollar question, Trace," Brina finally said, breaking the silence. "What do you love most about Zander?"

I shrugged. "I think I've been so hung up on the idea of keeping us together, I've lost sight of what attracted me to him in the first place."

Brina turned from Dr. Phil to Dr. Freud right in front of my very eyes. "Ahhhh. And what do you think that means?"

"Are you saying I should break up with him?" I asked, cutting directly to the chase. I wasn't necessarily going to do it if she answered in the affirmative—just take it under consideration.

Brina slung her arm around my shoulder and stared up at the sky. "I'm not saying anything, really, other than you owe it to yourself and Zander to figure it out. And whatever happens from there happens."

I gave her a squinty look, trying to find the catch. There didn't seem to be one. "And what if we break up again?"

She shrugged. "Then you know what they always say."

I actually had no idea what they always said. Or who *they* were, for that matter. "No, what?"

"There's tons of other fish in Lake Michigan."

I rolled my eyes, though I'm sure she couldn't see it in the darkness. "Yeah, a bunch of smelt. I have to tell you, I'm not all that attracted to smelt, Brina."

"No worries. I'm sure the guys at Fairfield wear deodorant. It eliminates smelt, don't you think?"

I punched her lightly on the arm and laughed. "So what you're saying in your very strange way is that either way, things will work out?"

"That's right."

I turned and gathered that crazy girl into a big-ass hug. "Thanks."

"For what?" Her voice was all muffled from being smushed into my shoulder.

"For knowing and loving all of me, not just the easy parts."

Brina broke free and smiled. "You've always done the same for me, you know? It's a two-way street."

"It's a pretty amazing gift," I said, the tears we talked about shedding over our separation finally breaking free.

"Trace, you might be amazed at how many other people out there are willing to do the same for you," Brina told me. "If you'd only let them."

"Since when did you get so smart?" I asked, sniffling loudly.

"Since you convinced me to give love a chance, no matter who slp turned out to be," she said. "Thanks, by the way. You were totally right."

CHAPTER
18

After such a great night, you can only imagine how psyched I was at the thought of driving seven hundred and fifty miles in a beater station wagon on no sleep with my feuding grandparents.

But at least my send-off seemed like it was going to be pretty cool. Everyone was already up by the time I crawled out of bed—having been prompted by my nerve-shattering alarm clock several thousand times—and trudged downstairs. Bebe had my favorite songs cranking in the kitchen from the iPod iStation, as opposed to her crappy playlists that usually accompanied our morning routine, and was making my most favorite childhood breakfast ever while Mr. Steve carried load after load of my stuff out to the car.

"So, when are you guys heading off for your honeymoon?" I asked Bebe as she set a huge stack of blueberry pancakes in front of me.

"Didn't I tell you? We're postponing our trip until Thanksgiving. Steve's got to get back to work this week, and I've got a book proposal due. So we just thought, fall is so nice here, we'd wait until the weather started turning colder before we took a little tropical getaway."

"Thhhssnssss," I said, my mouth so full of food the words all mushed together. Translation: That's nice. And also a great way to stop feeling guilty about my plans for not coming home for Turkey Day and heading to Shamus's instead. I'd been worried about how Bebe might react to the news; I saw now I'd been stressing over nothing.

"Yeah, I guessed you'd probably want to spend it in California with your dad," she said, giving me a knowing nod. "To work on getting to know him better. And that made it the perfect time for Steve and me to grab a little R & R together. Not that I won't miss you or anything."

"I'll miss you, too," I said. Leave it to Bebe to know what I was planning to do almost before I did sometimes. "But we've always got the phone, and e-mail, and IM until we see each other again, right?"

"I who?" Grandpa wanted to know.

"Ay yi yi," my Grandma said, shaking her head. "It's such whack when a silverback goes all dillweed on you, ain't it?"

"Rise up, foo!" Grandpa said, actually getting up from his chair to prove how serious he was. Any second, I thought those two might start a rap off or challenge each other to a break-dance contest or something, but eventually Grandpa sat back down and an icy chill settled over the table as they stopped talking to each other altogether.

"Trace, could you please pass the syrup?" Grandma asked me. It was pretty childish, since Mrs. Butterworth's was sitting right in front of Grandpa.

"Trace, could you please hand this to your grandmother?" Grandpa said, handing the syrup to me to hand to her.

"Could you guys stop acting like babies?" Bebe said. It sounded like a reasonable request. "And start talking like normal human beings while you're at it?"

"Not until I get an apology," they both said at the same time.

I'd have to figure out a way to make that happen, or the only sounds I'd hear on the ride to college would be either of the gaseous, nauseous type or the sleep-induced, log-sawing variety.

"What does either of you have to apologize for?" Bebe wanted to know.

Grandpa stuck out a thumb and flicked it in Grandma's direction. "Ask her."

She turned and faced the other direction. "Oh, no. Ask him."

"I take it back. You two are worse than babies," Bebe said, throwing her hands up in the air. "Good luck, Trace. I don't envy you."

"Me, neither," I said, pushing my chair back from the table and patting my belly. "Looks like it's gonna be a looooong ride."

"Whoa." Zander had suddenly appeared in the kitchen, and now he was just standing there completely dumbstruck.

I flashed Z a humongous grin. "Hey, baby, what's up?"

Z didn't smile back at me. He just stood stock still, his mouth hanging open.

"Something the matter?" I asked, an edge to my voice this time. The guy was staring at me like I was some kind of weird *Girlfriends Gone Ugly* museum exhibit. Or, even worse, like the time he finally showed up after I'd come home from Cali last year and unceremoniously dumped me.

"What happened to you?" Zander finally asked when he regained his power of speech.

My hand flew to my hair and patted a random spike. "A little emergency disguise so no one at Fairfield figures out I'm the infamous Earl," I told him. "Like it?"

"I—I—" Zander stuttered, clearly hating it. I knew it without a doubt, just like I always knew the first time I listen to a CD whether I'm going to play it relentlessly until every measure becomes a part of me or never listen to it again. "You—I—I mean, you just look so different."

"Thanks for the glowing endorsement," I said, feeling hurt and wanting to lash back out at him. "And you look like you got hit by a train. What gives?"

Z ran his hand through his unkempt hair and tried to turn his attention anywhere else but on my hair. "Crazy night. I partied with the cast and crew of *Kandy's Room* and then went straight to the airport to catch the red-eye. And now here I am. I feel like I could sleep all day."

I wasn't sure I wanted to know what kind of crazy he was referring to. Did he mean swinging-from-the-ceiling-with-some-hot-wannabe-actress crazy, or laugh-a-minute crazy, or busy crazy, or what? It was like Pandora's box—I knew once I opened the subject, I'd never be able to stuff it neatly back into the unknown. I decided we'd get back to it later—after I had a chance to get the real scoop from K.C.—and focused on practical items instead. "Ditto. Do your parents need any help loading your things into the car?"

Zander shook his head, staring at the coffeepot like it was the most fascinating thing in the world. "Nope. Me and my dad and Mr. Steve already did everything. My mom, of course, just stood there and sobbed. It was so pathetic, I just had to say good-bye outside and send them on their way. I hope they're not too lonely without me."

"Uh, I think they'll do just fine," I said. "You know, they've still got your little brother. A mansion on the lake. A successful business. One fine hot tub. Each other. It'll be hard, but they'll survive."

"Nerves getting to you? Or maybe all that hair dye fried your brain?" Z said, scrunching up his face like he'd smelled something bad.

I tried to shoot him my best dirty look but it's totally not effective when you can't catch the intended recipient's eye. "What are you trying to say?"

Zander shrugged. "You seem a little snippy this morning, is all."

"And you seem a little deluded," I told him. "Thinking your parents' entire lives revolve around you. Don't you think that's kind of funny?"

"No," he said, examining his fingernails.

"Well, I do."

"Knock it off, you two," Bebe said. "The car can't take any more fighting couples."

After Zander had polished off a million and two pancakes—not once looking in my direction—we all piled out into the driveway for the big good-bye. It was actually a lot less emotional that I expected. Bebe gave me a huge hug, whispered, "Stick to your guns," in my ear—whatever that meant, I filed it away in my brain under F for *Figure it out later*—yawned, and announced she was going inside to take a nap. Mr. Steve slipped me a fifty-dollar bill and told me to buy some cool posters for my dorm room. I thanked him profusely, never once mentioning I pretty much thought posters were an early-eighties phenomena that was totally over and that I'd probably use the cash to buy a couple of CDs or stock up on decent food if the caf proved too toxic.

After all the hugs had been bestowed, Grandpa instructed Zander to get up front with him because he needed a decent navigator, not the crazy woman who got them lost on the way out to Chicago. Grandma, for one, did not appreciate that comment. But still, we stuffed ourselves into the jam-packed backseat while Z rode shotgun, with me wrestling blankets and bedding and Grandma trying to subdue a herd of stuffed animals and wild floor pillows.

During the first few minutes of our drive, Zander deigned to turn around and make small talk with me. Well, at least I think he was talking to me. His focus was slightly to the right and over the top of my head, so there was a possibility he was actually conversing with the dried bird poop on the window.

"Do you really hate my hair that much?" I finally asked him. "I mean, so much you can't even look at me?" It seemed pretty extreme. I'd like to think if Z went bald or got a Mohawk or even a mullet, I'd accept it and go right on liking him without all the theatrics.

Z sighed. "Trace, really. You look great," he said, his gaze coming to rest on his hands. I can always tell when he's lying because he bites the skin around his thumb. I swear, he was seconds away from drawing blood this time. "I was just a little caught off guard."

"So then why are you having such a tough time looking at me now?" It was completely unnerving to have him staring everywhere—anywhere—but in my eyes.

"I get carsick when I ride backward," he said with a shrug, as if that covered just about everything. It didn't begin to skim the surface, in my opinion. But apparently Z wasn't in the mood for talking. He stuck headphones in his ears, twirled the dial on his iPod several times, and promptly fell asleep, his jaw falling slack and a soft *zzzzzzz* punctuating every breath.

"See, now that's a noise I could live with," Grandpa said, glaring at Grandma in the rearview. "One that's not able to wake the dead."

"I'll show you who's dead," Grandma said, raising her index finger in the air and then curling it slowly down.

"I beg your pardon!" Grandpa yelled, two bright red spots burning up his cheeks.

"And I'm begging you two to stop it," I butted in. I wanted to stick two huge cotton balls into my ears and not take them out until we hit Connecticut. I mean, how gross. I did *not* want to know a thing about my grandparents' sex life, or lack thereof. It just wasn't natural . . . or normal . . . or necessary. At all. And I mean ever.

Grandpa turned the boring talk-radio show he'd been listening to up to decibels more appropriate to a Mudvayne concert. Miraculously, Zander slept right through the right-wing racket, and I wondered how I was going to survive the trip. "Only seven hundred and thirty more miles to go," I muttered, staring out the window at the Sears Tower. "What joy."

I started digging around in my messenger bag, trying to find my iPod or cell phone or anything that would keep me occupied for an hour or two. Grandma's hand covered mine before I could come up with anything.

"Can I tell you something?" she whispered.

I winced. I wasn't sure I would ever be ready for whatever information Grandma was about to blurt out, especially if it had anything to do with the finger-crinkling implication. "I guess so," I said, bracing myself for the worst.

She leaned over to me and said in a low voice, "I was never interested in learning how to dance or talk crazy. I was just trying to make sure your grandfather didn't do anything stupid."

I wasn't quite sure what could be more stupid than two senior citizens spinning around on their heads on the floor or calling each other "foo" and "boo," so this conversation was turning out to be an interesting little surprise. "You mean you didn't do all that to impress me and my friends?"

Grandma waved away my assessment like it was so much foolishness. "Of course not, dear. I did it because Grandpa seemed to be having something of a late-life crisis. Started using Grecian Formula, squirting himself with Binaca and Polo cologne all the time, doing sit-ups every day. The man even bought himself a pair of Lucky jeans!"

I had to admit, it sounded a little weird, even for my grandparents. "I take it you weren't happy he was trying to update his look for you?"

Grandma pressed her lips together and stared out the window. "Oh, it wasn't for me, honey. It was for that little harlot teaching all those classes at the senior center."

I clutched her hand, trying not to smile. It was seriously cute how jealous she could still get, thinking her man was looking at other women. "Grandma, no. There's no way Grandpa was doing all that for someone else."

Grandma shook her head. "I know the signs Trace and they were all there. So I decided I'd just take up rapping and breakin' as my hobbies, too. Your grandfather was none too happy about it, either, believe me. Said I should find my own interests and stop following him around like a puppy dog."

"I bet all Grandpa wants is for you to be yourself."

"But—" she started to protest.

"No buts," I told her. "Just be yourself—the real you, not the you who's trying to be like that slutty teacher he thinks is hot—and you two will be just fine."

Grandma looked at me hard. "You really think so?"

"Yeah, I really do."

"Hmmpphh," Grandma said, not committing either way.

"Just out of curiosity, what classes would you have wanted to take? I mean, if you hadn't felt like you had to tail Grandpa all the time?"

"Oh, lots of things," Grandma said, looking faraway and dreamy. "Poetry. Photography. Japanese. French pastry making The list goes on and on."

"And you can't do that because . . . ?"

I was horrified to see tears welling up in my grandmother's eyes.

"Because if I do, your Grandfather will run off with that hussy and leave me in the dust!"

"It's way more important to be true to yourself than worry about what ifs," I told her, continuing to spout advice I hadn't quite been able to put into action myself. "And anyway, I'm sure Grandpa would never do that to you."

"Well, I'm not," she said, folding her arms over her chest. "Do you know I caught him asking her for private lessons? You know what happens in those, don't you?"

"The teacher teaches her student stuff?" I guessed.

"Yeah, sex stuff," Grandma hissed.

"Come on, now," I said, feeling more like her mother than her granddaughter. "You have nothing to worry about. Grandpa wasn't soliciting her, just trying to learn how to dance better."

"That's what you think," Grandma said.

"That's what I know," I told her, patting her hand gently.

There didn't seem to be anything more to say about the subject, and when Grandma quickly added her heavy-metal snoring to Zander's easy-listening sounds it became clear she wasn't looking for any more amateur counseling. The cacophony was enough to kill me, though, so I dredged up my iPod, stuck the headphones into my ears and cranked up my tunes high enough to block it all out—the noise, the family feud, even my nagging doubts about me and my boyfriend making it many more miles together. My last thought before I joined those other two in slumberland: Only twelve more hours till we get there.

I woke up who knows how long later to find we weren't moving anymore. I rubbed my eyes and blinked, trying to figure out where the heck we were. It finally became clear that we were at a particularly skuzzy-looking rest stop, and I was all alone in the car. Didn't these people ever watch *Cops*? And didn't they know this was the number one place for young women to get abducted and lopped to bits in a wood-chipper before anyone could even dial 911? Clearly, no one loved me anymore. I was debating whether to head into the store or wait it out with the ice scraper as my only weapon when Grandpa and Zander slid back into their seats.

"Do you have to go pee-pee, Trace?" were the first words out of my grandfather's mouth. Z tried to cover up snortfuls of laughter by pretending to cough.

"I think I'll just get out and stretch my legs," I said, giving Zander the hairy eyeball. He certainly was not among my favorite people today.

"Hurry up, then. We're trying to get to State College before dinner and Wilkes-Barre before we pack it in for the night."

"Did you guys already stop for lunch?" I wondered if they'd left me in the car then, too, with the window cracked just a little like I was the family dog or something. Not to mention a sitting duck for that same wood-chipper.

"Hours ago. You were sound asleep, and we didn't want to wake you." Zander said, staring at a falling-down barn perched precariously close to the gas station. Anything but me, of course.

I couldn't believe they'd been so inconsiderate, no matter how hard it had been to bring me out of my coma. "I'm ravenous. I'm going to pick something up so I don't starve to death before dinner."

"Women," I heard Grandpa mutter as I got out. "So damn dramatic all the time."

"Yeah," I heard my annoying boyfriend agree.

Inside the convenience store, I cruised the aisles for something halfway healthy that might tide me over until our incredibly chichi dinner at Denny's or whatever foul place awaited us. Chips? No. Chocolate? No. Fruit? Maybe. I picked up an apple and turned it over in my hands. It looked like it could've been sitting there since Woodstock. And I mean the original one in '69, not the '94 Green Day mud-throwing fest. I put it back and moved on.

In the last aisle, I found several ancient-looking Balance bars and grabbed two chocolate peanut butter ones, figuring they were pretty nuclear and couldn't really go bad. I was about to move on when I spied something called Charcotabs sitting next to a bunch of random over-the-counter drugs covering a variety of traveler's maladies: diarrhea, constipation, heartburn and the ever popular pounding headache. I picked up the box, thinking it might be an antidote for drinking too much—urban legend had it that if you went to the emergency room totally shitfaced, they made you eat charcoal to soak up the excess alcohol—and that it might be a funny thing to break the ice with my new roommate at Fairfield.

After reading the instructions on the box, though, I found out Charcotabs were actually an antiflatulent. In other words, the pills supposedly put the kibosh on any excessive burping and farting. Suddenly I knew without a doubt how to get Grandma and Grandpa back together. I grabbed one more thing from the medical aisle—Breathe Right strips—got myself a bottle of water, and then smacked right into the hottest man I'd seen in ages just as I was plunking the whole mess down on the counter. The guy laughed and gallantly swept his arm to let me go ahead.

I glanced at him out of the corner of my eye. He was a dash of Adam Levine from Maroon 5, a pinch of Gavin DeGraw, and a whole lot of stubble and tattoos and biceps and gorgeous hazel cat eyes. The effect was devastating. "Sorry. I didn't see you there at first," I said, trying to act cool even as my whole body was vibrating with nerves.

"No problem," he said, giving me a wink and a smile. "You go first."

"Thanks," I mumbled, trying not to let him see how much I was blushing—or what kind of weird stuff I was planning to buy.

"You from around here?" he asked, extending the expiration time of our conversation well past the few sentences I would've expected.

"Nah," I said, unconsciously reaching up to touch my hair. When it was long, I used to have a habit of twirling it around my finger. Now the best I could do was run my hand over it to give it that newly messed-up look. "I'm from Chicago, on my way to college in Connecticut."

"I should've known," he said, leaning casually back against the counter. "No way a chick as hot as you would live here in—where are we, anyway?"

"I have absolutely no idea," I said, giving him a full-on grin by this point. He'd just called me a hot chick. Even with my new look. Or maybe because of my new look. I was clearly hanging with the wrong people. It seemed beautiful, slightly dangerous, extremely tattooed guys actually liked me better like this. Halle-freaking-lujah, there was a God after all.

"I'm on my way back to UMass," Mr. Growing On Me By The Second informed me. "Care to hook up with me and my friends later on tonight? We're almost ready to pack it in for the day."

"Not unless you're planning to pack it in around Wilkes-Barre," I said, disappointment landing in my stomach like an anchor, even though I'd never had a chance of hooking up with the guy in the first place. "Because I've just been informed we're not stopping till we get there."

"Not even for me? C'mon, tell your wingwoman not to be such a buzzkill. Meet us at the Keg."

If he only knew my wingwoman was Grandma, and I was also being accompanied on this trip by my grandfather and boyfriend.

"She's a tough cookie, believe me," I flirted right back. "But I'll try to wear her down."

We were just standing there grinning at each other when I glanced over at the magazine rack and saw something that nearly made my heart stop. Staring back at me from the cover of *The Streak*—a hip new weekly magazine that was kind of a cross between *In Touch*, *The National Enquirer*, and *Maxim*—was me and my plumber's crack lying on top of K.C. Even worse, right alongside that mortifying picture was another one, and it was basically my biggest nightmare come true: Zander and K.C. dirty dancing. The headline screamed: *Kandy Kane Caught in Gender-Bending Love Triangle.*

"Hey, what happened to that gorgeous smile?" I vaguely heard Mr. Hottie asking me. "Was it something I said?"

I was about to answer when I noticed Zander at the door looking totally pissed off. I ignored him, running my finger over the Superman tattoo on my admirer's arm. "No, I love what you're saying," I told him. "Keep going."

And I'm sure he would've, if the semiretarded counter guy hadn't started yelling to his half-cousin-sister-girlfriend who was busy stocking the shelves, that is. "How much is this here gas reducer?"

"What do you think you're doing, Trace?" Zander asked from the doorway, his hands clenched in fists at his side. He was staring at me full-on for the first time since this morning.

"Just buying some stuff," I said, turning my attention back to Mr. Hottie and trying to pretend both Z and the counterman didn't exist.

"Which one?" the stock girl yelled back in the meantime. "The one for tooting or belching?"

The counter guy consulted the box. "Both," he yelled back.

"I gotta run," my new boyfriend said, lightly touching my arm. "Try to come tonight. I mean, if you're feeling better."

Oh, my God. He thought that stuff was mine. "It's not for me!" I yelled after him, but he took off so fast, I swear he left skid marks and burning tire smell in his wake.

"Who was that?" Zander asked. "And why were you talking to him for so long?"

The counter guy finally found the price on the Charcotabs box and rang up my sale. I helped him shove everything into a bag and marched over to the magazine rack. "I'll answer that just as soon as you tell me why you and Kandy decided to practically have sex in front of everyone the second I left California."

Z peered at the picture, then back up at me. For real this time. "Trace, I agree that it looks bad, but there's actually a simple explanation—"

"Yup," I said, completely fuming. "The simple explanation is you completely betrayed me. And that you guys totally suck."

Z looked bewildered. "Sometimes I feel like I don't even know you anymore."

"Believe me, you don't, buddy," I said, poking a finger into his chest and pushing him back out toward the parking lot. "For example, did you know I absolutely detest country music? That I'm so sick of foosball, I've considered setting the table in your game room on fire just so I never have to play again? That every time you crack your knuckles, you might as well be sending an ice pick through my eyeballs? Did you have any clue about any of those things at all?"

"Calm down," Clem, the counter guy, said, picking up the phone like maybe he was going to call the cops.

"No, *you* calm down," I shot back at him. "I've had it up to here with being calm."

Zander, who had gone totally silent during my speech, suddenly regained his voice. "Trace, how could I have known any of that stuff when you never said a word about it?" he asked, not unreasonably. "I already told you I can't read your mind. And you know what else? I don't think I'm into having a total liar as my girlfriend."

"Hey, cheater? I don't think you have anything to be so self-righteous about over there."

"Fine," he said, glowering at me. "Just tell me one thing. Was anything about our relationship real? Or was it all a lie?"

"No lie, what was real was that all I ever wanted was to make you happy. And what's even more real is that now I just want you gone. Poof. Out of my life."

"But—" he said.

I held up my hand. "No buts."

"But—" he tried again.

"Talk to the hand." Yeah, I know—totally juvenile, quoting *Master of Disguise*—but I was on a roll. I couldn't have stopped if I tried.

"But—" he started, giving it one last shot.

"Forget about it, Z. I know I already have."

Zander shot me a pissed-off look and stalked back to the car. I watched him slump down in the front seat as I paced the sidewalk outside Clem's convenience store and started dialing madly. Number one on my hit list: K.C. She picked up on the first ring.

"Hey, bitch." I said.

"I think you mean beee-yotch," she bantered back, not realizing I was dead serious.

"Nope, I definitely meant bitch," I told her.

"Wha—?"

"Just listen," I said, not giving her a chance to say anything else. "I'm calling to thank you for keeping such close tabs on my boyfriend while I was gone. I mean, I loved seeing those pictures of you two practically doing each other on the dance floor. It's so comforting, knowing you're so willing to put yourself out there like that for me."

"Trace, I have no idea what you're talking about—"

"Sure you do," I said, a deadly calm taking over my whole body. "Too bad Caden's out of the picture and Zander, your dirty dancing partner, is back here, though. Because I guess now you're just going to have to go fuck yourself."

"Trace—"

"Real friends don't do things like that to each other, *Kandy*," I told her, deliberately avoiding the friendly acronym I normally used when addressing her. "I hope you have a crappy—with a K—life."

Click.

After spewing that much vitriol, you would've thought I was done, but no. I had one last call to make, and it was going to be a doozy. I pulled Mrs. Kane's card out of my wallet—the one she'd tossed at me when she was screaming about having our lawyers contact each other—and dialed quickly. Mrs. Kane picked up on the third ring.

"Mrs. Kane, I have something important to say to you."

"No apologies necessary," she told me before I had a chance to launch into another tirade. "Kandy already explained that you were just trying to help her."

"That's great, Mrs. Kane, but what I actually wanted to tell you is that your daughter's a total fraud. My only consolation is the fact that she's been lying to you for a lot longer than she's been lying to me. I mean, did you know she hates being a pop star? And that all she wants in this world is to go to Columbia and be a psychologist?"

There was a long stretch of silence. "You still there, Mrs. Kane?"

"I can't believe what you're saying is true," she finally managed to stammer, sounding as shocked as if I'd slapped her in the face.

"Well, it is. So put that in your pipe and smoke it."

"What pipe?" Mrs. Kane said, definitely not knowing where to take our conversation next.

"A peace pipe, maybe? Now that the truth is out, maybe you can do something good with it. Maybe you can even think of what your daughter wants for once, and not how much money she can make you."

"I beg your pardon?"

"It's not my pardon you need to be asking for. It's K.C.'s."

Click.

"Trace, get in the car this instant," Grandpa yelled from the driver's seat of the Country Squire.

By this point, no one was exempt from the wrath of Trace—not even feuding senior citizens in the midst of a late-life crisis. "Keep your pants on, Gramps," I yelled back. "I'll get there when I get there."

I sauntered over to the car and knocked on Grandpa's window. When he rolled it down, I threw the Charcotabs in his lap. "Try these. Maybe they'll help you get a handle on all that foul burping," I said, leaning on the door. "And while you're at it, try telling your wife you love her and not your stupid Slanguage instructor. Take off your Lucky jeans and put back on your Habands. Forget the Grecian Formula and the Polo cologne and get freaking real. Grandma has stuck by you for decades. Don't throw that away now because you're so scared of getting older you'll do anything—even throw yourself at a girl young enough to be your granddaughter—to pretend it's not happening."

"Trace!" Grandpa said, shocked. "I am totally appalled by your behavior."

"Oh, yeah?" I said. "Well, Grandma is appalled by yours, too, so I guess we're even."

"What she said," Grandma butted in.

"And don't you even start with me," I shot back at her, tossing the Breathe Right strips in her general direction. "You should know by now trying to be someone you're not is totally useless—it only confuses the hell out of the people who love you and it's a one-way ticket to self-loathing. So why not let Grandpa know how you really feel—that you're scared of losing him—instead of pretending to be interested in things you're not, and let the chips fall where they may? And for God's sake, use those things in your lap to stop snoring. I guarantee you he'll be one hundred percent more affectionate if he gets a good night's sleep."

"Well, I never," Grandma harrumphed.

"And you know what? You should," I said, feeling totally self-satisfied. "It feels really damn good."

Zander, who had been watching in silence from his copilot seat, chose now to butt back in. "You're real good at telling other people how to solve their relationship problems, aren't you, Trace?" he said. "But real crappy at following your own advice. Did you know that if you had only done the things you just lectured your grandparents about, we'd be fine right now?"

In my mind, I had to admit he was right. Not that I was about to say it out loud or anything. I mean, it was too late for any of that now. So I stuck my fingers in my ears instead and got even more childish than before, when I was quoting bad kiddie movies. "Lalalalalala! I can't hear you."

"Real mature, Trace."

"Did someone say something?" I asked. No one answered. Probably because no one in the car was talking to me anymore. Finally, I broke the silence. "I didn't think so."

As liberating as it was, this complete and utter honesty thing was definitely turning out to be an individual sport.

CHAPTER
19

The uncomfortable silence lasted all the way to State College, throughout dinner at—yup, I'd guessed it—Denny's, and continued even after we'd stopped for the night at a hotel in Wilkes-Barre, Pennsylvania. The only tiny glimmer of hope I could see in the situation was that I caught Grandpa taking one of the Charcotabs after he brushed his teeth in his half of our two-bedroom suite, and Grandma came out of their bathroom with a strip across her nose. So at least they were trying.

Z and I were an entirely different story. Though we were all hanging out together in the living area of the suite, I'd stopped looking up whenever Zander directed a comment at my grandfather, and he'd stopped looking at, or even around, me altogether. The moment I'd been dreading for months—our second and final breakup—was turning out to be completely anticlimactic. I wasn't even horrifically sad or mad like I'd expected to be. In fact, probably the most depressing thing about it was how much time and energy I'd wasted worrying about this moment.

As everyone else was getting ready for bed—my grandparents not speaking in their room, Zander and I not speaking in ours—I stepped outside to see if there had been any backlash from my sudden leap into over-the-top honesty. Flipping through my missed calls, I saw Mrs. Kane had called once, K.C. twice, Brina three times. I was glad I'd made such an impact, but wasn't about to listen to the Kane women grovel. They hadn't earned it yet, I thought, and dialed up the one person I still trusted.

When Brina picked up a second later, all I could hear was sobs. "Brina, what's wrong?" I asked.

"It's Sully," she hiccuped through her tears.

"I know you're going to miss him, but don't worry. You guys will be OK."

This brought on new wails. "That's where you're wrong, Trace. He says he thinks we should keep a special place for each other in our hearts, but that we should be free to see other people while I'm away."

I gasped. If something like that could happen to the perfect couple, was it any wonder Z and I hadn't even made it through the first day of freshman year, much less the first semester? "No way."

"Yes way. He said it was the hardest thing he'd ever had to do, but he wanted me to be able to fully experience college, or some crap like that. Oh, and that he loved me enough and was confident enough in our relationship to do the right thing."

So maybe Sully really was giving Brina a gift, I thought, albeit a painful one to receive. "So are you still going to see each other when you're home on break?"

Brina gave a big sniffle. "Yeah, supposedly everything's going to be the same, except we're allowed to hook up or whatever if we want when I'm at school."

"So maybe that's not such a bad thing," I told her.

"I won't, you know," she said vehemently. "I won't *ever* want anyone but Sully."

"Maybe he won't ever want anyone but you, either," I said. "It could easily happen, knowing how happy you guys have been together this summer. You're just going to have to wait and see how it all turns out."

"So you're telling me things will work out either way?"

"Yup," I told her.

"And wasn't that the same advice I gave you on the beach last night?"

"Yup," I said again.

"How'd you get so smart?" I could hear the beginnings of a smile in her voice.

"It comes from hanging around smart people," I said. "Like you."

"Oh, Trace, I'm going to miss you so much." She sighed.

"Me, too," I said. "But, hey. We can IM and call and e-mail and all that other stuff so we always know exactly what's going on in each other's lives. And then when we're home on break, we can just pick up where we left off. OK?"

"Yeah," she said, undoubtedly smiling now. "That's definitely OK. Thanks for always being there for me, girl."

"Right back at ya, Brina."

Buoyed by the one relationship in my life that was going right, I decided to actually listen to my messages rather than erase them unheard like I'd been planning to. Connecting into voice mail, I was greeted with an in-box full of people who wanted further clarification about why I was so pissed off, to tell their sides of the story, but most of all, to fix our communication breakdown. I resolved to call everyone back in the morning, listen to what they had to say, and try to find a middle ground. For now, though, all I wanted to do was go to bed.

Back in the motel room, I found Grandma and Grandpa huddled on the couch in the living room, head to head, hand in hand.

Their conversation appeared to be pretty heavy and very respectful. They occasionally nodded in agreement, occasionally shook their heads to signal opposition, but were seemingly always on the same wavelength.

Wanting to give them some privacy, I moseyed into the bedroom where Zander was lying on one of the double beds, iPod on his stomach, earphones pressed in place, tapping out a beat on his legs. If he knew I was there, he didn't let on. So I assumed the same position as Z, only on the other bed, and cranked up my Todd Carey playlist. When "Sing Me Home" came on, I was surprised to find tears spilling out of the corners of my eyes. I figured it was due to a combination of relief from finally telling everyone how I felt and realizing I was headed for a whole new home—where things would probably turn out just fine, but they would never, ever be the same again.

"Are you OK, Trace?" Grandma gently shook me, and I opened my eyes back up.

"Yup," I said, trying to quickly wipe any telltale drips from my cheeks.

Too late—she'd already noticed, and was looking at me with concern. "Are you sure?"

"I'm totally cool, Grandma. Even better than cool, but thanks for asking."

She leaned over and whispered in my ear. "Me, too. Thanks for setting me and Grandpa straight. Now don't go doing anything I wouldn't do, OK?"

"Don't worry, Grandma, I won't."

"OK, then. Goodnight, darling."

Grandma headed back to her own room presumably to cuddle up with Grandpa, and I shut my eyes, trying to lose myself in the music again. I'd almost achieved rock 'n' roll nirvana when I felt

Zander lying down next to me on the bed and slowly folding his hand into mine. I turned to look at him and he pulled one of the iPod headphone buds out of my ear. " 'Guitars and Tiki Bars'," he said simply.

"Actually, I was listening to 'Somebody's Miracle' by Liz Phair." At least we were talking again, even if we still weren't quite connecting.

Z shook his head and tried again. "I meant the picture that got you so pissed off," he explained. "I was just teaching Kandy the 'Guitars and Tiki Bars' dance at the wrap party. Nothing happened, Trace. I swear."

I wasn't sure exactly how to feel about the news. Sorry for refusing to listen before now was the first thing that came to mind. Relieved that my boyfriend and new best friend hadn't sold me down the river like I'd thought, a close second. And maybe a third was happy, plain and simple—which really was amazing, since earlier in the afternoon, I had thought I might never be again.

Instead of getting into all that, though, what I said instead was, "I have a confession to make."

"What?"

I stared at the ceiling and chewed on a hangnail. Maybe I'd waited too long to reveal what was about to come out of my mouth. "You're not going to like it," I said, prolonging the inevitable.

"Tell me anyway," he said, squeezing my hand. "I can take it, I swear."

"Tikis only have one face on them," I finally blurted out. "When you made up that dance, you must've been thinking of a totem pole."

Instead of being ripshit like I'd expected, Zander let out a huge rumble of laughter. "You're kidding."

I shook my head and gave him a little half smile.

"Why didn't you tell me sooner?"

I gave him a look like, *You know why*.

"Trace, I never wanted you to be anyone but yourself," he said, shaking his head. "I don't know where you got that idea, but it wasn't from me."

"I guess when you broke up with me, I kind of freaked out," I admitted, letting everything fly now. "And when we got back together, I figured the best way to keep us that way would be to try and be the perfect girlfriend."

"I never expected you to be perfect," he told me. "I mean, sometimes I even felt like I had to force myself into a good mood when I wasn't because you were always so happy and perky. It was actually pretty annoying."

"I know," I said. "It *was* kind of a trap, wasn't it?"

"Yup," he said. "So, where does this leave us? Are we still stuck in it, or do you think we escaped relatively unharmed?"

"I don't know," I told him. "One thing's for sure, though. We're definitely in a better place than we were earlier today. Or even all summer, now that I really think about it."

"I guess you're right," he said, planting a little kiss on my cheek before rolling over.

I snaked an arm around his side and snuggled up against his back. The future was looking brighter every second, even if it was pitch-black in the room.

Not to mention silent.

I was definitely going to have to invest in the companies that made Breathe Right and Charcotabs when I got to school, that was for sure. Both products were obviously one hundred percent effective. I hadn't heard a belch out of Grandpa's room in hours, and as far as I could tell, Grandma wasn't even humming in her sleep. And when you added it all together—my grandparents finally giving up the street lingo and break-dancing to go back to being a (basically) normal, happy couple, me and Zander being on better terms than we had been in three months despite the fact that we'd just broken up again, and a road trip devoid of burps, farts, or snores—well, it was nothing short of a miracle.

CHAPTER
20

Though I'd planned to call K.C. first thing in the morning and apologize for going off on her before I knew the whole story behind the photo of her and Zander, I kept getting sidetracked. First, it was way too early—we'd set out at six a.m. Eastern time, which was something like three in the morning on the West Coast. Then I was assigned copilot duties—from the backseat, of course, because Grandma and Grandpa were too busy getting all googly-eyed with each other in the front to deal with any old maps. And then I got so preoccupied blabbing to Zander—agreeing with him when I agreed, disagreeing when I disagreed—that I totally lost track of time.

The vibration of my phone finally got me to shut up for a second. I flipped it open and saw it was K.C., so I launched into an apology before she had a chance to say anything. "I am so sorry I jumped to conclusions when I saw that picture in *The Streak*," I said, talking as fast as I could. "And also for those hurtful things I said, and for not having enough faith in you to listen to your side of the story. I'm the crappy friend, not you. But I still hope you'll forgive me."

"Just let me talk," K.C. said, throwing back at me what I'd thrown at her yesterday. Only somehow, she sounded like she was playing with me, not serious like I had been. "Didn't I tell you being friends with Kandy was going to be a lot less fun than hanging with K.C.?"

"I don't care," I interrupted, willing to take the good with the bad. "Maybe things are a little more complicated with Kandy, but it's definitely worth the extra effort."

"You still didn't let me finish," she said. "First, I wanted to thank you for having that little talk with my mom yesterday. Second, for injecting a little *real* reality into my life. And finally, for putting the last nail in Kandy's coffin, so to speak."

I gasped. "I didn't mess things up for you that much, did I?"

"Let's not ruin this thing with a lot of talk," she said. "I'd rather just show you how much you actually did."

I hung my head even though I knew she couldn't see the depths of my remorse. "I'm so sorry, K.C."

"Don't be. Just make sure you get your grandparents to drive by this address after you drop off Zander and before you head to Connecticut," she said, reeling off numbers and letters that I dutifully wrote on my hand in the only pen I could find in my messenger bag on such short notice, a black Sharpie. "You'll get the picture then."

"What's this all about?" Maybe a billboard in Times Square declaring me the world's worst friend, or a newly taped shout-out on *TRL* where K.C. tells everyone I was Earl, or—well, the list of disastrous possibilities went on and on.

"All I can say is, I think you're going to like it."

"Really?"

"Really and truly."

Somehow, despite Grandpa's nervous Nelly driving in Manhattan, we made it to Zander's dorm and deposited most of his bags on the curb before the cops started screaming through a bullhorn that they were going to boot the car if we stayed parked there for any longer. Just as my grandparents pulled away in search of a legal space, Z's mother called, wailing so loud about missing him I could hear her five feet away. After a few minutes I got really bored listening to him placate her, so I did a goofy series of made-up hand signals to tell Zander I was going to start lugging his stuff up to the room.

After the elevator let me out on the tenth floor, I wandered down the hall in search of room 1010, dragging Z's humongous yellow L.L. Bean rolling duffle behind me. There were guys, guys everywhere, of every shape and size, color, nationality, and affiliation. It was like this cool rainbow of humanity, and the thought crossed my mind that maybe I'd chosen the wrong school. I let the idea bounce around in there for a while before deciding whatever would be, would be. If I loved Fairfield, great. If I didn't, I could always transfer.

I had just found Zander's room when a random rainbow man— I never found out which one—sent a radio-controlled truck whizzing by me. Not noticing it had parallel parked in front of my left foot, I went to reach for the doorknob, tripped over the damn monster wheels, and tumbled headfirst through the door.

"You OK?"

I looked up to see a dark-haired guy sitting on one of the beds, cross-legged and shirtless with a professional-looking camera lying across his lap.

"I didn't know it was unlocked," I said, as if that explained why I'd come skidding over the threshold on my face.

"I could see that," he said, a mysterious Cheshire cat kind of grin pulling up just the corners of his mouth. "So, are you my new roomie?"

"Unfortunately, no," I said, wanting to eat the words back up the minute they flew out of my mouth. What I meant was, going to

NYU looked like it would be fun, not that I wanted to bunk with Cheshire cat grin man. Although now that I took a closer look at him, it wasn't like that would be such a bad option, either.

"I was just thinking the same thing," he said, climbing off the bed and bending over to offer me a hand up.

Something about Z's new roommate hit me—and I mean this in the best possible way—as slightly dangerous. Unique. Not to mention completely alluring. Maybe it was the juxtaposition of such a buff body belonging to a guy whose fingers were so long and tapered they could only be described as elegant. Or the fact that his skin was completely hairless, whereas Z practically had a rug growing on his chest and even sometimes—*ewwww*—his shoulders. But mostly, I think it was the uniquely placed tattoo, written in script over his left pec like he was wearing a uniform permanently announcing his name to the world.

"Sweet," I said once I was back on my feet, face-to-face with it.

"You're welcome."

"Uh, no," I said, pointing at the tattoo. "*Dolce*. It means *sweet* in Italian, right?"

Mr. Sweetie stuck his hands in his pockets. The sudden motion made him rock forward involuntarily—and made my hand lightly graze the writing above his heart.

"That it does," he said, seemingly unaware that touching him had sent a jolt of pure electricity throughout my body.

"So you have a sweet heart, is that it?" I'd forgotten all about Zander by this point and was flirting with reckless abandon.

The guy gave me that cocky half grin again. "Now that's where you're wrong," he told me. "I'm actually a total hard-ass."

"So then why not have *duro* tattooed on your left butt cheek and leave it at that?" *Duro* means *hard* in Italian. Get it? *Duro* on his butt cheek? *Hard ass*? Finally, a witty comeback had come to me while I was still in the moment, not hours after the original conversation had taken place.

Z's roommate threw his head back and laughed. The genuine, uncensored gesture was *soooooo* attractive. Clearly, this guy was completely comfortable in his own skin and had no problem letting everyone know it. "Actually, Dolce is my last name."

"Well, then, it's a pleasure to meet you, Mr. Dolce."

"Oh, no. The pleasure's all mine." The guy reached for my outstretched hand and brought it up to his lips for a kiss instead of a regular old shake. "That's how we greet beautiful women in Italy."

At this rate, he was going to have to get the maintenance man to come mop me off the floor, because I had pretty much already melted into some sort of strange love/lust/crush goo. "You're from Italy?" I asked. By now, I'd remembered about Zander just enough to wish he'd talk to his mom for another half hour.

"Nope. Lots of my relatives live there, but I just visit whenever I can," he told me. "I'm from right here in NYC. You?"

"Chicago. I'm Trace, by the way."

"Darius," he said, plunking himself back down on the bed. "Want to see some of my latest photos?"

"Sure," I said, sitting down next to him instead of heading right back down to get more bags. I mean, I deserved a little break, didn't I? I don't know who I thought I was kidding with my *Oh, I just need to rest a bit before I pick anything else up* thoughts, anyway. I mean, it had to be crystal clear to anyone with half a brain that what I really wanted to pick up next was the hard-assed, sweet-hearted (despite his protests) Darius Dolce.

"I've been working a nighttime series recently," he said, flipping through shot after shot of starry skies. "So, what do you think?"

"I think you're really talented." It felt like such a personal thing to say. Even if I'd already touched his bare chest and he'd kissed my hand with those pillowy lips.

"Hey," Zander said as he appeared at the door, loaded down with bags and books and CDs and random Yaffa cubes full of junk. "A little help here, Trace?"

Darius and I jumped off the bed and made a beeline for Z. As we were taking things off his hands, our arms accidentally touched. Sparks flew, but I guess they were all in my imagination, because Zander certainly didn't seem to notice. "Thanks, man," Z said to Darius. "I'm your new roommate, by the way. Zander O'Brien."

"Darius Dolce."

"Cool camera," Z said, nodding at the equipment on Darius's bed.

"Cool axe," Darius said, nodding to the guitar Zander had just plunked in the corner.

All the magic seemed to fly out the window once the caveman conversation started. From that point on, no matter how hard I tried to maneuver things to catch one more minute alone with Darius, it didn't happen. Bummer, but whatever. It's not like I could exactly make a play for my ex-boyfriend's roommate or anything. It was just going to have to be one of those things I looked back on forever and wondered, *What if*.

"So, I guess this is good-bye," I said to Z after the last bag had been dumped unceremoniously on the floor.

"I guess so," he said.

"And I guess this is my cue to take a walk or something," Darius said, closing the door behind him as he left the room.

As soon as we were alone, Zander took my face in his hands and kissed me. It seemed like a fitting end to what had basically been my first grown-up relationship. My first love, really.

"I'll miss you," I said, savoring the bittersweetness of the moment. On the one hand, it was going to be hard letting go of something I'd held on to so tightly for so long. But on the other . . . oh, my gosh, if there were guys like Darius at Fairfield, it was going to be a hell of a fun year.

"What's all this talk about missing each other?" Zander asked, staring right into my eyes. "We're still going to give this thing a shot, aren't we?"

"We are?" I hadn't even thought of it as an option. But now that the idea was out there, I thought it might be worth a try. If things didn't work out, it wouldn't be a total loss. I'd still get to spend some time in NYC . . . and see delicious Darius again. Not that I should be thinking about him or anything, but still. It never hurts to have a backup plan.

"I think we should," Zander said. "Don't you?"

"Yeah," I said, standing on my tippy-toes and giving him a quick kiss. "I do."

I was just getting out of the elevator on the ground floor when I bumped smack into Darius, who was on his way back up to the room. "We've got to stop meeting like this," I said, slipping right back into flirty Gertie mode.

"Or maybe we don't," he said.

"Or maybe we don't," I agreed, smiling up a storm.

"See you soon, Trace." Was I crazy, or had he just winked at me when the doors were sliding closed?

"You can count on it," I said, a second too late. The doors were already shut.

CHAPTER
21

Hopping back into the Country Squire, I had to break up a geri-atric make-out festival. "Gross, you guys," I said, covering my eyes with my hands.

"Sorry, Trace," Grandpa said. "Grandma just wanted me to check if she had anything stuck in her teeth."

"With your tongue?" I asked, still afraid to look up.

"Looks like we're off to Connecticut, then," Grandma said, sliding back over to her side of the bench seat of the car and patting her helmet head back into place.

"Actually, could we make one stop before Fairfield?"

Grandpa glanced at his watch. "I don't know, Trace. We're running late as it is."

"Please?" I meant for it to come out like an impassioned plea, but the reality was, I sounded more like a whiny five-year-old. "It's really important to me."

"Why?" Grandma asked.

"I'm not quite sure," I said. "I just know it is."

The address I'd scrawled on my hand turned out not to be in Times Square or the MTV studios or anything close to either. As we drove farther and farther uptown, I got more and more curious about where we were actually headed. Not to mention why.

The last few blocks before our destination, I actually found my-self wondering if maybe K.C. had been so pissed off at me she was hoping we might get lost in the ghetto or something. We seemed to be in a really sketchy area, where any moment maybe gangs would start shooting at each other from their pimped-out rides.

"Well, here we are," Grandpa said, pulling up to a rather nonde-script brick building. "What is it that you need to do here?"

"Not a clue," I said, checking the number on my hand one last time. K.C. wasn't sending me into a crack house, was she? "I'll be right back, OK?"

"You've got five minutes," Grandpa told me. "I can't stand pay-ing twenty more bucks to park for an hour like we had to at NYU."

Heading into the building, I was greeted at the front desk by a funky girl sporting a haircut just like mine. "Welcome to Columbia."

"Thanks," I said, grinning. I couldn't believe K.C. had actually pulled this one off.

Too impatient to wait for the elevator, I sprinted up three flights of stairs and ran screaming into K.C.'s dorm room. "No way!" I re-peated over and over. "No way, no way, no way!"

"Yes way," she said with a smile that seemed to envelope her en-tire body. Which was covered by normal, casual clothes, I might add. And no strange makeup. "Thanks to you."

Just then, Shamus and Mrs. Kane appeared in the doorway.

"Really, thanks for everything, Trace," Mrs. Kane said. "You helped me see I'd gotten so focused on helping Kandy achieve her dreams, I never stepped back long enough to see that they'd changed. That she'd grown up."

I couldn't say anything, only smile and clutch onto my used-to-be-a-pop-princess friend's hand like it was a life preserver.

"And I wanted to say thanks, too, Trace," Shamus said, leaning against the doorframe. "You've been an amazing addition to my life."

It suddenly hit me what an impact I'd had on all these people in the room. Sure, K.C. had gotten what she wanted—and I fervently hoped she did still want it after she found out what it was like to be a normal kid and not have a bajillion adoring fans surrounding her all the time—but that what I'd said also meant her mom was out a job and my dad wouldn't be enjoying his career pinnacle anymore. "Shamus, I'm sorry I made you lose the show," I said, feeling like I'd swallowed a big boulder. I certainly hadn't meant to ruin his entire life's dream.

"Lose the show?" he laughed. "I didn't lose anything. In fact, I've got two big shows now because of you."

"Huh?" I asked, totally confused.

"It seems you're my good luck charm, Trace. I don't know what I ever did without you."

I was grinning so hard my cheeks had nearly taken over my eyeballs when K.C. jumped in to explain before my dad could. "After you called my mom, we had a big long talk—"

"And cry," Mrs. Kane added. "And Kandy told me how she still had a place waiting for her here at Columbia—"

"And then we went to your dad with a proposal—" K.C. added.

"And that's how I ended up executive producer of two big shows instead of just one," Shamus said, rolling into the big conclusion of the story. "Now we're going to be filming *Caden's Crib* at the guesthouse in LA, and *Do Over* here in New York."

"You know, like the song Caden and I wrote," K.C. excitedly piped back in. "It's a cross between a talk show and a reality show where I'll be giving people another chance at doing something they've always wanted to do. Kind of like me and going to college, you know?"

"And me and you, right?" Caden said, sauntering into the room and slinging his arm around K.C.'s shoulder.

I hung my head one last time. "I'm so sorry about that oil incident, you guys."

"No worries," Caden said. "It brought us closer in the end."

"And your heart was in the right place, Trace," K.C. added. "Mostly. Anyway, *Do Over* shoots only once a week, so I can take a full load of classes, just like everyone else. And I'll head out to Cali to visit Caden every month or so."

"That's so perfect, you guys," I said, gathering everyone into a group hug. "I'm so happy I didn't screw everything up like I thought I did."

"Everything's going to be better than ever, Trace," Shamus assured me. "I'll be here in New York all the time, so we're going to be able to get to know each other without trying to cram everything into a week here or a long weekend there. Sound good?"

"Sounds great," I said. Tears were just streaming down my face by this point and I wasn't even trying to pretend to be tough anymore. I was just so happy.

"Nice hair, by the way," Shamus said.

"Yeah, Trace, it's totally edgy and cool," K.C. added. "Maybe you could even be my guest host on *Do Over* every once in a while, like for the episode we're doing on surviving embarrassing moments or extreme makeovers without plastic surgery."

I laughed through my tears. "K.C., you know how freaked out I get in front of an audience."

"Just stick with me," K.C. said, grinning. "I'll cure you of it yet."

Shamus called to me from K.C.'s window just as I was ducking back into the Country Squire. "Bye, Trace. I love you."

I smiled up at him and waved. "Me, too." And I did. I truly did. It had been a long time coming, and it sure felt good.

* * *

An hour later, Grandpa took a right into campus. I sucked in a deep breath as I tried to sort out everything that had happened over the past week or so. Before I started my new life at Fairfield, I wanted to make sure I'd reconciled everything in the old one.

I was finally able to exhale when I realized the retro mix that had been spinning my head around all summer had faded into black. And the new playlist reverberating in my brain was completely current. It was my life, right? And that meant I could choose my own direction, along with the tunes that would be cranking right along with me.

First up on my mix, "Trust," by Dakona. From here on in, I was simply going to trust myself—that I'd chosen the right school, friends, path in life, whatever. As my dad told me back at Kandy's dorm room, no snowflake ever falls in the wrong place. He said it was an old Zen proverb, and who am I to question ancient wisdom like that?

Second, "I Just Wanna Live," by Good Charlotte. So what if I had no idea which big thing I was going on to do next with my life? Figuring out what I wanted to major in, making new friends, acclimating myself to Fairfield, and learning how to do my own laundry was going to be plenty for now. The gotta-do-it-before-I-die stuff could wait until I was a little less busy.

Next came The Killers ripping through "Everything Will Be Alright." The way I saw it now, either things would work out between me and Zander . . . or they wouldn't. Only time would tell, and no matter what, we'd both be just fine. Plus, there were always other smelt in the sea, or whatever Brina had told me a few days ago, waiting out there if Z and I crashed and burned—especially that hottie Darius Dolce.

And that brings me to the big finale, the final encore, the curtain dropper: "One Step Closer," by U2. From here on out, Shamus and

I could let things—including making the leap from being merely biologically related to spiritually connected—happen one step at a time. It would all work out eventually, I was sure of it. And so, it seemed, was my dad.

Oh, and just for the record: Shamus hates mushrooms on his pizza and likes ketchup on his hot dogs. Just like his daughter.

Trish Cook is a freelance writer who lives outside of Chicago with her husband and two daughters. She's obsessed with Green Day, Led Zeppelin, her pink paisley Fender strat, not acting her age, running, wacky memoirs, and Laguna Beach (both the show and the actual place). Her first novel, *So Lyrical,* was published in May 2005. For more, go to www.trishcook.com.